# W.C. AUGUSTINE

# BACK ★ TO THE ★ WEST

DEFIANCE PRESS
& PUBLISHING

BACK TO THE WEST

First Edition: April 2024

Printed in the United States of America

10 9 8 7 6 5 4 3 2 1

ISBN-13: 978-1-963102-21-5 (Paperback)
ISBN-13: 978-1-963102-20-8 (eBook)
ISBN-13: 978-1-963102-22-2 (Hard Cover)

Published by Defiance Press & Publishing, LLC

Bulk orders of this book may be obtained by contacting Defiance Press & Publishing, LLC. www.defiancepress.com.

Public Relations Dept. – Defiance Press & Publishing, LLC
281-581-9300
pr@defiancepress.com

Defiance Press & Publishing, LLC
281-581-9300
info@defiancepress.com

*"Men have been taught that it is a virtue to agree with others. But the creator is the man who disagrees. Men have been taught that it is a virtue to swim with the current. But the creator is the man who goes against the current. Men have been taught that it is a virtue to stand together. But the creator is the man who stands alone."*

Howard Roark in *The Fountainhead*, by Ayn Rand

# ★ CHAPTER 1 ★

Adam counted four teachers monitoring students in the hallway during the change of classes. Loitering, loud talking, off-color joke sharing, teasing, hints of bullying, or flirtation were nipped in the bud. Adam often wondered what differences separated the control at the state prison and the Peoria High School hallway.

Adam Duval's high school locker was next to Terresa Davis's. Because of their names, they also sat side by side in the two classes they shared. The school had adopted a policy of seating students in alphabetical order. Doing so broke up the stereotypical rule of trouble-prone boys sitting in the back of the room and obedient girls in front. The policy also eliminated self-separation based upon race, gender proclivity, social groups, intelligence, or adherence to rules.

Earlier in the day Adam had noticed Terresa wearing tight black leggings and a white top. She had worn the combination two weeks prior on a Tuesday and a month earlier. It was his favorite outfit on her. And, in his mind, put her a step above the factory-holey jeans most often worn by girls. She wasn't hard to miss in a crowded hallway, at five feet seven, taller than most girls with her abundant brunette hair rising above the hallway cluster of students.

Adam made sure his glasses weren't sagging on his nose, then turned, and smiled at her as they opened their lockers. He was tempted to start a conversation, but his friend John had been reprimanded by the principal last week for harassing a girl. Earlier in the week he'd asked Terresa whether she enjoyed working at her dad's hardware store. Prudence said not to initiate a conversation again. Any kind of what could be construed as flirtation had to be kept to a minimum, but prudence was not his middle name.

Adam decided to go for it and ask her about her history essay when her towering boyfriend walked up. He was six feet two, and a forward on the basketball team. Those girls in his high school who chose to date guys preferred tall ones. Because he was only five feet six, finding a girlfriend was as difficult as getting around the gas allotment for your car.

For short guys, the pool of dating-interested girls was small. Some girls sought cultural acceptability by becoming super friends with another girl. Other girls sought independence and solitude, avoiding the hassle of befriending the hormone-plagued masculine gender.

"How ya doing' there, Adam?" asked her boyfriend.

"Good, you had a great game last night," Adam answered.

"Yeh, I scored fifteen points. Coach said I was great."

The boyfriend whispered something in Terresa's ear. Adam smiled at her. He was sure Terresa smiled back at him and seemed to ignore her boyfriend, at least that was his hope. With Adam following, they headed for history class.

The history class was primarily for seniors as were Terresa and her boyfriend. Adam was a junior, or a third-year student as wokesters called them. It was common for Adam to be placed with older students. As a freshman, he was placed in a geography class with seniors. Getting an A in the class among upper classmates cemented his reputation as weird.

"Take your seats and quiet, please," Ms. Johnson-Corinth stated, as always, like a recording before she previewed the reading of essays.

"Historically, the definition of theft has changed, although it has always been used to describe the socially unacceptable seizure of lands or goods. For instance, in pioneer times, stealing land from indigenous people was acceptable, while someone taking a chicken from their neighbor to feed their starving family was not. Your history assignment over the weekend was to write an essay with an example of how the definition of theft has changed over time."

Ms. Judith Johnson-Corinth was in her fourth year of teaching American history. Her mission was to prepare students for successful lives in an enlightened society. She found her biggest obstacle was parents who clung to archaic ideas. Her home partnership was with a man, but she chose to keep her mother's preferred name. It was often whispered around school that she spent a lot of time with the principal, but Adam ignored the gossip.

Ms. Johnson-Corinth was troubled this morning. Her mother had called the previous night, casually, but obviously to make a point, mentioning her neighbor babysitting a new granddaughter. Judith ignored the hint. Her mate and she agreed—the teeter-totter of environmental balance on planet Earth could not handle more humans. And how would they balance their mortgage payments, club memberships, and humanist donations with the cost of soccer camp? No, she had eighteen adolescents in her history class—they were her children and responsibility. The mission that had been drilled into her at the university was to teach children what to think, not how to think.

Terresa was the third student called upon to stand before the class and read her essay.

> In olden times, the mode of transportation was sacrosanct. Your horse was not only your means to the general store but often the animal became your pet. Punishment for taking another person's horse was brutal, sometimes the penalty involved a rope.
>
> Today we see the need for transportation differently. Often the person who would take your car has greater

need than you do. Cars can be tracked; they will be returned, and don't become pets. If you can afford the car payment, you can probably afford a bus ride. Low penalties and no bail for car theft are signs of the enlightened times in which we live.

"That was very good, Terresa. I particularly like your use of a word some may not know, *sacrosanct*. For tomorrow's assignment, everyone shall write a sentence containing the word. Now, Adam, you are next."

As Adam stepped to the front of the room, he heard a few snickers. Many looked forward to his essay, knowing that his independence sometimes would get him into trouble. Others admired the courage he often displayed.

We studied last week in class that Israel stole land from Palestinians, but there never was a nation of Palestine. And we ignore that Israelites had the land first and it was taken from them. Who is the thief and who is the victim depends upon the politics of the day.

As a boy, my dad and grandfather traveled out of state to hunt and fish, should they not have a claim to the lands they went to? Nomadic Stone Age Indians, we are told, had the land they traveled through stolen from them, but in virtually all cases Indians were paid for land they claimed. They traveled through areas to hunt and fish like my father. How can the National Park Service steal the hunting and fishing lands from my father with no compensation?

Boys and girls from my neighborhood loved to play in a nearby area with trees and a creek running through it. The city turned it into a dog park. Now you must have a dog to go there. Is that not theft from boys and girls?

We often hear today that thieves are the modern-day Robin Hoods. Nothing could be further from the truth. Most thieves today do not give to the poor but sell their plunder for gain. Robin Hood returned to the people loot which had been taken from them by the government.

When Adam sat down, the teacher took a deep breath before saying, "Adam, in this class we respect out-of-touch points of view, but besmirching groups will not be tolerated. We do not use the derogatory term *Indians*; we say *Indigenous Americans*. And we do not exclude children by the binary term *boys and girls*. You will attend a series of sensitivity training classes after school starting next Tuesday."

Although a few students tossed Adam approving glances as they left class, they kept their distance. It was as if he had acquired a new variant of COVID-19. Terresa hurried away from her locker as Adam approached at the end of the day. At the Friday night basketball game, it was like he was a pariah with the history teacher observing the student section. Empty seats surrounded him. Terresa's boyfriend again excelled on the court. At halftime, he wondered why he was at the game when he preferred to be at home reading his dad's old western novels. He left.

Adam enjoyed Connie's Sunday School class. In many ways, it was like being in a different world. The day's lesson was that one should obey authority, but only if it did not conflict with God's will. Connie taught truths that made sense, although the students knew taking what they learned in Connie's class to regular school had consequences.

Although no seating assignments were given in Sunday School, Adam sat down beside Terresa, not necessarily out of habit.

"I really enjoyed your essay," she said. "I agreed with all that you said and wish I could speak as courageously."

"Why can't you? I'd love to hear your real ideas."

"Just too dangerous. If I don't get into the right university, my parents will be devastated. All their country club friends' children got into a good school. And Dad says my behavior in school might influence whether his hardware store is audited by the IRS."

After church, Adam helped his mother clean the kitchen table when his dad left for his auto body shop to catch up on paperwork. Adam announced, "I'm biking to the stables for the afternoon to ride Chester."

Adam's dad grew up on a farm where his parents kept a horse, not for farm work but it was part of the farm, he often said. Although their home was on a double lot, no way could they keep a horse. Five years earlier, Adam's dad had purchased a horse and kept it at a stable south of town. When Adam took up riding also, his dad bought half interest in another horse so they could ride together. Sometimes his parents would go riding together, but his younger sister had no interest in riding.

"No, you are not. It's over ten miles away," his mother declared.

"Why not? I've ridden my bike there before?"

"Not anymore. In February, you'll get your driver's license. Until then, someone must take you and I can't today."

"I'm fifteen. When Davy Crockett was twelve, he was indentured to a cattle driver and found his over a hundred miles way home from Virginia."

"Well, you're not Davy Crockett and times are different. Remember, a neighbor turned in the parents of two children who were allowed to walk unaccompanied three blocks to a park last year. They were forced to spend thousands on legal fees to keep custody of the children from DCFS."

"I thought when I got older I could do more, not less."

"That's just the way it is. Learn to live with it as we all must."

Adam huffed, but knew it was fruitless to argue. Changing the subject, he asked, "Do you think I have the Napoleon complex?"

"Who told you that? You are not that short. Ignore them, but I must ask, how did you respond to that?"

"I told them that although Napoleon was generally described as five feet two, French inches were longer than English inches. He was the equivalent of five feet six in English measurement, no shorter than the average Frenchman of the time."

With that answer, she understood why some would say he had the Napoleon complex. It had nothing to do with his height. Nevertheless, she was proud of her son and hugged him.

"What are you going to do this afternoon?"

"I found another book in Dad's library titled *Sin Killer* by Larry McMurtry."

"What's it about?"

"It's about an aristocratic Lord Berrybender who finds life boring in England and travels up the Missouri River in 1830, two hundred years ago. He encounters the *Sin Killer,* a part-time preacher, who Berrybender's daughter, Tasmin, falls for."

Monday morning Terresa was early at literature class. Adam sat and immediately asked her how her weekend was. He thought their discussion in Bible school class had broken a barrier and they could become friends. He was wrong; she turned and ignored him. He could feel his heart sink; he scolded himself having mistakenly raised his hopes.

Mx. Bellamy, the teacher, did not ignore him as she/they entered the room. Her eyes immediately focused on Adam. She taught part of the sensitivity training curricula he was to start Tuesday after school. Adam immediately jumped to the conclusion Ms. Johnson-Corinth had advised Mx. Bellamy of Adam's essay. He was right—*There would be hell to pay starting Tuesday.*

Samantha (Sam) Bellamy at her prior school had gone by the honorific of Ms. She felt like it was as generic as it could get, but it felt jarring when someone called her Ms. It was her mother who found a more appropriate nonbinary honorific used in California, Mx. She was in her second-year teaching literature at Adam's North Peoria high school.

Mx. Bellamy wore her dark hair in a crew cut, shorter than most boys. Her clothes were always two sizes too big for her like she'd lost weight, she hadn't. Adam and two friends had bet whether Mx. Bellamy had her hair trimmed at a woman's salon, barbershop, or did it herself. The answer had not been determined.

Once situated at her desk, Mx Bellamy said, "As always, your first assignment Monday morning is to tell us what book you read from last weekend. We'll start at the back of the room."

After a few students named books Adam had never heard of, a boy stood and said he read more chapters of *The Life and Death of Lenin* by Robert Payne.

Mx. Bellamy asked the boy, "What year did Lenin return to Russia after a decade of exile?"

The boy hee-hawed, then answered, "I guess, I haven't got to that part yet."

"He returned in 1917. Next week be prepared to answer more questions about the book," she replied igniting a few muffled snickers. Most knew the boy likely hadn't gotten close to the book, and his effort to impress the teacher with his choice of books had backfired.

Terresa was next and reported she had finished Mitt Romney's *No Apologies.*

"What did his dad do?" Mx. Bellamy asked.

"He was President of American Motors and ran for US President," replied Terresa.

"Very good, Terresa, for choosing to read sanity instead of extremist propaganda. Adam, you are next."

"I'm halfway through *The Sin Killer* by Larry McMurtry."

"Have you read others of the author?"

"Yes, I read *Lonesome Dove* and *The Last Picture Show*."

"How often have I advised students to read a variety of genres? You are stuck in a grove. You are limiting yourself to stories slighting Indigenous Americans and women. To set an example for the class, I'm deducting five percent from your grade."

Adam expected something was coming but not this. He was livid but rational as he controlled his temper well. It struck him that he had nothing to lose but his dignity which he would protect. "May I ask you a question?

Mx. Bellamy didn't answer but kept her eyes on him as he spoke. "Are you a descendant of the Bellamy who was a socialist hypocrite flag salesman and wrote the Pledge of Allegiance?"

She froze standing behind her desk, a pin dropping would have sounded loud in the room until she walked to the door, held it open, and said, "Properly, you say *salesperson* instead of *salesman*. And now you can follow me to the principal's office."

Adam was sure he could hear laughter in the room once the door was closed. He had no regrets.

*"When the road looks rough ahead, remember the 'Man upstairs'*
*and the word 'HOPE.' Hang on to both and 'tough it out.'"*

John Wayne

# ★ CHAPTER 2 ★

The principal had no paddle, could no longer isolate a student for bad behavior, and was restricted from expelling a student as doing so looked bad on their record. He could, however, make note of Adam's behavior on his file to which any university registrar would have access.

"Your parents will be notified of this misbehavior," the principal said.

"I know," Adam replied, showing no regret at having kept his pride.

Adam surmised the reason the dinner table was unusually quiet. After he helped his sister clear the dishes, his sister was told to go to her room and Adam was summoned to the living room.

"Your mother and I received both texts and emails about your behavior at school today. Tell us what happened," his father stated as if talking to a shop employee.

Adam explained in detail what had happened.

"I don't disagree with what you said, but doing so violated the rules. You and I enjoy a game of Ping-Pong. The game has rules; you can't hit the ball twice or after it bounces from the floor. We may not like the rules, but they are there.

If we are to succeed in this culture, we must bite our tongue at times. I should have fired an employee for showing up drunk this morning, but doing so would have cost me God only knows what in legal fees. We must weigh the costs of our actions, whether right or wrong. We may know what is right, but, unfortunately, right does not set the rules."

His mother chimed in, "Son, you must think about college. If your background smells of trouble, you will not be accepted regardless of your grades and high SAT score. If you do get in, you can kiss a scholarship goodbye. Yes, you can get a student loan, but given your father's business, will it ever be forgiven?"

Adam's dad ended the conversation. "You've much to think about. You'll find God throws much at you in life, some you'll consider great gifts, others will be challenges. How you handle them is up to you and will define who you are. It is you who decides what to do with that given to you. Go to your room and ponder your future for the rest of the evening."

It was only seven when Adam's dad sent him to his room for the night to contemplate his situation. He knew his parents were right. He had to stifle the restlessness inside him, which seeped out and got him into trouble, under control.

Rather than kneeling, he lay in bed and looked up asking for guidance. He didn't speak or mouth the words but thought hard and clearly.

> Lord, I know you challenge us and I'm sure it is all for a reason. You have given me the buzz inside but also knowledge that I should control it. Is it like the person with an addiction to alcohol or drugs who struggles to control innate desires? Or is the buzz for telling the truth as I see it part of a gift I must not stifle and use for your glorification?
>
> Please help direct me on the right path.

Adam closed his eyes seeking a sign. *Would he miss it? What if he couldn't interpret a message properly?* So many questions. *Would life always be so confusing? When he was older would all be clearer?*

When he opened his eyes, he saw the Dallas Cowboys poster on his wall. He had hung it there last year. It was a Christmas present from his Uncle Allen who lived in Texas. In a way, it had gotten him in trouble.

Ms. Kelly, his sophomore history teacher, had asked that students wear a t-shirt of their favorite sports franchise and tell the class the history of the city. She set the example by wearing a shirt that had Washington Commanders emblazoned on it and said it was a gift from her cousin who was an FBI agent.

Terresa wore the most common worn Chicago Bears t-shirt and explained that a bear was an image meant to represent market pessimists as their basketball team, the Bulls, represented optimists in a town known for commodity trading. Adam was relieved when Ms. Kelly didn't go into a rant about capitalistic symbols.

When Ms. Kelly had called on Adam, he said the cowboy nickname for Dallas was obvious. He was relieved when she didn't ask him about all the bad things cowboys did.

Then he asked her that given the week prior they had learned Abraham Lincoln said in his Gettysburg Address that the government was of, by, and for the people, how could Washington call themselves *Commanders*. He suggested that *Servants* would be a more appropriate nickname given the intent of our founders.

He was held after class and informed by Ms. Kelly that he received an F for his presentation and was told he needed to follow instructions.

His mind drifted to Terresa. Something about her was confusing to him although he was attracted to her. She obviously had better control of herself than he. Her boyfriend, an average student, only had his height going for him, but it was all he needed. *Would she ever get past the desire to be 'in' among culturally astute girls by having a tall boyfriend, regardless of his intelligence?*

Perhaps once in college she would see boys differently. But she aspired for a better school than the state university he likely would attend. *Would he see her after high school graduation?* They started a great conversation in Sunday school class. *Would they take it a step further on their trips home from college? Would she do the culturally normal thing and drop church like a hot potato once away from home?*

He suddenly realized that his question to Mx. Bellamy about a potential relative was an attempt to impress Terresa. Inadvertently, it was his attachment to Terresa that had gotten him in trouble. He would force thoughts about Terresa from his mind and focus on what was important.

*Was he assuming too much that entrance in the state university was a given for him?*

Adam reached beside the bed for his laptop. He binged the state university entrance requirements. He found the state university was required by the legislature to admit any in-state student with a SAT score of above 1200, the 75th percentile, or with a grade point average in the upper third of the class unless extenuating issues existed.

He could find no listing or definition of what extenuating issues might be. He assumed drug use, violence, felony conviction. *No, drug use would likely not be a disqualification, but thinking outside the accepted paradigms likely was.*

His score on the fall SAT was 1510, which put him in the upper two percent. The high score was not reflected in his grades because of his propensity to challenge teachers, making his class rank uncertain. He was sure his grades were in the upper third; whether they were in the upper ten percent, he was uncertain. Although his high SAT score would normally guarantee entry, the stickler was what admittance personnel might find undesirable traits in his file.

Research confirmed Adam's fear that acceptance at the university would require much more than his high-test score. He had what remained of his junior year and the next year to stifle any intellectual curiosity and become a docile lamb among woke wolves—he would wear a figurative muzzle. He would resolve not to disappoint his parents and do what he must.

His first step would be symbolic. He would take down the Dallas Cowboys poster and replace it with a Cleveland Guardians poster. As Cleveland had dispensed with the improper nickname of Indians, he too would become correct. Perhaps, it was a sign from God when he opened his eyes after prayer on an inappropriate poster.

Then it struck him that one and a half years of compliance might get him into the university, what then? From all he had heard, free thinking at the university was more forbidden than at his high school. It wasn't a year and a half; it would be at least five and a half years, before he could freely speak his mind.

*Would it be over then? Would he need to sift through woke companies to find employment? Had God given him an inquisitive mind to challenge the status quo only to waste it? Or was it a challenge God had given him to avoid the temptation to speak his mind as he was to avoid sinful behavior? Was telling the truth sinful behavior? What kind of a message might he send the culture that enough was enough?*

The more he contemplated his situation, the more depressed he became. Adam sought escapism. He reached for a McMurtry western novel only to reinforce an analogy. In the frontier, wolves feasted on young calves and colts; now it was students away from the influence of their parents who were prey.

Adam's mind wandered. *In pioneer times, and up until a few years ago, it was hard work, creation, and innovation that propelled people upward in society. It was called meritocracy. Now all was stifled, success meant keeping your mouth shut and never questioning proper thought. If people could be programed like a computer, why have people at all? Let AI do it all. Challenging a paradigm meant they would break you. He had great parents but given a chance he would live in a different time. If only he could be one of many characters in a McMurtry novel.*

It was an hour later; the print became blurry as he thought of an escape. He drifted toward unconsciousness, and the book fell from his hands on his lap. He was partially awakened by a bump. Half asleep, another bump –was he dreaming while on his bike? A dream fantasy would be better than the real world. Slowly, he realized the motion wasn't his bike encountering a rough road, but more the motion of a gentle horse lope. The dream had him on a horse not a bike. *The dream was replacing his disappointment of being denied an afternoon at the stable.*

It then struck Adam how the realization that a dream was a dream as it was happening was beyond anything he had ever experienced. If you knew you were dreaming, how could a nightmare ever scare a person?

Gradually, another sensory function was added to the feeling of a horse's lope. A cotton- filled view opened before him. Dense fog was obscuring what lay in front of him. But it was daylight, and the fog was lifting. He expected to soon see the familiar riding trail around the stable before him.

The view became clearer from the sky down. First, he saw blue sky sprinkled with cirrus clouds, then a distant tree line. The trees were tall pine and birch with a purplish mountain range on the far horizon. Neither existed around the stable near Peoria. Then a vast expanse of prairie opened before him, speckled with mysterious dark spots. As the contrast in his vision sharpened, the dark objects became clearer. It was a herd of cattle spread across the prairie, most with their heads down meandering in no pattern in methodic consumption of grass.

It was as if he willed his conscience knowledge of reality, in which he had sulked in bed, away in an inaccessible part of his mind and he fully entered a new reality. Slowly, worry about the trauma of high school not only dissipated but left his memory.

He found himself sitting on a western saddle mounted on a chestnut horse, not his dad's bay gelding. The horse on which he sat stood on a slight rise. Looking down at a herd of cattle, he saw six riders on horseback surrounding the cattle.

Adam felt vibrations of a rider approaching from behind before he heard a cowboy stop beside him. The last remnants of what was his past disappeared when he saw the rider wore a hat, not a riding helmet. The hat was not a Hollywood western hat with the sides turned up for lighting effects. It was a broad-rimmed faded brownish hat with the rim frayed and sweat stains around the headband. A scabbard hung from the saddle with a rifle handle protruding from it. The cowboy wore not jeans but beige corduroy pants. What Adam assumed was a six-shooter rode high on a belt around his waist, not hanging halfway down his leg as represented in legend.

Suddenly, Adam realized he should take stock of himself. A hat was on his head. The size and shape he couldn't see, but by the way it blocked the high sun, it was ample.

Gray heavy pants covered his legs, the material he didn't know, but it was safe to assume it wasn't polyester. On his left side, hung a pistol of some kind. It was real and on the correct side, he was left-handed. Looking further down, he saw the toe of a worn brown boot in a stirrup. He wiggled his foot. It was his.

The cowboy beside him, having caught Adam gazing at his boots, gave him a strange look and said, "I warned you to have that bootmaker make you a bigger size."

"Where's my dad?" Adam asked, not knowing why.

"He said to tell you he left a day early before snow came in. Think it's time to get this herd to a fresh pasture in the next valley?"

Adam didn't answer but took in the expanse of the valley before him.

The cowboy prodded Adam, "Remember what your dad told you last night, *It is you who is in charge of what you've been given.* I was spectin him to leave me in charge, but he didn't. I spect it had something to do with whiskey and me."

"Looks like enough grass left in this valley for a couple days. We'll move the herd then," Adam answered.

"You're the boss. I'll spread the word."

As the cowboy trotted off, Adam rode around the perimeter of the valley in which the herd was spread. The first two cowboys he rode past nodded at him. He nodded back. The third cowboy wasn't wearing a broad brimmed hat but a bowler type, the style the piano player in a saloon wore in western movies. The smallish hat accentuated hair hanging to his shoulders.

"We've not met. I'm called Hairy, because of my…well, you can see…and already figured, I suspect. Foreman Hank hired me yesterday," the man said to Adam.

Adam had now learned that the cowboy who rode up behind him was Hank, the range foreman. Hairy was a new hire, and he was the son of the owner and now boss in his dad's absence. It was a start, but he needed to learn more before he was found to be the fake intruder he was.

"Thanks, Sky, see you at supper time," another cowboy hollered at what appeared to be a chuckwagon as Adam rode up.

Adam climbed down from his chestnut, and although he couldn't see anyone, spoke into the wagon, "Sky, any coffee left?"

He was shocked when the tallest ebony-skinned man he'd ever seen crawled out of the opening. The cook's name fit.

"Yep, get you some. Morning okay? Any strays last night?"

"None that I know of," Adam cautiously answered.

With a tin cup of coffee in hand, Adam sat on one of two boards placed over wooden barrels. He took a big sip of lukewarm coffee and got a mouthful of coffee grounds. From reflex, he spit.

"Sorry, I shoulda warned you, end of pot," Sky said, as he picked the other board up and started to put it in the wagon.

"Why are you loading the wagon?"

"Hank says we're movin to the next valley."

"Not for a couple days," Adam answered, hoping he hadn't made a telling mistake.

"I'm all for that, move enough," Sky replied.

Sky sat on a barrel without saying more. It gave Adam an idea.

"Sky, no one has more interaction with the cowboys in this outfit than you do. I've got an opinion of all. Be good to have another viewpoint. Tell me what you think of them one by one."

Sky, who obviously loved to talk or perhaps gossip, went on to give his impression of each cowboy. To Adam's delight, each time Sky gave his impression of a cowboy, he glanced in the cowboy's direction. Adam hoped he could remember it all and keep each description linked to the cowboy and horse Sky nodded toward.

*"Experience is not what happens to a man. It is, what
a man does with what happens to him."*

Aldous Huxley

# ★ CHAPTER 3 ★

After terrible-tasting coffee and gleaning information from Sky, Adam rode to the ridge around the valley and looked at each cowboy surrounding the herd, replaying in his head their name and Shy's description of them. Beside Sky, there were six: Hank, Fancy, Herman, July, Clint, and Hairy. It was not unlike remembering numbers on some game starting with S, sodka or something he played on a lighted box. *Where did that thought come from?* He wondered. *Games on lighted boxes—what a crazy thought.*

A rider was approaching Adam on a sorrel. Sky had identified him as July who had suffered a major family tragedy. He was dressed better than the rest of the hands. At least his clothes were less worn— a buckskin jacket, and a low rodeo style hat which looked new with no sweat stains. The low crown and large brim tended to be worn by those who wished not to be noticed.

Adam wondered how he knew that. *Perhaps, he was well-knowledged in cowboy attire from experience, and he'd just had a memory lapse, maybe fallen off his horse and struck his head.*

His speculation was interrupted when July asked, "Do you think the winter will be much tougher here than in Casper?"

*Ah,* Adam thought, *we must be north of Casper, Wyoming, but how far? In the northern part of the state? Montana or possibly Alberta or Saskatchewan?* "I suspect we should prepare for a somewhat harsher winter," Adam answered.

July turned, inspecting the blanket rolled behind him. "I hope I brought enough blankets. What is Sky fixing for supper?"

"I didn't ask him, but it was starting to smell good."

"Hank said we're not moving for a couple days."

"That's right."

"I hope we move to that valley further from town. It'd prevent some problems," July stated.

"We'll see," Adam answered before riding off to avoid more questions.

All but two of the cowboys, who were tending the herd, were lined up for chow when Adam rode up. He had already decided that the need to check the right flank of the herd would cause him to leave if he became uncomfortable. Ample amounts of beef were in the bean stew. It was better than Adam expected, and the vigor with which the cowboys ate prevented conversation.

July was the first to put his plate down and pull a gold pocket watch from his vest. He opened the cover and stared at it.

Hank gave him a dissatisfied look and said, "If'n I'd lost a wife, and two children like you in a house fire, I'd be sad too, but don't bring the rest of us down every chowtime. Go sulk elsewhere."

July ignored Hank and kept his attention on the watch cover, which Adam rightly assumed held a picture of his family.

Hank continued to address July, "You being a banker en all, how about a loan when we move closer to town tomorrow?"

"Yeh, I could use one too," Fancy added.

"I told you, I'm no longer a banker. But if I was, I wouldn't loan you two money. You'd both blow it on gambling and women."

"That right," Herman jumped in the conversation. "They are both sins. It says so right here," he added holding up the Bible.

Fancy ignored Herman and said to Hank, "I think we made a mistake nicknaming Horace Covington, the uppity banker, July just because he showed up here in July.

"Enough, enough," Adam declared. "Leave him alone. And don't worry about going to town until Sunday because we're moving to a valley further from town tomorrow."

"Some girls in Great Falls will be greatly disappointed," commented Fancy.

"I think they can wait for the weekend," Adam answered, having discovered that they were in Montana with the mention of Great Falls.

Before breakfast the next morning, Adam saw Hank, Fancy, and Clint milling around the town side of the herd looking at the ground.

"Looks like there were two of them and they got dozen head and are heading off yonder," Hank pointed.

Adam circled the tracks, having no idea how Hank determined rustlers got away with a dozen head rather than six or twenty.

Hank stated matter-of-factly, "Fancy and me better head after them. Your dad tolerates no rustlers. We'll give them a proper hanging."

Adam didn't ask what entailed a 'proper' hanging but suspected it didn't involve a sheriff. "No, we need you to stay with the herd as we move them. Fancy, you and Clint go after them."

Hank said nothing but galloped off in frustration. After they successfully moved the herd to another valley, still peeved that he had to stay, Hank complained at supper, "You should know that I'm heading to town late Saturday afternoon since Great Falls is farther now. Likely won't be back until Monday morn."

"Just make sure you're back in condition to work," Adam replied.

All had mounted after breakfast the next morning, when Hairy was heard hollering, "Yee Haw."

At a distance, two riders could be seen bringing in cattle. Adam counted twelve head as Hank predicted.

"Did you get them hung?" asked Hank.

"No, the cattle were spooked. We were afraid we'd lose them and had to let the rustlers go. Expected getting the cattle back were our first charge."

"So, what did you do for the night?" Adam asked.

"It was dark, too dangerous to drive them. We put them in a ravine."

"And what did you do?" asked Hank.

"We were so close to the falls and hungry, thought we better get nourished."

"What happened to the right side of your face?" Adam asked Clint, noticing a bruise covering half of it.

"I've told him an old man like him should watch his mouth at a bar, but he doesn't list'n," Fancy answered as Clint hung his head.

"And where were you, Fancy?" Hank inquired.

"Susie and I were getting reacquainted."

Adam, at fifteen years of age with no experience in cattle, saloons, or women, knew not what to say. Clint was old enough to be his grandfather. Why he would pick a fight with a younger cowboy Adam didn't understand. He simply shook his head and told them, "You got the cattle back and didn't get in much trouble. Go have some breakfast now."

"When do you think your dad will be back?" asked Hank at supper.

"I don't know. He hardly told me he was leaving," Adam answered, knowing he wouldn't recognize his dad if he rode into camp.

Sky added, "The boss man said he wouldn't be back until late spring. He was looking forward to a Texas winter for a change."

"If he doesn't get back until late spring, he'll miss the branding and work on the young bulls. It is a tradition that the boss man ropes the first calves. I guess that's something you'll need to carry on, Adam," observed Hank.

Adam had seen Hank rope a stray calf from a distance while galloping. It was a feat he would expect to see at a Wild West show. If his dad had set the example, he would have been better than Hank. And Hank had ten years' experience cowboying. Adam had never tried throwing a rope.

*With winter setting in, how many months did he have to master roping?* Adam wondered. If not exposed as a tenderfoot know-nothing before, roping would be the telltale sign he was out of place. He had noticed a rope hanging from his saddle. He would discreetly practice when he had an opportunity.

"Just to remind you, tomorrow is Saturday. I'm heading for town mid-afternoon and need my pay by then," Hank announced.

"Me too," chimed in Fancy.

"I'll take care of it," answered Adam. All he had learned from Sky was that his dad said Adam was to be in charge, and he expected the herd to remain intact. Sky had handed Adam the key to the box under the chuck wagon seat, but what to pay to whom, Adam had no idea.

The next morning after breakfast Adam opened the lock box. He was shocked by the combination of coins and bills. It was more than he expected, but the best find was a note from his dad with each of the hands' wages on it. The note also told him to be courageous, learn quickly, and fear not. By the sun's position—what he assumed was a couple hours after noon—he gave Fancy and Hank their wages. They rode off in a hurry. He would pay the others at suppertime.

Winter was setting in. How long they would be in the valley, Adam didn't know, but he gave Hairy, Clint, and Sky the task of setting up tents, then climbed on his chestnut, not wanting to disclose that he knew nothing of tents.

Out of sight, he pulled the rope from his saddle. He fumbled with it until he had a loop and tried tossing at nothing. It got tangled halfway to nothing and fell. *It would be easier for a beginner off the horse,* he thought. For an hour, he got nowhere attempting to rope an old rotten stump.

When Adam returned to camp, two tents were set up with the openings facing each other. In the short space between the tent openings, the trio were in the process of ringing a firepit with rocks. One fire to warm both tents, Adam thought it was ingenious. He would have never thought of it, but he had no experience with tents anytime, let alone in a Montana winter.

As they sat around the fire at suppertime, July opened his pocket watch.

"You know the time, but do you know the date?" Adam asked.

"I do," Herman answered for July. "I keep a calendar in the back of my Bible. Today is the fifteenth day of November. I suppose it'll be another couple of weeks before we move into winter quarters," he added, giving Adam another clue about the operation.

July hadn't taken his eyes from his pocket watch cover.

"Mind if I have a look?" Adam asked.

July handed Adam his pocket watch. The miniature photo was of a woman sitting with a child on her lap and a six to eight-year-old daughter standing close. "You were blessed with a beautiful family, you were lucky to have had them," Adam remarked, not knowing what to say.

"I wouldn't say blessed. The Lord stole them from me, the opposite of blessed."

Herman chimed in, "Be careful what you say, The Lord doesn't take blasphemy well."

"Shut up, you religious retard. You're not living my shoes," July retaliated.

"Hey! Hey. Hey, stop it now. We'll have no fighting in camp," Adam interjected.

Herman picked up his Bible and went into a tent.

Hoping talk about the disaster would show compassion and lessen July's grieving, Adam asked, "Do you know how the fire started?"

"Chimney fire, my fault. I should have had it cleaned. Guess I killed them. Told the sheriff, but he wouldn't arrest me. Couldn't stand to be in the town any longer, thought cowboying would help."

Adam didn't know how to reply and got up to gather more wood for the fire. When he returned, Hairy had picked up his ukulele and was humming a tune. Although Adam didn't recognize the tune, it was soothing to all.

Sunrise wasn't early in mid-November Montana, likely 7:30-plus guessed Adam. It was at least two hours later; he saw riders approaching the valley. It was Fancy and Hank. They looked unusually happy having partied and done God only knew what for two nights.

"Well, I see you made it, and neither appear to be beaten up. Should I congratulate you?" Adam teased.

"Yes, you should. Fortune was with me at the poker table," he said, patting his saddle bag. "I turned one week's wages into a half year."

"Where did you spend the night?"

Fancy answered, "A few miles outside Great Falls. Susie and I were watching the game when a couple players got concerned the cards were marked and started inspecting them."

"Were they?" Adam looked at Hank.

"They couldn't find any markings, but once players get suspicious it's a good time to pack up."

"You didn't answer my question."

"No, they weren't."

Fancy added, "We rode into town separately so no one would guess we knew each other. When Susie nodded me about the guy's bluff hand across the table and I tipped Hank, it was helpful, right Hank?"

Adam gave them both a frown. "Hopefully, I don't have to bail you two out of jail someday, and don't expect me to pay for your burial."

"Hank tipped Susie and I both well, well enough Susie said she could take a couple days off." Fancy reached over and slapped Hank on the back. "Thank you, buddy."

It was mid-afternoon when two strange riders rode in. "We tracked a couple guys here. Did you have a couple hands in town last night?" one asked Adam.

"Why?"

"We found out one was a friend of a saloon girl who stood behind me at the table last night after I bought her a drink. Then she pretended she was with me."

"So?"

"Must I spell it out for you?"

The cowboys could tell from expressions exchanged that all was not well. Fancy and Hank rode up joined by Hairy and Clint. Two positioned themselves on each side of Adam facing the intruders.

"Looks like what we have here are a pair of sore losers," stated Hank. "It's a shame you rode all the way out here only to chance losing something else."

The pair, who had ridden in, noticed the hands of four cowboys they faced moving closer to their pistol handles. Nothing was said for some time as the pair calculated their odds. The reality of the standoff determined a loss of money was more tolerable than the loss of something irreplaceable.

Finally, one said, "Better get back in town before dark."

At supper, Hank asked, "You okay with me putting a bag of winnings in the box? Better than carrying it around."

After eating Hank grabbed a shovel from the wagon and started digging a hole a hundred feet from the tents. "What are you doing?" Adam asked.

"A few years ago, I had a big winning and boss man suggested we have a hole available if riders came in. We could toss the box in and cover it quickly if need be."

*"You must train your intuition—you must trust the small voice inside you which tells you exactly what to say, what to decide."*

Ingrid Bergman

# ★ CHAPTER 4 ★

Adam and the cowboys had finished Sky's breakfast. It was unusual as the breakfast included a sage hen that Hank had shot the day before instead of beef. They were saddling their horses when Adam noticed July riding at a gallop toward the chuck wagon. It was not strange for whoever was assigned night watch duty to be anxious for breakfast, but his pace drew everyone's attention.

"Five gone," July exclaimed as he rode in camp.

"Five gone where?" Adam asked.

"Over there," July pointed. "Tracks show five head driven off by one on horseback and a man on foot."

"Eat your breakfast, July. Clint, you, and Hank come with me, and we'll check it out."

"Guys don't be late for supper. I'm fixin biscuits and beef gravy," declared Sky.

Adam noticed before Hank mounted, he reached into the chuck wagon for a rope and laid it on top of his lariat.

Adam picked Clint because he was the best tracker among them. After riding around the tracks, he declared, "July was right. Five head herded off by someone light on horseback and a big man by the size of his footprints. He must be well over six feet tall."

They followed the tracks over the ridge across a depression along a stream. No effort had been made to conceal their tracks; even inexperienced Adam could follow the tracks.

"It appears they want to be followed," observed Clint. "They are purposely riding on soft ground when they could be riding over the stream-side gravel and make tracking more difficult."

"Why would they do that?" Adam asked.

Hank answered, "They's wantin to be followed. Ambush. I advise we spread out and move carefully, check behind each tree."

Their pace slowed by half as they moved with caution, following the meandering stream what must have been a couple miles, until it branched into two streams. "Over here," Clint hollered.

Both Adam and Hank drew their six-shooters and trotted to a clearing. Adam had no idea why he drew his gun, never having shot one, but it seemed the thing to do. Instead of finding rustlers, four head of cattle were lazily grazing in the clearing's tall grass.

Cautiously, they rode the perimeter searching for the rustlers and found nothing. When Hank joined Adam back at the clearing, Adam said, "Maybe Clint was mistaken and there were only four head taken and the rustlers thought better of their theft and left."

"Clint knows what he seen," Hank answered.

"I got something," they heard Clint declare from the other side of the stream. It looked like a heavy tree branch had been dragged from the water. "It's an attempt to cover tracks of one cow brute, a rider, and a man on foot. They left the four head hoping we'd be satisfied and not look too hard."

Adam got off his chestnut and knelt by the water, studying the tree branch scratches in the mud as they came from the stream. The water was still, like a mirror. In the water reflection, a cowboy was looking at him. He realized it was himself.

"Are you going to stare at your reflection in the water all day or are we going to get these rustlers?" Hank asked.

Unlike their earlier trail, the rustlers now were traveling in hard-to-track places, over rock beds and hard ground. Clint's sharp eye for turned rocks, a twisted leaf, or a low-hanging branch broken kept them on the trail. After a couple miles of meandering trail with the rustlers sometimes doubling back to confuse any trackers, the tree limb they were dragging lay beside the trail. Their path became apparent as they obviously had assumed anyone following them had given up. Without Clint's eye for details, Hank and Adam would have abandoned the pursuit.

A few hundred yards from the discarded tree limb, Clint, who was riding ahead of Adam and Hank, stopped and held his hand up. "I hear something," he whispered. Neither Adam nor Hank could hear anything, but they all dismounted, tied their horses, and cautiously walked forward. Adam glanced at the rustlers' encampment from behind a tree.

He saw a big man lying with his head propped up on a saddle. He was humming a tune that Adam didn't recognize as he sipped from a whiskey bottle. A smaller man was in the process of butchering a steer. Adam's family brand, the rocking D, was apparent on the steer's hind quarter. A lean-to consisting of a canvas was draped from a log suspended by two tree branches. From the debris scattered around and a well-used firepit lined with stone, he surmised that they had made camp there for some time.

All three men backed away from the camp to strategize the capture. "Just two, one is distracted butchering, and the other is on the way to being drunk, let's just walk in and take them," said Clint.

"Must use more caution. We don't know who may be under that lean-to. I won't walk into a trap," said Hank.

"All right let's be careful. I'll circle around behind that big Ponderosa Pine. You guys spread out here," strategized Adam.

"No, we'd be forming a circular firing squad. We can spread out, but all stay on the same side facing that lean-to," Hank corrected Adam.

Adam knew immediately Hank was right.

Once all three were in position, Hank hollered out, "You with the steer drop the knife. You with the whiskey bottle keep it in your hand. Movement behind that lean-to canvas will cause us to poke it full of holes. Any other activity will save us using a rope."

When the small man dropped his knife and the big man held his bottle to his side and quit humming, the three stepped from behind trees. As they had planned, Clint kept his focus on the small man, Adam on the canvas lean-to, and Hank on the big man.

"Anyone in that lean-to?" Hank asked the big man.

The man jerked his head toward the lean-to, hoping to draw Hank's attention to it, and frantically reached for his Winchester Model 1866 which lay behind him. Hank did not fall for the distraction. Hank's first shot struck him in the shoulder, causing him to drop the bottle, but he continued to swing the rifle in front of him as Hank's second bullet entered his right ventricle.

In shock, he looked up at Hank, now standing above him, as the life spark left the man's eyes. His corpse appeared to stare out at nothing, perhaps it was regret for the life he had lived. In the afterlife, he entered eternal damnation for many infractions of which rustling was only one.

"Glad he went for it, cause I only brought one rope," Hank said.

The smaller man's hat rested low on his ears covering much of his face. Clint reached for it and tossed it aside. As he did, a flock of long hair fell halfway to the person's waist. It was a woman.

"Explains why the horse tracks were shallow. She was riding and he was walking," explained Clint.

Keeping his gun on the lean-to, Adam walked up to the woman. Her left eye was blackened such that it covered half her face.

"What happened to you?" Adam asked.

She didn't answer, but looked at the big man whose body was in the process of assuming the cool air temperature.

"Let's get on with it," Hank said. "I don't want to be late for supper. Sky is fixin my favorite—biscuits and beef gravy."

Clint lifted the woman by her arm and led her to her horse. Hank had the rope he picked up in the chuck wagon in hand and was ready to toss it over a hickory limb.

"No, she's a woman," Adam stated the obvious and following a voice inside of him that said hanging her was wrong.

"Yeh, and a cattle thief also," Hank replied, as the rope fell over the limb.

"No, please," she pleaded, nodding toward the canvas lean-to when Clint hoisted her on her horse. Clint tied the horse to a limb and the three men guardedly approached the lean-to with guns drawn.

Adam picked up a stick in his left hand and was preparing to lift the canvas when they heard a dog growl. "If anyone is in there, better come out before we start a shootin," Hank stated.

Hearing nothing, Adam lifted the canvas with his stick. Sitting with their backs tight against a tree were two children. A rat terrier sat in front of them intent upon protecting them. The girl had bushy fiery red hair that didn't appear to have ever seen a brush. Adam guessed her at thirteen. Something about her seemed familiar. What appeared to be her younger brother huddled close to her.

"Are these your parents?" Adam asked, waving his hand toward the dead man and woman on the horse.

The girl mumbled and pointed to the woman they'd put on the horse to hang. "Just Mommy."

"Enough, let's get on with it. We've a long ride back to camp," insisted Hank as he hastily tied a loop at the end of the rope, not bothering to properly give it thirteen wraps.

Adam caught the mother's gaze at her children—it signified resignation to her fate and concern for her children. It was a glance to remember them by. The children seemed oblivious to what was about to happen to their mother before their eyes.

"No, we will not do this," protested Adam, now following a louder voice inside him.

"Are you willing to signal to all wildering ruffians that stealing cattle from our herd is fine? Your dad wouldn't tolerate it."

"Haven't you noticed there are two children here, and this is their mother?"

"She should have thought of that before wearing men's clothes, thieving, then butchering our steer."

Adam felt his back straightening ready to step out on a limb. "My dad left me in charge here, not you. You may hang her under one of two conditions. You take these children east until you find the nearest orphanage and leave them with your poker winnings to pay for their keep, or you bring them into our camp and take full responsibility caring for them, which means no weekend trips to town for you."

The glare from Hank was hard for Adam to take, but he drew on what was festering inside him and met it until Hank broke and pulled the rope from the tree, coiled it, mounted, and left.

Clint's look shifted from Hank to Adam and back. "Go ahead, but save some biscuits for me," Adam told him. "I'll finish here."

The woman was still shaking as Adam pulled her from the horse. "What's your name?"

"Mildred."

"Get your knife and finish cutting the hind quarters off that beef," he told her as he picked up her man's Winchester and put it on his saddle.

"You can come out now. No one will hurt you," Adam said to the children. He stopped himself from asking their names. *It was better to keep his distance*, he thought.

With the hind quarters separated from the carcass, he tied the hoofs together, then tossed one over the back of his horse and mounted.

"Don't ever do that again," he told Mildred.

She glanced at the remainder of the carcass. He responded to her unsaid question, "I can't carry that, so take care of your children."

He had started away when he heard a wolf howl. Adam reached for the Winchester, unloaded it in his hand, dumped the cartridges on the ground in front of the woman and tossed the rifle toward her. "Use it wisely."

It was past dark when Adam rode into camp. "Any biscuits and gravy left?"

"Sure, I saved some for you," Sky answered then asked, "Are those beef hind quarters you are carrying?"

"Yep," he answered. "I thought you could find a use for them."

Hank didn't look at Adam, said it was his night to watch the herd, mounted, and left.

When Hank was gone, Clint said to Adam, "Just want you to know. You did the right thing. He'll get over it."

*"All life is an experiment. The more experiments you make, the better."*

Ralph Waldo Emerson

# ★ CHAPTER 5 ★

"Got a list in my head of supplies we need next week when you head to the falls," Sky said at breakfast.

Adam had learned that Sky and Hank couldn't read or write. He retrieved a graphite pencil, which later came to be called a lead pencil, from his bag and made note of the supplies.

"Where'd you learn write'n?" Clint asked.

"Dad taught me some," he answered before thinking.

"Couldn't have teached you much, could hardly write himself."

"I had some schooling," Adam answered, trying to be vague.

"I suppose your mother sent you there in those years you were away with her," Clint observed, giving Adam a big piece of his missing life puzzle.

"We should start marking the twenty head we will take to the railroad pens. When are we taking them?" asked Hank. It had taken a few days, but Hank was over his frustration at being refused use of the rope on the woman rustler. It was not that he would have gotten pleasure from hanging a woman. It was just the way he was accustomed to protecting the herd. Although he was not the boss, ten years with the herd had made it an unreplaceable part of his life.

"We'll leave tomorrow," Adam answered.

"Do you want to mark the animals to go?" asked Hank.

"You know what we usually take—go ahead and mark them. I'm going to ride and check out any herds that may be around us," Adam answered.

"Last month I had to stay with the herd; this month I get to go to town with y'all," Fancy reminded Adam.

"Yeh, the devil has you for sure. You not wait to sin more," Herman responded.

"Bible man, you ever wonder why God gave us horses and legs? It was so we could move. We were given other parts too," Fancy replied to agitate him.

"He also gave us the ability to make guns. That doesn't mean we should all shoot each other," Herman answered.

Adam stopped the conversation that was bound to escalate. "That's enough, get mounted. We've work to do."

As they started saddling horses, Adam asked Herman, the date keeper, "What do you have today?"

"Twenty-sixth of November," he answered.

Little by little Adam had acquired details of the outfit's routine. At every month's end, twenty head were driven to the railway in Great Falls and sold to a buyer for shipment to the packing houses in Chicago. Culled were the fattest steers and oldest cows. His dad had been adamant that the herd be kept at its present size so they wouldn't over graze their winter quarters.

The men were looking forward to the winter quarters move which was usually made in the first week of December. Early cold was starting to set in and the fire between tents in the present valley was not ample. The move was twenty miles in an arc around Great Falls to a valley not grazed in the summer, allowing cattle to consume tall grasses through snow cover. A log cabin identified the winter grazing valley as belonging to the outfit. On the way back from selling cattle and resupplying in Great Falls, Adam planned to check out the cabin and winter quarters. He deemed it better to acquaint himself with winter quarters while alone to avoid revealing his newcomer status. But a problem remained—he did not know the location of the winter quarters.

The cowboys saw Adam ride off to check their perimeter. What they didn't know was he doubled back and behind a cluster of trees and watched the hands mark and cull twenty head they would take to town the next day. Some information about how things were done could be gleaned from conversations at camp; other information he had to see. Watching, he learned how the monthly twenty were separated from the herd. Out of sight, he tried his hand with the lariat again. He had been watching others rope but was no better than the first time he tried it.

The next morning Hank, Fancy, Hairy, and Adam were mounted when the sun peeked above the eastern mountain top. Adam had made note that the sunrise and set were slowly creeping north from straight east.

Adam let Hank ride lead on the twenty head they had separated, and he rode drag leading a pack horse. If Hank thought it was to make up for their disagreement about the woman rustler, he was wrong. Adam wouldn't have been able to find his way into town, but Hank would show him.

Fancy rode up as Adam was using his graphite pencil on parchment from the saddlebag. "What are you scratching there?" he asked.

"Just making notes of our activity. Dad will appreciate a good record when he returns," Adam lied. He was drawing a map of the surrounding mountain tops relative to their position for future reference.

By the time they reached the railway pens in Great Falls, the cattle were docile and easily driven into a pen. Negotiations hadn't changed, Adam assumed. He asked for ten percent more than the first buyer offered. Within an hour, he accepted a lesser offer.

He put the cash in the inside pocket of his vest and led the pack horse to the general store.

"Haven't seen you around here before," the shopkeeper's daughter asked.

She was dressed as properly as could be seen in the town, wearing a calico green patterned dress with her hair perfectly rolled and bunched under a small bonnet. Her demeanor was as straight and proper as her dress.

Adam decided on next month's supply trip he would pay more attention to the condition of his clothes. Once all on his supply list was sorted and placed by the door, she started tallying the bill as he viewed the display cases.

"Can I get you anything else?" she asked.

"What must you have for this pocket watch?" he pointed to one in the case.

She pulled it from the case and handed it to him. "This is the latest high-quality watch from the best maker in the country, Elgin Watches, made near Chicago, Illinois. It is a treasure for any man who chooses to carry it. If you have family, a picture can be placed under the gold-plated cover."

"And?" he asked again.

"For you, since you bought all these supplies, it'll only be eight dollars. It's usually ten."

"What is the tally with that?" Adam reached into his vest pocket and pulled out a roll of bills and counted out what she asked for. As she watched him, he could see her demeanor change. A stolid business facial expression became a smile.

"Oh, my name is Emily Doyle. My dad is Elmer." Her look nearly demanded he reciprocate.

"I'm Adam, Adam Duval. Glad to meet you, Ms. Doyle," he answered nervously, given her flirtatious smile.

"I'm sure we'll be meeting again, Mr. Duval."

With all the supplies loaded on the pack horse, the pocket watch in his right-side pocket and less money in his left, he was focused on his next stop instead of on Emily. As he started down the street, she stood at the door and said, "Now you come back anytime you are in town."

He wasn't looking forward to the next stop at the saloon in which he had no experience. Hank, Fancy, and Hairy had taken off to the saloon as soon as the cattle were penned. Avoiding the saloon was not the image he wanted to convey. He took a deep breath as he stepped into the saloon.

Hank and Hairy were sitting at different poker tables. Adam learned later that cowboys from the same outfit at the same table were forbidden. It was a temptation for cheating. Fancy was whispering sweet nothings into a saloon girl's ear at a corner table. Adam stepped up to the bar at a distance from a well-dressed man.

"What'll it be?" the woman behind the bar asked.

"Whiskey, Ms. Kitty," he answered, before he caught himself not knowing why he had called her that and fearing that he would be asked for something about his age. He knew not where either thought had come.

"Whiskey it'll be. My name is Betsy but call me as you wish."

Not knowing a shot of whiskey cost only a bit (twelve and a half cents), Adam tossed a silver dollar on the bar and said, "Refill Hank, Hairy, and Fancy," while pointing at each.

Betsy picked up the dollar and started to say, Boy, that'll do it, but caught herself and said, "Thanks, man."

With his glass of whiskey in hand, he held it up catching his three cowboys' attention. They nodded at him and raised their own. *How bad could it be?* he thought before raising the glass to his mouth and taking more than he intended. It was a nasty taste. Nothing pleasant about it. Mistakenly, he swallowed quickly, thinking doing so would rid his mouth of the taste. It burned all the way down as if it were on fire, and the burn lingered in his stomach. Adam turned quickly back to the bar hoping his watering eyes had not been noticed.

He cautiously took two more sips before he asked Betsy where the outhouse was. He took his whiskey to the alley and dumped the remainder before entering the outhouse he didn't need.

Back at the bar, he heard Hank holler to Betsy, "We're ready for another round." Without asking, she also filled Adam's empty glass.

Adam noticed the floor was filthy. He wondered if ridding himself of whiskey on the floor would be noticed, then decided it was too risky.

Betsy noticed his inspection of the floor and said, "I see you looking at the floor. I know it's a mess. Can't find someone to clean around here, and I don't have time for it. Don't suppose you know of anyone?"

"No."

"Well, if you run into anyone, they could stay in the lean-to by the alley, and I'd feed them."

Adam had only taken two small sips from the refilled glass and was thinking of the outhouse again when Betsy reached for his glass, poured it back into the whiskey bottle and said with a wink, "From experience, I know the look of dislike for whiskey. A little sarsaparilla with water looks like whiskey which I can provide on the QT if you pay for it as whiskey."

He was pleasantly stunned looking at a newly filled glass when the well-dressed man from down the bar slid toward him. "How about a toast to our similar drinks?"

Guardedly, Adam clinked glasses with the man and took a sip. It wasn't bad. In fact, pleasant compared to rotgut whiskey.

"I'm Nate Clements, a new lawyer in town. You are?"

"Adam Duval, I'm running a herd east of town." Immediately, Adam wished he could take his words back. He didn't know where Duval came from. *Was that really his last name?*

"The regulars here think I can handle as much whiskey as anyone, but they don't know the secret of our drink. I'm here to drum up business. There are only two other lawyers in town, both old and one is the county prosecutor, and doesn't defend criminals. Perhaps I can help a fighter get out of jail or help a rancher like you sue a poaching herder."

"So, what brought you to Great Falls?"

"My brother Bob has a law practice in Iowa, but not enough business in the small town for both of us. Besides, if not adventure now, when?"

Twice Betsy refilled their glasses as Nate and Adam visited. Adam stood such that his cowboys could see his refills. On his second glass, he noticed Fancy and the saloon girl had gone, and the table Hank was at was getting rowdy.

"Betsy, I may know someone who needs work. I'll let you know," Adam said, "but from the commotion at that table I better get my hands out of here."

He was offering Nate a goodbye handshake when they heard a bang as a chair hit the floor and words not heard in church were bellowed. Hank and another cowboy were at each other with limbs flying. Most of the wild swings were blocked, but some short punches were landing. The other cowboy's friends were egging him on. Hairy had left his table and was standing by to enter the brawl if need be.

Unwilling to exchange more blows, Hank lunged at the cowboy, sending them both to the floor. As they rolled, chairs were toppled, and tables moved. They were under a table scrambling, hidden from view when a man wearing a silver badge burst through the door.

The sheriff knelt beside the table and held his revolver on them. "That's enough—get out from under there."

Hank stood spitting blood from a cut lip on the floor, which did little to soil the filthy floor. Hairy handed Hank his hat. The combatants exchanged a few nasty glances.

After surveying the place with Betsy, the sheriff said, "You both are lucky—only two broken chairs. What will it cost to fix them?"

"Five dollars apiece," she answered. All knew that it would cost much less, but she would set the rate for damaging her property.

"Each of you will render Betsy five dollars now or end up in jail."

Hairy had gathered Hank's money from the table and handed it to him.

Hank counted his money and handed it to the sheriff. "Here's three dollars and two bits."

"Looks like you're going to jail," he answered.

Adam stepped forward. "I'll pay the balance."

"Who are you?"

"I'm the outfit owner's son. Hank's our trail boss. We don't want to be without him."

He started to reach for his inside vest pocket and caught himself. Too many cowboys of what character he did not know were watching. He pulled two silver dollars from his pants pocket and handed them to the sheriff.

"Fine, but I suggest you control him or jail it will be next time."

Between the other combatant and his friends, they handed the sheriff five dollars. Betsy was delighted with ten dollars for chairs it might cost her a dollar to fix. Fights plus the business they brought were not all bad. It was a good night for her.

The sheriff warned, "Now, here's the deal. You both have two minutes to be on your horse and out of town. And forward, next time you come to this town you will leave your firearm with me or go to jail, understood?"

Hairy was already mounted when Adam followed Hank and his adversary outside. Their horses were tied adjacent to each other. They glanced at each other and stepped toward the other. Adam moved quickly toward them hoping to break up a continuation of the fight. But at three feet apart, they both shook hands.

For the cowboys, the fight accomplished three things: they had maintained their dignity, showed others a price would be paid for trifling with them, and earned respect from the others. The next time they met in a saloon, they would buy each other a drink.

As they rode off, Adam wondered where Fancy was. He found him coming down the stairs without the saloon girl and wearing a smirk on his face heading for the bar. Adam put on a slight stagger, approached him, and said it was time to get back to the herd.

"As much as I saw you drinking, can you ride?" Fancy asked.

"Sure, just tell me which way to our winter quarters, the whiskey made me forget. I got to check it out before we move there."

Adam's plan to play drunk and obtain directions to the winter quarters worked without revealing his naivety. In the street, he gave Fancy his packhorse to take back to camp and headed in the direction Fancy had pointed.

*"It all comes to this: The simplest way to be happy is to do good."*

Hellen Keller

# ★ CHAPTER 6 ★

Following Fancy's directions, Adam rode a little east of due north toward the outfit's winter camp. He guessed it was a little after three by the sun's position; by checking his newly acquired watch he found it was nearly four. His learned estimation of the time by the sun was close. Having the pocket watch was helpful, but he should not depend upon it. The sun was now setting around six. He had two hours to cover twelve-fourteen miles, according to Fancy. He would need to maintain a trot.

The sun was close to the horizon when the three mountain tops to the west Fancy said to watch were nearly lined up, signaling his proximity to the camp. At the next ridge, he saw before him a valley with good grass interspersed between large clumps of bunchgrass. It was the abundance of tall bunchgrass rising above a winter's snow cover which made the valley ideal for wintering a herd.

On the west end of the valley stood the log cabin. Beside it was a longer low-roofed structure Fancy described as a barn. It didn't look like a barn to Adam. To the east of the cabin was a large cattle pen made of birch logs. Before moving on, he made record of all landmarks in route on parchment paper.

Adam dismounted and was stretching his legs from the long ride when he heard noise in the cabin. Noticing the cabin door ajar, he tossed rather than tied his horse reins over a birch log on top of posts which served as a hitchrack in front of the cabin.

Instinctively, he pulled his six-shooter and peered through the open door. Later, he wondered what he would have done had rustlers inhabited the cabin. But two-legged rustlers, they were not. *Marauders* would be a more appropriate term for the family of racoons. When they saw him enter the doorway the mother and five half-grown coons stopped their plundering and froze as if being caught with their paws in a pickle jar.

Adam moved toward the mother. She hissed at him, and he answered with his pistol sending a round through the floor. Inside the cabin, it was louder than he expected. Later, it struck him as funny, seeing all six scampering for the door and knocking each other over as they all tried to escape through the narrow door at the same time.

He heard his horse give a stressful neigh. Standing at the door, he saw coons running one direction and his frightened horse the other. Concerned about the cabin and thinking the journey had tired his horse, he had not tied the reins. The spectacle of wild beasts exiting the cabin had sent the horse galloping away.

All his tack remained on the horse. In near darkness his horse disappeared into the blackness of the coming night. Adam had no choice but to follow the horse. It was pitch dark soon, and he wasn't sure he was headed in the right direction until a full moon rose above a mountaintop, and he saw the horse at a distance.

Back at the cabin he unsaddled the horse, brought his tack inside, and tied the horse securely to the hitch rail with his thirty-foot lariat, giving him ample room to graze the nearby grass for the night.

With dry kindling he found inside the cabin, he pulled a match he purchased from Emily. Then realized she hadn't given him a safety phosphorus-coated strip to strike the match. He struggled starting a fire with his wheel-lock tender. On second inspection of the match, he saw a light blue tip on the match which made it look unlike any he had seen. Frustrated, he scraped it on a rock, and it burst into flame, surprising him. A thought crossed his mind, from where he didn't know, that *some things worked better in the past*. With the kindling ablaze, he added a few split logs from outside the door.

Light from the fire allowed him to survey the sixteen-foot square log cabin. Double bunk beds sat on both sides of the fireplace, a table by the door, an equipment rack along one wall and a counter along another. Up a ladder to a loft, he saw three jail-grade mattresses in disarray, likely from the intruders.

Cramped quarters for sure, but it would keep him and the crew warm in the coming winter. How would Fancy, with few morals, and Herman, the Bible reader, cope with each other in tight quarters? It would be chaotic, but maybe interesting.

Adam had pulled his boots off and stretched out on a lower bunk when the bed count struck him. Seven places to sleep, six hands, and his dad. *Where had he slept, if not here, where was he*? As mysteries were solved, more arose.

Sleep did not come easily, but when it did it was sound. The sun was up when he woke. His search of the cabin found no food, as if anything left since March would be fit to eat. From his saddle bag, breakfast was hard tack, and beef jerky Sky had made from the hind quarters of the rustled steer. He was able to wash it down and fill his canteen with water from a well near the cabin. The hand dug well water was sweet tasting, which would be a plus for the winter.

Adam found the door latch was faulty, likely having allowed the wind to blow it open for coon occupation. With piggin strings, thin strips of rawhide, he secured the door. He updated his map and studied it before loading and mounting his horse. His travel, mostly west, would allow him to inspect the remainder of the winter grazing valley on his way to camp, but he planned a diversionary stop.

He sought a stream but approaching it from a different direction caused him to become lost twice. When he finally found the stream he sought, it was mid-afternoon. He made corrections to his map and found the location where Hank, Clint, and he had followed a trail leaving the stream.

Close to where he thought his destination lay, he heard movement in the brush. He reached for his Winchester. Bear, or wolf, he was ready to defend himself. Deer would be food for someone. Holding the rifle in his left hand, he nudged the horse easily. He saw it. It was not what he expected but a young bare foot, bushy redheaded girl with an armful of firewood wearing a worn smock soiled such that it was nearly camouflage.

She was a slight thing, hardly five feet tall. Her attention was alternating between him and the ground in front of her. She walked backward a few steps, dropped the firewood, and took off running, weaving around trees.

Adam rode into the former rustler's camp shortly after the girl arrived.

"We've not bothered your herd again," the mother declared.

"I'm not suggesting you have."

The boy huddled behind his mother. The girl stood brazenly beside them ready to stand her ground. Adam glanced at the remainder of his steer's carcass. "Looks like you've finished what was left of the steer. What are you eating now?"

"Late season berries, trying to get a rabbit with the rifle you left but a bad shot I am and about out of ammo."

"So, Mildred, what are you going to do? Winter's coming on. It is Mildred, isn't it?"

"Still looking for the gold nuggets he stole from my husband," she answered, glancing at what appeared to be a shallow grave.

"Mind if I get off my horse?" Adam asked.

"I guess you can do as you want. I owe you for not hanging me."

Adam sat on a stump across the shallow rock-lined firepit from Mildred.

"Lori, you were supposed to be getting firewood, get at it," Mildred told her daughter.

"Sorry I scared you, Lori. My name is Adam."

"My name is not Lori, it is Lorraine," she corrected him.

"Sorry, what is your brother's name?"

"It is Gerald, not Jerry," she answered looking at her mother.

"I named you both to start with; I can nickname you as I please," Mildred responded. "Now gather firewood while I find out what this man wants."

As Lorraine left, Adam couldn't help but admire spunk in her as fiery as her red hair.

In conversation with Mildred, Adam found that the rustler Hank shot was not her husband but the man who killed her husband for his gold nuggets and used her while tolerating the kids.

"He was scared I would kill him while he was sleeping and get the gold back. So, before he slept, he unloaded his guns, slept on the shells, and hid the gold somewhere around here. We've looked for days, why we're still here, and haven't found it. I expect we need give up finding it and move on, but I know not where to go."

"Other than tending your children, can you do anything else?" Adam asked.

"I'm a seamstress of sorts, but I'll do most anything to provide for my children. I guess after that man had his way with me, anything includes all."

"Great Falls is a day and a half ride that way," Adam pointed southwest. "There is a saloon keeper who needs someone to clean and otherwise help her keep up her saloon. The woman says she'd provide quarters and meals. You might do sewing on the side."

"Even though that man...I'm not that kind."

"That's not what she is looking for."

"Why are you telling me this?"

"Why did I not let my foreman hang you?"

Lorraine arrived with an armload of wood. Adam broke some branches and added them to the fire. It was clouding up and dark would come early.

"Where are you headed?" Mildred asked.

"Half of a day's ride that way," he pointed southeast.

"Rain is coming. I can feel it and it will be cold. You may stay with us. We'll be eating the last of the beef. It is yours after all."

Mildred scraped mold off a scrap of front quarter that was hanging from a tree, speared it with a stick, and placed it above the firepit. Adam offered his remaining hard tack. As they ate, Adam caught Lorraine often making eye contact with him. There was something about her he couldn't quite grasp.

It was soon dark and starting to rain. Gerald and Lorraine scampered to the canvas lean-to. "It's going be a cold rain, you're welcome to share the lean-to with us," Mildred offered.

"Thanks, but I've got a blanket and a long duster," he replied.

Adam put his saddle beside the fire. He laid half his oil-coated canvas coat on the ground, put his blanket over him, and wrapped the remainder of the duster around him. As he was only five feet six while standing, the duster nearly reached his ankles. The long duster served him well. With his hat covering his face and boots below the bottom of the duster, he was rainproof.

It was in the middle of the night Adam felt himself shivering and heard activity around the firepit. Someone with an old, soiled blanket over their head was rolling a firepit rock onto a rag. He reached for the pistol he had put beside him. The person turned toward him causing light from the fire to show bushy red hair protruding from under the blanket. It was Lorraine.

*Was she going to bash him with the rock?* He would not shoot her until he knew. *But could he?* Near him, she lifted his duster and rolled the warm rock beside him, went back to the fire, gathered three more rocks, and disappeared in the lean-to. With warmth from the rock, his shivering soon dissipated.

The rain stopped before daylight. Adam had added kindling to the fire and was readying his horse when Lorraine came out of the lean-to.

"Mom says we are headed to that town you spoke of. Will we see you again?"

"I make it there monthly, so I expect you will. How old are you?"

"I'm fourteen, be fifteen on February the sixth, if a rattlesnake doesn't get me before then." She continued after his inquisitive look. "Before you rode up yesterday, a rattlesnake was under a piece of wood I lifted. He was coiled and ready. I think he must have felt your horse approaching and chose to slither off instead of biting me. How old are you?"

Adam, surprised she was nearly his age, attempted to partially answer the question, "I was also born in February," but her look forced him to continue. "I'll be eighteen in February," he answered adding two years to his age.

"Mom says I'm going to be ten next year," Gerald added emerging from the lean-to.

"When is your birthday?

"April, Mom says."

Mildred emerged from the lean-to. "You kids talk too much. The man is wanting to leave."

"I'm Adam," he reminded her and gave her directions to Great Falls the second time. He opened his saddle bag, pulled out six 44 rimfire cartridges for her rifle and handed them to her.

"You said you were short on ammo. Be careful traveling to the falls and use them sparingly."

"Thank you, Adam."

The sun was high overhead when Adam rode into camp. Hank came riding up. "We were 'bout to go out looking for you. Trouble"?

"No trouble, just checking the winter camp. We'll be moving there next week."

*"The greater danger for most of us lies not in setting our aim too high and falling short; but in setting our aim too low and achieving our mark."*

Michelangelo

# ★ CHAPTER 7 ★

Although it was less than a day's ride to winter camp from their present location, driving the herd would require all the daylight hours. An hour before sunrise, the outfit, six cowboys, Hank, the head wrangler, and Adam sat around the chuckwagon for breakfast. Most had their sleeping blankets draped over their shoulders as snow was starting to fall.

"Can't wait to get to proper cooking quarters, and abandon this wagon for the winter," stated Sky, the tall cook.

"Does that mean our meals will improve?" asked July.

Adam was glad that July was thinking about something other than sitting quietly staring at a pocket watch image of his passed family.

"I've noticed your appetite has improved to some degree, chuckwagon or not," stated Fancy.

"Yeah, maybe he forgot about his burned family," Hairy added.

The former banker's reaction surprised everyone. He dropped his plate and lunged at Hairy, sending his plate of food flying, knocking Hank's coffee cup over.

July initially landed on top of Hairy and his fervor momentarily gave him an advantage, but Hairy was much more skilled in brawling and soon reversed positions. July would have paid dearly for his assault had it not been for Adam and Hank separating them.

"Enough, save your energy for our drive. If you still have a spark of fight in you when we reach the cabin, have it out then," Hank declared.

"July, you help Sky pack up the chuckwagon. Hairy, help the others tear down the tents. We'll be riding shortly," Adam ordered.

Adam had studied his map the prior day and was now familiar enough with the route he rode at the head of the outfit. At the top of a ridge, he looked down upon a valley they had to cross. It held a similar-sized herd. He was contemplating the time it would take to circle the valley when a rider approached.

"We're not hiring anyone now. But will have need when our herd expands," the rider said without introduction.

"I'm not looking for a job. Just taking my herd to our winter quarters," Adam replied.

The rider didn't answer but sped to the top of the ridge and looked down upon Adam's approaching herd.

"Lord Barnhouse has authorized me to buy any herd we encounter. What do you want for your herd?"

"I'm Adam and you are?"

"I'm Chance. What do you want per head?"

"Herd's not for sale. Who is this Lord Barnhouse?"

"He's an English lord, moving here in a year. He wants me to have all the herds in the area bought up, a big house built for his family, and more cattle moved in from Wyoming. It won't be to your advantage to hold out."

"We'll see," Adam replied as Hank rode up.

"Are you ramrod of this outfit?" he asked Chance.

When Chance didn't answer, he said, "Move your herd to that end of the valley," he pointed, "so we can cross and soon be out of your hair."

"And why would I bother doing that?"

"Because you don't want to waste your time separating our herds if they get mixed," Hank replied.

"Our herds will eventually be joined anyway." Chance resolutely stood his ground.

Adam nodded at Hank, beckoning him to follow. "Any alternative to taking our herd around the ridge will cause more delay than the extra travel," Adam said.

Herman rode up, "What's happening?"

Hank ignored him and said to Adam, "Yeah, know you're right, but don't like kowtowing to an asshole."

"My Bible tells me more liars and purveyors of foul language reside in hell than thieves," warned Herman.

Hank and Adam rode off ignoring Herman.

A light snowfall fell all day. It was after dark when the herd reached the winter quarters. Adam had sent Sky ahead with the chuckwagon through the Barnhouse herd, allowing him to have smoke moving skyward from the cabin chimney as the cowboys approached. It was a welcome sight as was his beef stew.

Mid-afternoon the following day the snow was melting, and cattle were feasting on native grass which hadn't been touched all summer. *Perhaps it was nature that made the native grass more palatable than bunchgrass, saving the latter for heavy snow cover*, thought Adam.

On Adam's mind was how his herd would survive the winter if another herd, like Barnhouse's, had grazed their winter quarters earlier and left little grass behind. It was open range; nothing prevented such happening. He spent the rest of the day appraising the size of the winter quarter's valley.

At supper that evening, Adam announced, "I'll take the empty chuck wagon into town tomorrow and load up on oats for the horses. I noticed a church in town. July, you can ride my horse and take the wagon back after church on Sunday morning. Maybe preaching will help you deal with your family tragedy. Herman, you come also."

"Why would I want to come?" asked Herman.

"I thought you'd welcome an opportunity to attend a real church."

"No, preachers are charlatans, all 'bout money, not the good word. I stay here," he answered.

"I'll come in his place," Fancy volunteered.

"And I expect you'd want an advance in pay, as you spent all last months on that pudgy light-haired saloon girl."

"She was not pudgy—just on the short side," Fancy answered. "I'll go to town after we're paid with Hank next week."

"Hairy, you haven't been in town for some time," queried Adam.

"Yep, I'll go but probably drink more whiskey than proper."

"Okay, but you'll need to be sober if you go to church with July and me. I'll have no bad examples set by our crew."

The three arrived in Great Falls late Saturday afternoon. Hairy headed for the saloon with two months' pay, and July went to the hotel to get the three a room for the night. Adam headed for Nate Clement's law office only to find a sign on the front door, *Be back on late Sunday stage.*

Assuming the general store would be closed on Sunday, Adam pulled the wagon into the alley near their feed storage. He saw Emily peering through an upstairs window but didn't acknowledge her and stepped around to the front door. He was nearly ready to leave when Emily's father answered the door.

"We close early on Saturday."

"Sorry for the inconvenience, but I hate to wait until Monday."

"You are Adam, aren't you, boss of the spread north of town?" the man inquired.

"Yes, I just need a few bags of oats and other supplies; it shouldn't take long,"

"Go around to the back, and I'll have my daughter take care of you."

Adam waited for what seemed to be a long time before Emily stepped out of the back door, wearing a brown dress, no bonnet, but her hair knotted on top of her head. "I'll show you where the oat bags are, but you'll need to load them yourself."

After loading the bags and picking up a few supplies in the store, Adam asked, "I'm staying at the hotel and assume this wagon will be safe if I leave it here overnight."

"Sure, we've never lost anything, and my dad keeps watch on the alley with his shotgun."

"Again, sorry for the late inconvenience."

"Quite alright, you just come back anytime, you hear?"

When she joined her father on the second floor living quarters, he said, "I saw his roll of bills. Why didn't you keep him longer, invite him to stay for dinner?"

"Dad, I can't be too forward, and he's younger than me."

"All the more reason to take charge," her dad answered.

"Guess I'm a little timid after Calvin left me for his swanky second cousin."

"Emily, you are what now, twenty-five years old? You're near spinster territory. Your days of playing hard-to-get are over. The doctor says I won't last another ten years. I'd like to see my grandchildren before then."

Adam walked to the hotel, found July, and ate at the hotel diner adjacent to the lobby. He contemplated going to the saloon, then thought better of it. The biggest room in the hotel had only a full-size and twin bed. Adam took the full-size. In the middle of the night, he smelled whiskey as Hairy crawled into bed with him. Within a few minutes, Hairy was snoring loudly, even louder than his cabin snore.

The snoring continued as the sun rose, causing July and Adam to rise earlier than they wished and don the clean shirts they had brought for church. On the dresser lay a quarter over a note that said, *Give to church.* Adam pocketed it. Anxious to get away from Hairy's likely hangover whining when he woke, they took their time eating breakfast in the dining room until they heard the church bell ringing.

The church sat on a slight rise at the edge of the town. With white clapboard siding, a cupola rising above the cube-framed structure and double doors at the entry, it matched Adam's idea of what a country church should look like. As he entered the church with July, he pondered where his stereotypical church recollection had come from.

At least half the people seated in pews turned their heads upon the men's entry. Except for the front two pews, few seats were left. Adam hesitated. The front two pews might subject him to easy access for punishment of his sins. He felt a shiver down his back as he contemplated a lightning bolt. His eye caught a blue bonnet covered head turning toward him. It was Emily. She nodded at the empty space in a pew beside her.

When Adam sat beside her, her head remained looking forward, but he could see a smile overtake her face.

Her father leaned forward and reached his hand out across his daughter's lap, "I'm so glad you could join us this morning. We couldn't be more delighted to have you with us," he said holding Adam's hand longer than normal, while thinking of a future wedding in the church.

"Sir, this is July. Emily, this is July."

The introductions were cut short when the pastor stepped to the podium and started singing, accompanied by the piano player Adam recognized from the saloon. Grinning, Emily relayed a songbook her dad handed her to Adam. Awkwardly, Adam and July joined the congregation in singing. Emily's pleasant voice was nearly drowned out by the shrill off-key voice of a woman behind them.

The sermon dealt on the mysterious ways of the Lord. "All has a reason," the preacher said in different ways using multiple examples. It was the perfect message for July to hear.

When the plate was passed, Adam added a dollar and Hairy's quarter. July a quarter. Emily's father thought the dollar donation from Adam was good, but an extra quarter was strange. *Why not either a dollar or two?*

When the service ended, Adam felt uncomfortably out of place.

He had been sitting with a near strange girl—no, she was a woman—older than he was, likely much more experienced, and he knew not what to say.

She broke the ice. "Next Saturday evening the town is having a citizen's get-together. It would be great to see you there."

"Oh, yeh, I may try to make it," he stumbled.

"I look forward to seeing you then," she answered as Adam left and ended up in a line waiting to great the preacher at the door. Emily joined girlfriends to the side.

As July and Adam waited in line, Adam heard one of the girls ask Emily, "Have you got a date for the dance next week yet? We both have."

Adam kept his eyes forward as if not hearing the conversation. Emily replied, "Yes, of course I have a date."

"Is he that young guy you were sitting with in church?"

"He's not as young as he looks," she replied.

*Citizen's get-together was really a dance,* thought Adam. He didn't know anything about dancing. *Had she purposely deceived him?* Next Saturday would require considerable thought on his part.

Hairy was sitting outside the hotel on a chair under the awning when July and Adam approached. He looked like he'd been ridden hard and put away wet. "You okay, Hairy?"

"Yeah, I'm great."

"Did you spend all your wages?"

"Yep, spent it all, but the good news is I made back half of it at the poker table. I see you found the two bits I left for church."

"That was good of you."

"Hopefully, make up for my sinful ways and propositioning Fancy's blonde girl who left with another guy."

"You and July take the wagon and head back to camp. I've must stay another day to see someone."

"Who?" asked Hairy.

"She wears a blue bonnet," July answered for him with a snicker.

"No, not her. Business. Now get going," Adam answered but glad July had shown some humor.

Adam had thought about killing time in the afternoon at the saloon, but on the walk back from the church saw it was closed for the day. *For the better,* he thought, although he wondered if the floor had been cleaned.

The hotel dining room had a few old newspapers on a rack, most were weeks old and well worn. Nevertheless, they were a great opportunity for Adam to familiarize himself with the era in which he found himself.

The first thing that struck him when he picked up a newspaper called *The Rocky Mountain News* published in Denver, was the date. October 4, 1883. It was a couple months old, but the year had to be right. *Okay, now he knew where he was in time, but from where had he come?*

He read an article about the passage about the Pendleton Act signed by President Chester Arthur which reformed federal hiring procedures. Arthur had become president after Garfield had been assassinated. Some way Adam knew that, but he did not know how.

The next newspaper he picked up was the *Chicago Daily Tribune,* dated from August 1883. It had an article about the prospect of the Dakota territory eventually being broken into two states, north and south.

His newspaper attention was diverted with he saw Chance, the foreman of the herd they had encountered moving to the winter quarters, and the short blonde girl Fancy had been with on a previous Saturday separate in the lobby. He appeared to be telling her goodbye and she left. Entering the dining room, Chance asked, "Mind if I sit with you?"

"Go ahead."

After ordering tea with Adam, Chance said, "See you're catching up on the news. Too bad most of it is history before we get it here."

"Interesting, nevertheless," Adam answered.

"Given anymore thought to selling your herd?"

"No."

"You'll find Lord Barnhouse can be very convincing once he arrives."

"Why would an aristocrat from England want to move to this wilderness? And how did he get such a name?"

"Interesting story, the lord's grandfather was a sergeant under the Duke of Wellington at the battle of Waterloo. Someway his squad flanked Napoleon's command headquarters and took the emperor's surrender. King George III knighted him Lord Barnhouse when he heard the sergeant's family was living in a barn."

"And why come here?" Adam asked again.

"Like his grandfather, he is prone to adventure. He finds life in England boring."

*"Time is too slow for those who wait, too swift for those who fear, too long for those who grieve, too short for those who rejoice, but for those who love, time is eternity."*

Henry Van Dyke

# ★ CHAPTER 8 ★

Monday morning Adam was up early and at Nate's law office at eight. The door was locked, but he soon saw Nate walking down the sidewalk.

"Adam, isn't it? I met you in the bar. We shared common drinks. You're here early. Got a cowboy or two locked up and need help?"

"No nothing like that. I need to talk to you about some property."

"Well come on in and have a seat."

"More herds are moving in, including one that seems very aggressive. My fear is that someone will graze our winter quarters during the summer and leave no grass for winter."

"It is free range. The only way to stop it is to purchase the land and place stakes around it."

"Tell me about the Homestead Act. Is it a possibility?"

"The Homestead Act enables citizens to claim land up to a quarter section, 160 acres, provided they live on it, cultivate it, or improve it. The problem in Montana is a quarter section isn't enough grazing land for enough cattle to sustain oneself."

"What if I homesteaded and bought a parcel next to it? What is the government pricing of land out here?"

"A dollar and a quarter per acre. How much would you buy?"

Adam thought then answered. "If I homesteaded 160, I could buy another 160 next to it for two hundred dollars, right?"

"But isn't that range you are wintering on much bigger than that?"

"Yes, the valley is around a mile and half wide and three miles long. I timed walking my horse around it last week."

"That would be four and a half sections, and you would only own a half section of it."

"But I would mark my claim in the middle of the valley from the cabin to a mile east. Owning land in the middle of the valley would make it difficult for any herd to graze around it. And the cabin, horse stable, and corral would meet the homestead requirements as improvements, wouldn't they?"

"Yes, they would. One of your wranglers, or preferably you, would need to be there constantly if a land agent showed up. Don't you move your herd all over during warm weather?"

"I or someone will be there constantly. Can you start the paperwork?"

"Will do. It should be ready at the end of the week."

"I'll be back Saturday."

Before he left town, Adam had to check on one more thing. He headed for the saloon. As he approached the swinging door from the wooden sidewalk, it flew open striking him mid-section nearly knocking the wind from him.

It was Lorraine carrying a bucket. Her red hair was as bushy as ever, but he could tell it had seen a comb. The wind caught her hair exposing her left ear and a mole a few inches below it. Compared to the wild look she had when he found her picking up firewood, she looked tame, but from the ferocity in which she swung the door open a spark remained.

"Well, you look busy."

"I'm taking this to the trash wagon behind the sheriff's office."

"When did you get here?"

"We rode the next morning after you left."

"Well, what do you think?"

"Our lean-to back of the saloon is livable. It sure beats the canvas one in the wilderness, and the food is much better than Mom fixed around the campfire. Mom says we owe you."

"You owe me nothing. I'm just glad it worked out. I hope to see you around here every time I come into town."

A blush overcame her, which she tried to hide by saying, "No rattlesnakes for you to chase away here." Before he could respond, she picked up the bucket and scurried across the street.

Adam walked into the saloon. "We're not open yet," Betsy told him while standing behind the bar and pouring water from a pitcher into a not full bottle of whiskey. Mildred was sweeping the floor and Gerald was loading a bucket with piles she had swept. The floor would no longer hide blood, or tobacco juice.

"I'm not here to drink—just wanted to say *hi* to a couple friends."

Betsy came out from behind the bar. "You're the guy who sent them, right?"

"I told them about your place."

"Well, when we open today your first couple special drinks are on the house."

"I can't stay today, but I'll stop by Saturday," he answered then stepped to Mildred. "I'm glad you took my advice."

"I'll thank you along with Betsy. Did you see Lori leaving? She talks about you all the time. How providence caused your approach on horseback to scare a snake away."

"Yes, I ran into her. Glad to see you made it here. Now I must get back to our winter camp." On the ride back, Adam had a hard time getting Mildred's last comment about Lorraine from his mind.

Riding through a clump of trees before he reached the ridge to the winter valley, Adam saw a stump. It brought his mind back to present reality. The stump was the same height as a calf's head, which he would never get a rope on in the spring roundup unless his roping skill improved.

A dozen times he tossed his rope toward the stump from his standing horse to no avail. Even if successful from a standing horse, he would need to rope a running calf from a horse in motion if he were to save himself embarrassment. *Why did cowboy tradition force the boss to lead the roping. Might he feign sickness or a sprained shoulder to avoid the ordeal?*

It was one step at a time, he decided, dismounted, and tied his horse to a low-hanging branch. He would practice until he got the rope around the stump in the simplest way, then increase the difficulty.

On his fifth attempt, the loop encircled the stump. Adam thought he heard a noise, then guessed it was his excitement at having finally snared something with his rope. He was winding the rope to repeat his success when he heard his horse let out a panicked neigh. The chestnut jerked the reins loose from the branch it was tied to, turned, and galloped over the ridge toward its winter home as if chased by the devil.

He had no Idea what had spooked the horse but was thankful to be within walking distance of the camp. As he started toward the camp, he heard a growl behind him. Adam turned to see a wolf standing thirty feet away barring his teeth. The growl was joined by another in front of him.

The talk in camp came to mind of strategies to fight off a pack of wolves while on foot—block off a side of their attack with a rock or big tree thus giving you only 180 degrees to defend. But no big trees or rocks to protect one's backside were in the new growth and brush. A third wolf tested him by running past him at only twenty feet distance. His horse with rifle was gone. Adam's side pistol was more for show than use. Although he was better with it than he was with rope, he had only shot it a few times.

Adam felt pounding in his chest as the fight-or-flight adrenaline pumped through his veins. Thoughts raced through his head at incredible speed. *Would he never meet his father? Never have children?*

*Crazy to be worried about his rope inability. Was his plight to be worse than the rattlesnake might have inflicted on Lorraine as wolves tore him apart.*

Hank was checking on the herd when he saw Clint waving at him and pointing to a chestnut mount with only saddle running for the stables. He recognized it as Adam's horse. *The boy was not the best rider and had gotten thrown* was his first thought as he started his horse in the direction the empty mount had come from. Then the desperate pace the horse was galloping struck him. It was not the leisurely pace a horse would move toward stable feed.

Hank added slack to his reins and flipped them on his horse's neck which brought his horse to a lope, which non-westerners called a cantor at eight–twelve miles per hour. When a gunshot echoed through the valley immediately followed by another shot, Hank dug his spurs into his horse's flank bringing him to a full gallop, around forty miles per hour for the working quarter horse.

Adam drew his sidearm, but it was more reflex than measured intent that caused him to draw down on the leader of the wolf pack which was rushing toward him with teeth bared. The wolf was struck in the head by the bullet sending brain matter into his throat. His head dropped to the ground causing the wolf's momentum to backward flip his body over within a foot of Adam.

Adam's attention was turned to the second wolf who followed in attack on the heels of the leader. Adam pulled the hammer back on his 1873 single action Colt 44-40 and inflicted similar damage on the second wolf.

The third wolf, sensing the folly of continuing the attack, turned, and started to leave when Adam's third shot hit him in the shoulder and pierced his heart. He collapsed and gasped for his remaining breaths. Between two trees, Adam saw a fourth wolf scampering away. He pulled the hammer back, raised his Colt, steadied it with both hands and sent a bullet on a long path to the wolf's exposed posterior. His hind quarters fell, and his front legs attempted to drag the remainder of his body as he howled.

The howling stopped when Adam heard a shot from where he did not know. The front quarters of the remaining wolf dropped as if slammed by a sledge from Hank's rifle.

Adam, trembling, injected his fifth and last round into the second wolf as a safety measure when it gave a death flinch.

"You alright?" Hank hollered from his horse.

Standing in shock with his Colt dangling from his hand, Adam didn't hear the question.

Hank dismounted and was inspecting each of the wolves when Clint and Fancy rode up.

"What happened here?" asked Fancy.

"Wolves here made a deadly mistake trifling with our boss, looks like," answered Hank.

"Did you shoot any?" Clint asked Hank.

"Just put one out of his misery—he'd have died anyway."

Adam said upon Fancy approaching him, "Did what I had to do."

"Yeh, looks like you did it pretty well."

"Two in the head and one in the heart—amazing shooting," declared Clint as he and Fancy inspected the three closer wolf bodies. Hank was taking long strides from the far wolf to Adam. "Sixty-five-yard hit on a running wolf from a pistol. Adam here can outshoot his dad by a mile."

Adam was reloading his pistol and ignored the comment, then said, "I'm tempted to add a sixth cartridge if shooting wolf packs becomes common."

"Wouldn't do that, a shell under the hammer is too dangerous. You'll shoot your leg if your horse pounces wrong," cautioned Hank.

Fancy found Adam's lariat on the ground and started coiling it.

"Why was your rope off the saddle?" asked Hank.

"He must have tried to rope the wolves first instead of shooting them," joshed Clint, drawing laughs from all except Adam.

Later as snow started falling, they sat around the fireplace. Fancy and Clint told of the feat Adam had performed, often exaggerating it.

Adam saw no reason to toss cold water on his newly earned respect.

It was not missed by Adam that Hank was looking at him differently. Hank had called him *boss*. It was the first time.

Lying in his cot, he thought of the time lapsed when he fired his rounds at the wolves. It was hard to remember. His mind drifted to providence. *Had there been intervention to cause him to aim his pistol beyond his capabilities as the rattlesnake had chosen not to bite Lorraine? Were he and Lorraine recipients of favor from above? Why? His past he did not know, but what would time bring to his future?*

*"And this I believe: that the free, exploring mind of the individual human is the most valuable thing in the world."*

John Steinbeck

# ★ CHAPTER 9 ★

Saturday morning Adam opened the money box they had hidden under a rock behind the cabin. Hank insisted on getting his prior poker earnings from the box which Adam gave him. Adam retrieved fifty dollars from the outfit's saving and added it to the fifty dollars in his vest pocket which he would supplement with over one hundred from the cattle they were driving to the Great Falls railway pens.

With the monthly twenty head of cattle sold, Hank and Fancy headed for the saloon, and Adam for Nate's law office. After signing the necessary paperwork, Adam handed him two hundred dollars, and they walked to the assay and land office. Enroute Adam saw Lorraine carrying a bucket to the waste wagon. He waved; she waved back.

"You know her?" asked Nate.

"Yeh, her, brother and mother were stranded on the range. I told them about the opening at Betsy's saloon." He didn't mention the rustling episode.

Once the paperwork and money were exchanged, Adam received a qualified homestead deed and a real deed for an adjacent 160 acres.

"I strongly advise you to keep the paperwork in a bank lockbox instead of your vest or some buried box," Nate advised.

They waited some time for the bank president to finish with a customer and another waiting. Finally, the banker got to them. "Sorry to keep you waiting. We're short on help here. Neither of you know anyone with bank experience, I suspect," the banker apologized, as introductions were made.

Adam thought of July, but July was still too distracted with his family loss and replacing July with another cowboy would be troublesome.

Leaving the bank, Adam told Nate, "I've a couple drinks coming at Betsy's; you just as well join me."

"And I've a fee due for the paperwork preparation," answered Nate, informing Adam that he didn't work for drinks.

Nate and Adam stood at the bar with their sarsaparillas in hand as Mildred came out of the kitchen and sat a platter of fried beef, potato, and bread chunks in front of them.

"We didn't order anything," Adam said.

"Besides cleaning, I'm now handling the cooking here and some discretion I have for my friends."

"I saw Lorraine earlier. Is she coming back?"

"No, I don't allow her in this establishment after six. It'd be asking for trouble. She will be helping Betsy cater beer at the dance later; expect she'll be safe there."

"Are you going to the dance?" Adam asked Nate.

"It would just be trouble for me. Any girl I danced with would cause her boyfriend or would-be boyfriend to get jealous and spread rumors about me. It would be bad for business."

As Adam left the bar, he stopped at a poker table and asked Hank if he was going to the dance. Hank replied, "I got my hands full here, and I expect Fancy is doing all the dancing he can handle upstairs."

Adam entered a building that had been built as a combination community center, schoolhouse, and courtroom. The desks had been pushed against the walls, and a ragtag community band was readying themselves. He scanned the room and saw Lorraine busy at a beer table with Betsy, then saw Emily wave at him from a school desk.

"Have a seat," Emily waved to an empty desk beside her. "I brought something for you."

She handed him a book. It was *Treasure Island* by Robert Stevenson, which had been published earlier that year. Adam opened the book giving it a once over.

"You said you liked to read and missed good books. I finished it last evening."

"I don't know what to say. I'll get it back to you after I finish."

"Where did you go to school?" she asked.

Not having an answer, he replied, "Here and there. We moved around a lot. How about you?"

"Dad sent me to Miss Wolcott's School for Girls. It is a finishing school in Denver. Besides reading at a higher level, I learned piano, watercolors, needlework, elocution, and etiquette. It was a wonderful experience for me."

Adam had no idea what elocution was and wasn't about to ask. "Sounds like you had a great experience."

"Would you care for a mug?" Adam heard someone say, turned and saw Lorraine holding a platter of beer mugs.

"No, no," Emily answered as if the mugs might be infectious.

Adam smiled at her and said, "Sure, why not?"

He pulled the mug to his lips as he looked at Lorraine. She wore a white apron with her hair tucked under a bonnet exposing the mole below her left ear. It was the first time he had noticed freckles on her face. Their eyes held each other until she moved on with the platter.

"Do you know her?" asked Emily.

"Yeah, she was traveling through the range with her mother, and I've seen her around town."

"Well, it takes all kinds. There is a place for us all, I guess," Emily commented, then added, "At least the council doesn't allow whiskey at these community events."

The band struck up a tune, although in tune were not some of the band members. "A gentleman who receives a gift from a lady, usually asks her to dance," Emily stated.

"I'm not good at this," Adam said as Emily led him to the dance floor.

"Just follow me—you'll do fine."

Over Emily's shoulder, Adam more than once saw Lorraine glancing at him. He tried to ignore her.

After two dances, given Adam's long ride back to the cabin, he said he must leave. Emily said she'd seen enough and asked him to walk her home. As they approached the general store door, Adam saw her dad trying to be inconspicuous in a second-floor window.

"See you in church tomorrow?" Emily stated more than asked.

"Not tomorrow. My turn to watch the herd, but I'll be around." He turned and walked back to his horse.

At the cabin in the morning, Adam found that Hank had spent most of the night at the poker table. For his many hours, his only satisfaction was he had left with the same amount of money he went with.

It was a long, but normal winter, cold, and snowy but occasionally interrupted by Chinook winds that blew and melted the snow from ridges giving cattle something besides bunchgrass to eat.

Inside the cabin, confinement from the frigid weather was sharpening tempers. More than once, Hank or Adam broke up fights. Sometimes it was Adam that pulled Hank from an antagonist. Escaping to town helped but riding for hours in zero-degree weather required a great desire to leave the cabin.

One morning Hairy came in from checking the herd and exclaimed, "Some son-of-a-bitch destroyed my varmint trap," while looking at Fancy.

Hairy was good with his hands building things. He had tied and wired birch branches to make a cage on the south side of the cabin. Baited with scraps from Sky's cooking, opossums, raccoons, and an occasional skunk were lured into the trap. Once inside, they tripped a mechanism that closed the entry door and trapped themselves.

"Too bad, probably a bear," Fancy answered.

Fancy was the practical joker amongst the crew. Getting a laugh at the expense of another cowboy often seemed a goal for him. More than once someone's saddle slid off as they mounted because Fancy had loosened the cinch.

"Don't give me that BS. There was a footprint amongst the damage," Hairy hollered as he lunged into Fancy.

Fancy, a jokester and provocateur—not a fighter—backed away from Hairy, frustrating Hairy more. Adam and Hank stood back as Fancy kept retreating.

"Fancy didn't do it. I did, for which I am glad as it brought out blasphemous language from you exposing the sin within your soul," announced Herman.

"Why would you do that?" Hairy inquired.

"Because God created those creatures as he did us. Killing for our eating is necessary; killing to amuse oneself is sin. What does a coon hurt?"

"I'll tell you what it hurts, one got into a flour sack we left in the wagon for lack of storage in here," declared Hank. "What the varmint didn't eat, he scattered everywhere."

Adam interjected, "I notice you both like to eat Sky's biscuits made from flour. Until Hairy apologizes for using profanity against one of us and Herman helps Hairy rebuild his varmint trap, neither of you will have biscuits."

Quiet returned to the cabin. Herman opened his Bible, and Fancy dealt cards at the table. Cabin poker was a common diversion to take minds off controversy. They bet wooden chips as Hank and Adam forbid money betting at the camp.

Looking up from his Bible, Herman broke the silence. "I guess killing a varmint that destroys our food isn't much different than killing an animal for food. Hairy, I have an idea to improve your trap."

A few minutes later after a winning hand, Hairy declared, "I ought not use profanity against one of us."

Later Adam lay in bed happy that a dispute among the cowboys had been resolved without blows being landed. Turning sixteen last month had given him more confidence in asserting himself although all who knew him thought he had turned eighteen.

The snow drifts were starting to recede with days of warmer weather. Mid-April was around the corner bringing on cattle processing and branding. His roping skills had not improved. *Because of his lariat ineptitude would he soon lose the respect he had earned dropping wolves?*

His mind drifted back to the varmint trap—then an idea struck him.

At breakfast the next morning, Adam announced, "Hairy, you and Herman rebuild the varmint trap. The rest of us are going to the woods for building material to add to the corral."

"The corral is ample size for our herd; maybe a little repair is all that's needed," Hank offered.

"No, we're going to add something that will make cattle processing easier for all. I'm the boss and starting the process by tradition is my job."

After a day cutting logs for fence posts and corral rails and hearing too many questions from Hank, Adam asked Hank if he'd be up for scouting grazing areas for the upcoming season.

"That was something your dad always did, and I expected you would do it," he answered.

"You know what we seek. I think it's time for you to take on the responsibility."

"I'd be gone at least a couple weeks and may have to crisscross town a few times."

"Of course, you will. I'll add a little extra to your pay, so you can get a room in town a few times and avoid spending every night on the trail."

With Hank leaving, Adam achieved two things. He avoided having to scout grazing areas himself for which he hadn't accumulated enough knowledge to do. And he got Hank out of his hair while he built what would be a monumental change in cattle processing.

With birch rails, Adam laid out where a fence would be built. It ran inside and parallel to the corral fence at a separation of only three feet. The narrow alley ran for twenty feet. It then flared out at thirty degrees for sixty feet creating a funnel into a narrow column.

With the ground recently thawed, fence posts were dug, and railing added. The fence on both sides of the narrow column was fortified with extra railing.

"Looks like an elaborate plan to force cattle into single file," July observed.

"I'm not finished," Adam replied. "Other parts, I'll get in town."

The next day at the general store, Adam handed Emily a list which included oak boards, bolts, and nuts.

"What are you building?" Emily asked.

"An addition to our corral."

"Dad and I would be pleased if you stayed for dinner."

"Wow, that's a hard invitation to pass, but I've much work to do. Might I get a rain check?"

"Perhaps next time you are in town I can fix a picnic lunch and we can take Dad's buggy out."

"That sounds like a great idea for next time."

That evening Emily's dad said, "Where's Adam? Don't tell me he turned dinner down."

"We decided next time he's in town we're going on a picnic ride. I might even let him spark me."

"I don't want to hear the details. Just get yourself married," her dad answered.

Although not a carpenter, Adam worked for two days until he got what he came to call 'a headgate' right. He attached it to the end of the narrow alley. The next morning a warm spring breeze was in the air as his cowboys drove a few dozen head into the corral.

Adam stood atop the headgate he built at the end of the narrow alley. He held an oak 2x6 board that extended five feet above the headgate. As instructed, the cowboys drove the cattle into the funnel forcing some to walk down the narrow alley.

When Adam saw a cow's head start through the headgate at the end of the alley, he pulled the 2x6 tight against her neck and kicked a lever over that fell into a notch on the 2x6 trapping her. She flounced back and forth but couldn't escape the trap.

Adam jumped down and reached for a stick. "Imagine this was a branding iron," he said as he pushed it to her flank. "A little easier than someone roping, two to three guys bulldogging her, tying her legs, and holding her down as she is branded, right?"

He slid a board behind her to prevent her from backing up and released the board opening the gate. She burst through, and he soon caught another, this time a yearling steer. After four animals were caught and released, Adam was satisfied with his invention.

Hank rode into camp late in the afternoon.

"What'd you find?" Adam asked.

"That Barnhouse herd has expanded. We'll likely need to move further north this summer for grazing. Don't know what the heck you did to the corral, but at least you gave the boys something to do and kept them out of trouble."

"You'll find out soon enough."

"Hope you got your rope in good shape—we better start processin em next week. It usually takes three weeks; then it'll be time to move outta here to spring grazing."

"I'm ready," Adam replied, thinking it would take a week at tops.

*"Success is a journey, not a destination. The doing is often more important than the outcome."*

Arthur Ashe

# ★ CHAPTER 10 ★

After supper, Hank sat at one end of the table sharpening his knife for the upcoming work as the others played poker. "Clint, did you get enough kindling stacked for two weeks of branding iron fire? Won't have time to cut more once we start workin the cattle."

"Got plenty of kindling cut, boss."

"And, Herman, did you get the coal oil barrel filled in town?"

"Yes, Adam says we can get it refilled in a few days."

"If it's full, it should be plenty for those we hogtie and work on."

"We may want to oil treat more than usual. They will bring more money at the yards without warble holes in their hides," Adam stated.

Warble flies laid eggs on the backs of cattle in the early spring. When hatched, they grew as a parasite then burrowed through the hide and exited in the fall, leaving a hole in the hide, reducing the hide's value. Coal oil poured on the back prevented flies from laying eggs.

"Where are you going to find the extra help, or you planning on processing lasting a month?" Hank asked.

"We'll see."

"I hope you can match your dad's roping ability. We'd all better get to bed early. It'll be a tough two weeks or more," Hank stated as he gave Adam a skeptical look, pulled off his boots, and got in his cot.

The next morning the cowboys drove the cattle around the valley twice, draining their excess vigor before they deemed the herd docile enough to be driven into the corral. With all cattle corralled, Adam started a fire on the outside of the corral adjacent to the alley he had built.

"Why there? You want us to climb the fence every time we need an iron?" Hank observed.

Adam ignored him.

With two branding irons in the fire, Adam said, "It's time," and climbed on top of the headboard.

"Going to rope from there? Where's your rope?" Hank asked standing on the ground ready for his role in processing.

"Bring them in boys," Adam hollered to his mounted cowboys. They headed the herd for the funnel they had built. Soon some were headed down the alley.

Adam caught the first entry in the chute. "It's a cow, if the brand is okay, oil its back and we'll go on."

An outside gate was swung open allowing the chute-exiting cow out of the corral, keeping the processed cattle separated from the others.

The next in line was a yearling steer from the previous year. "Touch up that brand and oil him."

The third entry was a bull calf. "Your turn, Hank," Adam yelled.

"But how will I?"

"Get behind him and do your surgery. July, hold his tail tight against his back just like you did while one was tied on the ground last year to prevent him from kicking Hank."

Often the cowboys called Hank's surgery brain surgery although he cut on the opposite end. The punch line was that it changed the bull's mind from ass to grass. When complete, the bull left the chute a steer.

"What do you think?" Adam asked Hank.

Hank shook his head and said, "We may have more cowboys than we need."

They soon learned that the cows could have the dipper of oil poured on their back as they moved single file through the alley without trapping them in the headgate.

When the day was over, they had processed over a third of the herd.

Hank was quiet at dinner until Adam asked him the second time, "What do you think?"

"You may not be roping but you created a whole new game. What will they think of next, a passenger train coming to Great Falls or puttin motors on buggies?"

The second day went better than the first until they ran out of coal oil early afternoon.

"Whew, we're usually exhausted working to dark, and here we're over half done, and the rest of the afternoon for loafing, which we don't need," Clint observed.

"Since you are opposed to loafing, Clint, take the wagon to town for more coal oil. But first find Nate Clement's office and have him follow you out here in the morning with the coal oil."

"What if he doesn't want to come? He's a slicker, you know?" Clint replied.

"Tell him if he wants any more of my business, he will. And I'll send enough money along so you can stay at the hotel tonight."

"Don't know if I can sleep on a real bed instead of a cot or my blanket."

"It'll be a good experience for you."

Emily noticed the familiar wagon pulling up to the general store without Adam. The next morning, she handed Clint a basket of freshly baked cinnamon rolls. "Give these to Adam and don't eat them all before you get to camp," she cautioned him.

As Clint left town on the wagon, a girl carrying a bucket stopped him as he approached her, waving him down. "Adam is with you?"

"No, not this time."

"Tell him *hi* for me, will ya?"

Clint nodded and moved on. Emily saw the wagon stop and conversation exchanged with the girl. She made note that she would eventually need to address any potential competition to her goal.

At the livery stable, Nate joined the wagon on a day-rented horse. He was not without experience riding but preferred a stage or train.

"Don't know what Adam wanted you fer," Clint said without being asked.

"I don't know either, but I hope to get more business from him," Nate replied.

Out of coal oil, the cattle processing had stopped, and they were eating when Clint arrived with Nate following the wagon. Adam had shown July how to handle the headgate and let him trap cattle by the neck while he talked to Nate.

"What do you know about processing cattle?" Adam asked Nate.

"Not much." Nate was distracted by a young heifer's bellow as the branding iron sizzled on her hide leaving the outfit's trademark D sitting on a rocking chair curve.

"Did you summon me out here to represent the heifer?" Nate teased.

"No, let me give you the short of it. We have 708 head of cattle, of which around 300 are cows, giving us 250–300 calves per year. The rest are yearlings and bulls. Each year all the calves need branding, and the bull calves need to be fixed, plus we try to coal oil as many others as possible. Sorting, roping, hog-tying, branding, and fixing takes two weeks doing it the standard way as all ranchers do. In the process, we're lucky if a cowhand doesn't get crippled by flaying hooves, and many get bruised. This year the job will be done in three days without anyone getting hurt."

"That's great to know, but how does that affect me?"

"It's happening because of the headgate contraption I built." Adam led Nate closer to the action for a better view as more cattle were processed.

"Great invention, but—"

"I want to patent it. Can you do the paperwork and get it filed?"

"I never have filed a patent for a client, but I had a class in law school on it. My brother in Iowa can help run me through the process."

Until they finished, Nate watched intently so he could accurately describe the headgate and its function in words.

When the last new steer was released from the headgate, July, standing on the headgate, raised his hat from his head, waved it, and cheered. He was soon joined by the rest of the crew in celebration.

"Looks like you have some cowboys in the mood to celebrate," observed Nate.

"Yeh, I promised them if all went well, they could all head to town tonight."

"You can handle the herd alone?"

"Yeah, unlike the cowboys after the processing, the herd will not be in the mood to wander off. And Herman will be with me. He has no use for town activity."

"I'll read up on patents and telegram my brother. Give me a couple days and stop in. I'll know more about patents then. And put out a few more stakes around your property. You can likely expect the government land inspector agent to drop by soon."

"So, this is the Montana Betsy's saloon I've heard so much about," July said to Hank.

"Yep, Betsy, come here," Hank hollered down the bar at her. "This is July. He's been with us nearly a year, had some family tragedy we're helping him past. Get him a shot on me."

"So very glad to meet you." Betsy held out her hand and clasped it longer than July expected. "His first drink is on the house." Betsy had learned that investment in new business prospects was prudent.

Hank was on his second shot of whiskey when Chance, foreman of the Barnhouse spread, walked into the saloon.

"I thought you guys would be processing for another week."

"Boss came up with a new way of doin it—we finished and now into fun."

"You must have taken many shortcuts. We start next week and need more help. My offer still stands. Be my assistant foreman for more money than Adam is paying you."

"Thanks, but no. Havin' one boss is enough."

"Lord Barnhouse will be here in June. You'll find him very hard to refuse."

"The answer will be the same to your Barnhouse fella."

"He prefers to be called Lord Barnhouse, calling him otherwise you'll regret."

"If he prefers his title, stayin in England might have been his better choice."

The Duval cowboys of Hank, Hairy, Fancy, Clint, and July planned to share a room at the hotel with two full beds. Although the room was smaller, sleeping in the same cabin room they were accustomed. Straws were drawn to determine who slept on the floor. Fancy lost. He protested and said for a dollar more than his share of the hotel expense, he would extend his frolicking stay upstairs in the saloon for the whole night.

In the morning, four left for the winter camp, while July was charged with picking up a few supplies at the general store.

"You are part of Adam's outfit, aren't you?" Emily asked.

"That I am."

"When do you expect him to head this way?"

"He said toward the end of week he'd meet with his attorney."

"You don't talk like the other cowboys. Where are you from?"

"I'm from Nebraska. I've been here a year."

"Well, you tell Adam I told you the next time you are in town to look me up."

"Yes, ma'am."

Emily's dad had been listening from the back room and entered when July left. "What are you doing, girl? You need to be focusing on Adam. Are you intent upon chasing him off like you did that other boyfriend?"

"No, Dad, not at all. But I must give him cause to not take me for granted."

Adam was out the next morning with stakes adding to the property corner stakes as Nate had suggested. Clouds were moving in from the west. Likely a spring rain would soon be upon the valley. He saw a buggy coming over the ridge from the south. He had expected his cowboys to be back soon, but no other company.

In a plain no-frills buggy sat a short man whose ample belly was such that he could rest his reign-holding hands upon it. "I'm from the federal land homestead department," he announced.

"Glad to meet you," Adam said climbing from his horse to shake the man's hand.

"My lawyer suggested I add a few stakes to outline the property."

"Good idea," the inspector said as his eyes scanned the sky then turned to the cabin. "Looks like rain is coming."

Adam got the hint. "Why don't you come in the cabin and wait the rain out? Our cook likely has biscuits left from breakfast."

Sky had baked extra biscuits thinking that the returning cowboys would be hungry. He hadn't expected a visitor to devour the biscuits. It seemed that the harder it rained the more biscuits the inspector ate.

"You have improved the property," the inspector remarked as he made note on a paper form with one hand while holding a biscuit in the other hand. Part of the biscuits often crumbled before entering his mouth making a pile of crumbs under his chair. "You've staked it properly and are on the homestead site. I see you have purchased adjacent property."

"Yes, I intend to do things according to rules," Adam replied.

"Able to purchase other property, you are obviously of means," the inspector said, as a statement rather than a question.

After a prolonged silence, he added, "Sometimes I find time to reinspect a homestead claim, but other times I'm just too busy with higher priority work. A man in my position must prioritize."

Adam again got the hint. "It's still raining outside. Do you play cards?"

"Of course," replied the inspector.

Adam had played poker with cowboys in the cabin often but never for money. He knew five-card draw well, but usually played to win. They agreed on a four-bit stake per hand. Three times Adam discarded one of a pair, enabling the inspector to leave the cabin happy with five extra dollars.

The cowboys returning from town were disappointed when they rode in.

"I expected biscuits," Hank exclaimed. "Who was in the buggy we met?"

"Looks like someone ground the biscuits by the pile of crumbs on the floor," July observed.

"The only words I can think of to properly describe him would upset Herman," Adam said.

*"A gem cannot be polished without friction,*
*nor a man perfected without trials."*

Seneca

# ★ CHAPTER 11 ★

"Did you guys see anyone in particular in town?" Adam asked the cowboys.

"Sure did," answered Fancy.

"The short blonde you left money with is not what I mean."

Hank said, "Chance, the Barnhouse foreman, was at the bar for a while, offered me more than you're paying me."

"So why are you here?" Adam asked.

"The Barnhouse fella sounds like a real ass, don't need that."

"Could you watch the language around here?" Herman's remark was ignored by all.

July cautiously said, "Don't take this wrong—just repeating what Emily asked me to tell you. She said I was to tell you she told me to look her up the next time I was in town. And, believe me, I did nothing to encourage her, but I thought withholding it from you would imply disrespect."

"Ha, ha, Adam. Looks like July is going to take your girlfriend," tormented Fancy.

"She's not my girlfriend, so what?"

It was time to drive the herd to spring pasture. Sky dutifully loaded cooking ware and supplies in the chuck wagon, knowing it would be seven months before he had the convenience of cooking in a cabin. All mounted with bedrolls and personal items on their horse or stored in the chuck wagon, they started the herd moving to the nearest valley. After the payoff to the land inspector, Adam felt safe leaving the homestead vacant for a time.

Once they were settled in the new valley with the chuckwagon and tents set up and the money box buried, Adam headed for town. Emily was sweeping the wooden sidewalk in front of the general store when Adam rode by headed toward Nate's office. It was the second time in the morning that she had swept the walk. From what July had said, she was expecting Adam.

Rudeness was not part of Adam, and to have ignored her would be rude. He would put what July had relayed out of his mind. "Good morning," he said.

"And a good morning to you although it is nearly noon. What are you in town for?"

"I've an appointment to see my attorney."

"You must have important business with a herd like yours."

"Not exactly about the herd."

"It's a beautiful spring day. I'm frying chicken for dinner. I promised you a picnic. Should I have the livery hitch up dad's buggy, and we can have an early supper picnic by the river?"

"That sounds great to me. I should be finished at the lawyer before three. Would that be too early?"

"Not at all," she replied with a coy smile.

Adam noticed it was the second time he'd stopped at Nate's office to find him unoccupied, and his schedule allowed him to come to the camp at short notice. Pretending to drink whiskey at the saloon had not yet brought him business. It seemed to Adam that his negotiating position was good.

"What did you find out about patent procedures?"

"I've been back and forth with telegrams to my brother's firm in Iowa. They have patent application forms. I can telegram the information, and he'll file it from there. Based on what we know it looks good but will be expensive."

"How so?"

"I already have twenty-two hours into working on it including the time I rode out to your camp."

"You are charging me for the trip there and back?"

"I only billed one way, giving you a break."

"How generous of you. I suppose it will be at your normal fee of a dollar an hour. With that many hours, I assumed a discount would be in order."

"Maybe I'll cut off a couple hours. The good news is that brother Bob thinks the headgate is a great invention and can be used all over the country. What would you like to call it?"

"Do you have any ideas?"

"How about *Adam's Chute?* Sounds a little biblical."

"Fine with me, but I do have an idea. I've noticed you are not very busy with legal work. Since you and your brother think it will sell, and frankly, I'm busy with the herd and don't want to market it and all else that'll go into it. Why don't I turn it over to you for 20% of anything that can be generated from the patent?"

"What about the twenty-two hours billed presently, which I'll reduce to twenty?"

"I'll pay that, but from now on you work for a percentage."

"It's going to entail much work. Perhaps we might consider giving a manufacturer exclusive right to produce your headgates. Since the patent will be in your name, I'd need you to give me power of attorney in matters relating to the patent. And I believe if I'm doing all the work, 40% would be more appropriate."

"It's my invention. Perhaps I'd be better off paying you by the hour." Adam rose from his chair, took a couple steps to the door, turned, thought momentarily for effect, and said, "I'll share 30 percent, no more."

Adam was halfway through the door when Nate said, "Thirty

percent it is. Now get back here because we have more to discuss. I need to get back to Iowa for business before the year is over. I'll head there next week, go over a strategy to produce, and market the head-gate with Bob, and visit a couple manufactures in the area. You are right, unfortunately—it's not like I'm inundated with business here."

"How long will you be gone?"

"I'll take a stagecoach to Billings and trains from there. Probably three days to get there and back. I should be back in ten days."

"All right, have a good trip," Adam stood.

"Hold it. I'll need that power of attorney before you leave."

Adam tied his horse to the hitching rack outside the general store, caught Emily looking through the second-floor window, and found Emily's dad behind the counter. "I hope it's okay that Emily and I take your buggy on a picnic with Emily."

"Why wouldn't it be? You are a good customer, and well….it is good that she gets out. You know what they say about Sally."

"What's that?"

"Never mind—the all-work-and-no-play thing. The stairs to our quarters are in the back room. She is expecting you."

"I didn't want to start packing before I saw you riding up," she said as he entered a kitchen den area. As she packed the basket, Adam looked around. More than one wall had framed canvases of flowers painted in oil. Near the kitchen table hung a still life of apples.

"You have some nice art. Who is the artist?"

"Check out the signature."

On the lower right-hand corner of each painting was "Emily Doyle" in neater script done with a brush than Adam could have with a pen.

"I can't believe it. You are a great artist. You could sell these."

"Maybe someday I will when I don't need to work at the store and have time to paint." Her plan to get him up upstairs to show off her artwork worked.

"Did you learn this at the Denver girls finishing school?"

"Yes, I'm ready to go," she answered handing him the basket to carry.

Adam helped her on the buggy, walked around, and started to get on the left side of her. She gave him a strange look.

"What?" he asked.

"You are getting on the wrong side. Haven't you ever driven a buggy with someone else?"

Adam didn't answer and switched sides. He could not understand why his spatial memory told him the left rather than right side of her was proper.

As they passed Montana Betsy's saloon, he saw Lorraine on a stepstool washing a saloon window. Like not understanding the source of an incorrect position on the buggy, he didn't understand his hope not to be seen by Lorraine, but it wasn't to be. Lorraine turned and seemed to glare in curiosity at the couple in the buggy. Adam did not see the smirk Emily returned Lorraine.

The buggy had frayed icicle cord frill around the edge of the canopy. It was prestigious while the land inspector's buggy was plain to convey a frugal image.

On the ride to the Missouri River, Adam asked many questions about her paintings, validating her plan and giving her another idea.

They avoided the shade of a tree and placed the blanket in the sun a few feet from the water's edge. The spring sun felt good. The chicken and conversation were good, only interrupted when a crappie occasionally jumped from the river making a splashing sound.

"What happened to your mother?" Adam asked.

"Dad says she didn't like it here and moved back to Ohio, but I heard rumors that she left with another man. Where is your mother?"

"She passed," Adam said not knowing whether it was a lie and changed the subject quickly. "Do you know how to swim?"

"No, not the thing a proper lady does," she answered.

"I don't mean skinny dipping, just swimming."

"I have no need to, and I prefer to clean myself in my private bath in case your deviant mind wonders."

"I'm sorry. I didn't mean to offend you."

"You didn't. Now before we leave, I'd be tolerant if you chose to spark me a couple times."

Adam had no recollection of ever kissing a girl. But his inexperience would not prevent him from giving it a try. The first kiss ended quickly. He backed off. She held steady and he leaned in for another kiss. This one lasted longer and he could feel a certain excitement. When they parted, their eyes held each other, and he leaned in again.

She backed away, 'Enough, you shouldn't get the wrong idea about me. I think it is time to go."

It was quieter on the ride back to town. The sun was near setting when he pulled up in front of the general store and told her he would return the buggy and walk back for his horse. They said their goodbyes.

She was standing at the store door when he returned. "I suppose I would blush at what you cowboys have hung on your cabin walls."

"Not unless empty walls cause you to blush. Such as you think would cause Herman to go on a tirade and sleep outside."

She reached around the door and handed him a framed small still life painting of a bowl of fruit. "Hope you enjoy it on your wall, although I know you will be out much of the season."

Emily could tell by Adam's inspection of the painting that she had successfully attached another string to her prey.

"Well? You were gone nearly three hours." Emily's dad asked as she entered the family's second floor living quarters.

"It went very well, although I have this feeling that he may be younger than he says."

"Why is that?"

"It seemed as though he wanted me to drive the buggy. Maybe he's never driven one and was just timid since it is your buggy, but it almost seemed as if he didn't know which side was which."

"You said he was eighteen; that's a seven-year difference. Does that bother you?"

"No, I think it is good. Although he seems smart and has ample resources, his inexperience at some things allows me to direct him. I don't think he's had any encounters at sparking."

"That's enough—some things I don't need to hear," her dad replied.

Emily stepped to the window and looked down the street. "I see his horse tied in front of that place of sin."

Elmer responded, "I've asked around and it seems he isn't into drinking and has never been seen at a gambling table. I suspect he just stopped to brag about his picnic with the most sought-after daughter in town."

"You may be right, but there may be another problem there which I will deal with."

Emily unsuccessfully tried to be discreet walking by the window every few minutes to check on Adam's horse. On the last pass, her father saw a smile emerge on her face.

"Well?"

"He's gone."

Before leaving town, Adam had stopped at the saloon. No one was at the bar and Mildred was behind it. "What can I get you?"

"A beer will do. Where's Betsy?"

"She's in back working on a supply order. She has me tending bar some now. Do you want me to get her?"

"No, no, just stopped. Where's Lorraine?"

"She's in the lean-to with Gerald. I don't want her in the bar when the sun gets close to the horizon. Men might get the wrong idea. But leaving her with Gerald isn't the best either."

"Why?"

Gerald's slow, what can I say. I hoped being around people and more age on him would make him right, it hasn't. I don't want his condition to hold her back. She has abilities."

"Have you thought about sending her to the school on the other side of town?"

"She's too much work to do here for that. I'm doing side seamstress business. The girls who work the tables and upstairs are always needing garment repairs. Lori is filling in for me cleaning during the day. The extra money I'm putting away. Maybe in a year or two we can get a proper place to live. My illusions about that great house my husband and I would buy with the gold are gone. I must live in the present."

"But what about Lorraine? She needs an education, or she'll end up like the girls you are mending clothes for."

"Oh, I'm working on that. She caught on well to me teaching her the alphabet and numbers when she was young. Now she can read and multiply as well as anyone her age."

"I better get back to the herd. Tell her *hi* for me."

There wasn't a cleaner, better swept sidewalk in the town than the section in front of the general store. A broom in her hand gave Emily an excuse to survey what was happening in town. For Elmer, her dad, sitting on one of two chairs under the awing over the sidewalk served the purpose, conveying an image of control. For Emily, besides knowing the town happenings, keeping the wooden sidewalk spotless would impress any would-be suitors that she would make a great housekeeper.

It was the second time in the morning Emily had checked the sidewalk for dust and debris when she saw Lorraine headed for the waste wagon with a bucket. On Lorraine's walk back from the wagon, she encountered a well-dressed lady twirling a parasol over her. She immediately recognized her as the store owner's daughter and buggy companion of Adam.

"Good morning,"

"Morning," Lorraine returned.

Emily stopped. "I don't think we've formally met. I'm Emily and you are?"

"Call me Lorraine."

"Well, it's so glad to meet you. I saw you yesterday as my boyfriend and I went on a picnic. Do you know him?"

"Yes, he helped my family when we were stranded in the wilderness."

"He is a great guy, experienced in much and very sophisticated, too much for most in this town, I suspect. We had a great time on our picnic, and I must say he is very skilled at sparking. It is so enjoyable making plans for the future with him. Now you have a good day." Emily moved her gaze forward and continued down the sidewalk without waiting for a response.

*"Remember, happiness doesn't depend upon who you are or what you have; it depends solely upon what you think."*

Dale Carnegie

# ★ CHAPTER 12 ★

In late summer it had been three weeks since Adam had gone to Great Falls. He needed the quiet of riding among cattle to sort things out. Time in town seemed to only complicate his life. It seemed at times like he had two lives, but one was unknown, nearly impenetrable, tucked away with a wall built around it.

His signature signified trust in his attorney to handle his invention. Whatever would become of it would happen. It wasn't as if he had a responsibility to preserve and maximize it, because it was his idea to do with as he pleased. He was not a custodian of it like he was the cattle herd that belonged to his father. His primary obligation was maintaining the herd. He was where he needed to be.

He had shown the cowboys the still-life painting Emily had given him. July said it deserved to be hung in a house, not a cabin. July was right. But on a trip to check out the winter quarters and make them appear inhabited, Adam hung it on the cabin wall.

Emily was so right for him in many ways. She was well heeled in the customs of the time in which they lived. A time that he often felt like an outsider in. He struggled to find from where the outsider feeling came just as he struggled to understand why he felt an obligation and affection for Lorraine. If he had not been with the crew that day, her mother would have been hanged and Lorraine and her brother left to the peril of the wilderness.

He had told Emily he was eighteen when he was only sixteen. She was twenty-five. *How would she react if he told her the truth? Would her patronizing attitude toward him increase or would she dump him because of his youth? Was the reason he felt comfortable with her because she was like a mother figure which he had no recollection of?*

"We've cattle to get to town. Are you going to sleep all day, boss?" Hank hollered standing at the tent opening. "Sky has breakfast ready."

"I'll be right there," Adam answered, pushing reflections upon his life in the background and pulling his boots on.

"Am I to go with to town with the culls?" Fancy asked before Adam filled his plate.

"No, it's not your turn. You were in town last weekend. Hairy is joining Hank and me."

"Well, that's not all bad news. At least I won't have to ride that nearly impassible trail."

"It couldn't have been that bad," Adam stated.

Hank added, "It was bad, a quagmire of ruts in the mud. The constant caravans of limestone-block-filled wagons from the quarry near Billings has destroyed the trail."

"Must be quite a house Barnhouse is building."

"From what I heard in the saloon last week, will be more like a castle. And roofers on top of the hotel. Seems to be they're adding a third floor. Hope all doesn't change the town."

With twenty head sorted out for the monthly cull, they headed to Great Falls. Two wagons loaded with limestone blocks worked their way through the herd with little difficulty but leaving deep tracks in the dust. Hot, dry weather for two weeks had eliminated what Fancy had called the quagmire of the trail, but heavy traffic evidence was obvious.

To Adam's surprise, because of the constant increase of immigrants in the country, the price of beef had gone up. Buyers from Chicago packers were paying one and a half dollars more for head than the prior month.

With the cattle in a pen and the price paid, the three cowboys rode into town. The third floor of the hotel had been framed with windows set. They also noticed two new houses being built on the edge of town. Great Falls was growing.

"We're going to check out the castle progress," Hank told Adam. "I suggest you join us."

Emily was with a broom on the sidewalk. Adam stopped and told the others he would join them shortly.

"I heard you were in town. Nice that you finally came back," she said with a hint of sarcasm.

"You know how it is—lot of work with the herd. We're needing to move more than normal as there is more competition for range grass."

"I see."

"I was thinking with business in town, I'd stay the night. Perhaps you'd like to join me for dinner at the hotel diner."

"Nice of you to think of me. What time?"

"I need to catch up with Nate. I'll pick you up here at six."

"I'll be ready."

Riding away it struck Adam that he had said he'd pick her up. He had no buggy. She certainly wouldn't double with him on his horse for two blocks to the hotel. He would, of course, only walk her to the diner.

About a quarter mile from town there was a flurry of activity. Limestone blocks two feet long, a foot wide and thick were being stacked with mortar. The walls were six feet high with gaps where Adam suspected windows would be put. The outline of the structure covered more area than any building in town. Hank wasn't exaggerating—it had the looks of a soon-to-be castle. At a distance, two wooden structures were being built. Future servant's quarters or barn, Adam did not know. Many tents were erected for builders he suspected; many of which were Chinese.

Any doubt Adam had about Chance overstating the means and resolve of his boss, this Lord from England, were erased. He would be a force to reckon with.

"It is what it is. We can't do anything about it, but makes you wonder what he'll do to the cattle range," Adam observed.

"I just thought you should see it, boss," Hank replied.

"You guys do your thing at the saloon. Try to stay out of trouble and don't get back to camp too late. I've business and will stay the night."

Adam tied his horse on the street and walked under the stairs which led to the town doctor's office. Nearly hidden under the stairs was the door to Nate's office with a small sign identifying it. Nate had the door propped open in hopes of getting a breeze. Adam knocked on the door frame before entering.

"Well, well, you finally showed up. Had you forgotten about Adam's Chute?"

"I've been busy on the range and details are what you will get thirty percent for."

"Let me bring you up to date. The paperwork has all been filed. We worked out an agreement with a manufacturer in Iowa to start production immediately. They will have exclusive right to produce the chute and do all the promotion for a fee."

"What's the fee?"

"Ten percent of margins."

"I expect that ten percent will come from your thirty."

"No, it will come off the top."

"I don't recollect that was our agreement."

"Were you prepared to spend a thousand or more on advertising and promotion? They will display your invention at the Iowa State Fair which starts this week and have reserved space for a display at the Texas State Fair in October. Contact has also been made with Ag schools around the country. The chutes will be priced at ten dollars, allowing a margin of five dollars. Broken down it will be fifty cents for them, one dollar and thirty-five cents for me and three dollars and fifteen cents for you per unit sold. Adam, you soon will be a wealthy man."

When Nate finished updating Adam, the fire in him hearing of losing ten percent had dissipated. "It does sound like you've made progress. Giving you thirty percent may have been sensible." Adam stood ready to end their meeting when curiosity caused him to ask, "You said family business necessitated your trip to Iowa."

"Yes, mother wanted us there to celebrate my brother's and my birthdays. We were born in the same month ten years apart."

"Not to be nosey, but how old are you?"

"I turned thirty last month. Speaking of age, it's a good thing you're eighteen. If you were younger the patent paperwork would have to have been filed under your dad's name. And that reminds me. The telegraph office delivered a telegram from your dad. They didn't know how to reach you."

The telegram was short.

> Business about finished in TX. Expect me back by roundup time next spring.
>
> Ted Duval

Now Adam knew his father's name. He folded the telegram in his pocket and started to leave only to be stopped again.

"You should know I purchased the building across the street. My office will be on the first floor, and it has three apartments on the second. In one, I will live. Funds were released from my inheritance at age thirty. I used the money to purchase the building."

"That was the startup general store building, right?"

"Yes, but the space was too small. They were not able to compete with Elmer and Emily."

Adam checked his watch before mounting his horse. It was a

quarter of six. The meeting had lasted longer than he expected. Emily was expecting him to take her to dinner at six, but he had another stop first. Not wanting to be seen by her riding around the corner of the block to the saloon, he walked the opposite side of the block and intended to enter the saloon from the alley.

In the alley, he heard discussion from inside a tin-sided lean-to.

"Is anyone there?" he announced himself and realized how ridiculous the question was.

Mildred stepped out. "Adam, I was just telling Lori she needs to stay here with Gerald and not be roaming around after dark."

Lorraine joined her mother. "Hi Adam."

"I'm glad to see you, Lorraine," he said unconsciously tipping his hat.

"I know the saloon is closed on Sunday. I'm staying in town overnight," he stated, finding himself fumbling. He turned his attention back to Mildred. "I just thought I might escort your family to church in the morning."

"I have given it thought. It would be a good experience for Gerald and Lori. It's just that…well living and working here and all."

"Phooey, church is at ten. I'll be here to walk you at a quarter of."

It was ten minutes after six when Adam tied his horse in front of the general store. Emily had been watching the mantel clock in frustration since it chimed six times.

"I apologize for being late. My appointment with Clements lasted longer than I anticipated."

"Rumors around town have it that you have a patent on that cattle contraption you built. My daughter understands that business is business," Elmer stated, taking the ire from Emily.

Her father's intervention worked. Emily smiled at Adam, reached for his arm to be escorted, and said, "Adam, I've been looking very much forward to our dinner. Let's go."

The hotel diner was the place to eat in town. The only other choices were a breakfast hangout that served the same meals all day and the saloon. Emily's dress flamed out below the waist more than Adam had ever seen as it contained many petticoats. With her arm tucked under his, he had to use caution to avoid tripping on her dress hem which brushed his leg with every step.

In the diner as they made their way to a back table, the dress hem purposely brushing against many guests' chairs announced their arrival.

"Did it go well with your attorney?"

"I believe so. He told me your startup competition in town closed and he bought the building."

"Yes, now we can adjust some prices."

"How so?"

"For us to serve the community well, we must make a decent profit." She then added, "As I expect you will on Adam's Chute."

"You know the name."

"It is a small town."

After small talk and flirtatious innuendos, Adam had to ask, "We are seven years apart in age. You are older than I. Do you see that as an obstacle if we continue to…you know…see each other?"

"Not at all. What is age? It's a number we seldom discuss. Do you know the age of Betsy, the saloon owner? Or the man who owns the livery stable?"

"I see your point but what if I were younger still?"

"Well, I do want to have children, but not marry one."

Her answer startled Adam. He was comfortable with Emily. She was good for him. But he had not contemplated where it might lead. He changed the subject.

"If you'll excuse me for a moment. I'm staying in town tonight. I should go to the lobby and get a room booked."

The desk clerk answered Adam before he asked, "I hope you are not looking for a room. We are full."

"Why, you've never been close to full."

"It's that Barnhouse building project. Many building supervisors are staying here."

"Did you get a room?" Emily asked on his return to the table.

"No."

"I expected such, with all the activity north of town. You may stay with us. Our sofa is short, but I can bring extra blankets if you prefer the den floor."

At the back door to the store, Adam stopped. "Can you save me a place in church tomorrow?"

"Of course, aren't you coming in?"

"No, like you say it is a small town and rumors…well you know."

"Okay, if you must," she replied but made no movement toward the door and waited. Sensing what she was waiting for, and desirous of the same, he leaned toward her and kissed her goodnight.

"Goodnight," he said as she opened the door.

"Goodnight, dear," she replied as she closed it.

Adam led his horse into a stall at the livery stable. It was known the price of stalling a horse for the night entitled the owner a place in the hay mow. Laying on his blanket in the mow, he decided he was eighteen, and he would not acknowledge sixteen ever to himself or others. However, the words *dear* and *marry* bounced in his head as sleep came.

In the morning, Adam washed himself from a bucket of water, put on a clean shirt, and jacket and brushed the straw from his pants as best he could. Gerald, Mildred, and Lorraine were waiting for Adam as he entered the alley.

Lorraine immediately captured his attention. She no longer wore a frayed dirty smock, but a lavender dress with a matching bonnet. The fit left no doubt that she was not a tomboy.

Blushing from his attention, Lorraine said, "Mom is a great seamstress, isn't she?"

"No doubt about it," Adam replied as they walked to the church.

Numerous heads turned toward them as they entered the church, including Emily's. Two back pews were empty. Adam waved toward an empty pew, inviting the family to sit. Lorraine accidentally brushed against him as she entered the pew. He was tempted to sit with them, but it was not to be, he told himself and walked to an empty spot toward the front saved by Emily.

The sermon was on charity and all God-fearing people's obligation to help the poor.

The family in the back row was gone when Emily and Adam left the church.

"You must have had a premonition about the sermon today, bringing that poor family," Emily said to Adam.

*"The soul that is within me no man can degrade."*

Frederick Douglass

# ★ CHAPTER 13 ★

Adam went through different scenarios of how he could learn more about his dad without exposing himself. One day riding around the herd he took a chance and asked Hank, "Do you think Dad went to Texas for a reason other than he said?"

"I think he was afraid to admit he was homesick."

"Really?"

"Yes, and throwing responsibility on you, forcing you to grow could have been part of it also."

Adam asked no more. He had learned his dad was from Texas—that was enough to digest. The rest of the summer and fall they moved the herd more than normal seeking grass. A combination of a hot, dry summer and more herds on the range left them no choice. Winter came early, and all were happy to get to their winter quarters.

Once the herd and cowboys were settled into winter quarters, Adam headed for town with Sky following in the wagon for supplies. Every two weeks Adam traveled to town to check on the chute sales. Money was being sent to a bank account he had opened. Each time he checked, the amount surprised him. He now had plenty of money to expand the herd. *Would that impress his dad? And where would they find the grass?*

Although Adam hadn't met Lord Barnhouse, his arrival was the talk of the town. According to Chance, the lord was adamant upon expanding their herd, which meant less grass close to town. Even without another hot, dry summer, Adam's herd would need to graze in valleys further away. Expanding his herd would only increase the distance he had to travel.

Emily and he had become a regular item whether dining at the hotel or eating dinner with Elmer and her at their place. She was the guide and mentor he needed in an era which still felt strange to him. She was easy to lean on, but at some point, would her constant initiative on most matters become too much? Because he was forced to travel further with the herd next season, seeing Emily would become more difficult. The last time they went for a picnic, she asked if he was ready to leave the herd and move to town. It was a thought.

Adam had planned to stop and see Lorraine and family before meeting Emily, but his meeting with Nate lasted longer than he expected. Most times in town he checked on Lorraine. She was not in a good situation, but he did not know what to do about it. He gave up checking on Lorraine before he met Emily as being late at Emily's would raise her ire.

It was an unusually warm November day. Emily had insisted on taking advantage of it for their last picnic of the season. As was becoming custom, he kissed her twice, more than a peck each time. To his surprise she let him lean in for a third that lasted longer than any until she backed away.

She drew a deep breath and said, "I shouldn't have let you kiss me the third time. It was breaking the rules I've set for myself. Until our situation changes, two kisses are enough."

When he didn't reply, she continued, "From what you've said about chute sales, you've now more than enough money to buy a house in town. I'll be twenty-six soon. I don't want to live with my dad forever."

"Are you suggesting something?" Adam asked.

"All I'm saying is a girl's got to wonder and consider her future."

"I think we each should give that much thought before we discuss it further."

Emily didn't stop and turn at the back door to the store. "Come on in, I'm sure Dad has the carrom board out. Frequently, before Adam left for his hotel room, they had a carrom tournament. Emily and he would strike their shooter dice with a flip of a finger attempting to knock other dice in a corner board pocket. Elmer would play the winner. He always won.

When the clock struck ten, Emily escorted him to the door. After a goodnight kiss, she said, "You will think about our discussion."

"Of course, I will," he answered.

Lorraine put her book down. She had been reading by lamp light in the lean-to for three hours. Her eyes were tired. "I'm thirsty and we are out of water. I'm going to the well," she told her brother.

"Mom said we're not to leave here after dark," Gerald cautioned.

"You don't need to tell her everything," Lorraine answered as she picked up the water bucket and left the lean-to.

Jake and Dirk had been at the Barnhouse spread for three months. Chance was apprehensive about their demeanor, but available, experienced cowboys were in great demand and hard to find. Nearly out of money and frustrated by their night at Montana Betsy's they mounted their horses. As they left town, they saw a smallish redheaded smock-covered girl at the well.

Lorraine felt a shiver as two riders slowed and took notice of her. With the water bucket filled, she headed toward the alley shortcut to the lean-to. Out after dark it was better to avoid the sidewalk where her mother might see her.

"What do you think?" Jake asked Dirk.

"Why not?" Dirk answered. He pointed to the end of the alley Lorraine had entered, then himself and gestured in the other direction.

Lorraine was halfway through the alley when she saw a moonlit man standing at the end of the alley. She slowed. He didn't move, staring at her. She turned to see another man behind her.

"Hi, sweetie, want to have a good time tonight?" the man in front of her said.

She felt the man behind her lay his hand on her shoulder. Reflex caused her to turn and swing the bucket striking him midsection. Nearly, knocking the wind from him and drenching him with cold water.

"You little bitch," he hollered.

She replied by bringing her knee up hard to his vulnerable area. He yowled and fell to the ground in fetal position. Suddenly, two hands grabbed from behind and spun her around, then pushed her against a brick wall.

"Wow, a little fighter, I like that," he said as he pressed against her, filling her nostrils with foul body and whiskey odor she would not soon forget. Her hands slapped his away as he attempted to grope her. Rather than making him angry, he snickered at her defense. "You know I'll get what I want."

Adam left his horse at the livery stable and walked to the hotel. He hadn't time to see Lorraine before meeting Emily. He contemplated going to the saloon and talking to Mildred but thought better of it, preferring to avoid the late-night havoc in the saloon. He had stopped at the lean-to and chatted with Gerald and Lorraine before after dark but never this late.

A full moon made it easier to move around the town than normal. Lamppost lanterns were talked about by the city council but had not been approved. Adam stepped down from the wooden sidewalk onto the entrance to an alley and heard a muffled scream. At first, he thought it was two alley cats fighting, then realized it wasn't.

Turning into the alley, moonlight passing over a building highlighted two figures struggling against brick wall. Adam nearly passed it off as two drunks from the saloon having an alley squabble. He was starting to turn away when he heard a *NO!* He recognized the voice.

In strides faster than Adam could remember, he was upon a man attempting to get his hands under Lorraine's smock as she struggled. The man was too focused on his pursuit to notice Adam's approach.

With his left hand, Adam pulled his pistol from his left-handed holster, raised it, and swiped it across the man's head. The man knew not what hit him and dropped at Lorraine's feet. Adam reached for Lorraine steadying her when something slammed his chest hard, knocking the wind from him. The hit caused him to fall beside the man he'd knocked out pulling Lorraine down with him.

He turned to the sound of the shot and saw another man on the ground with a gun pointed at him. Adam quickly lowered his head as the second round from the man entered the leg of fallen man he laid behind. The man now recovering from a blow to his head flinched from the bullet.

Adam raised his pistol, pulled back the hammer, and squeezed the trigger. The Colt erupted close to Lorraine's ear deafening her. The barrel explosion sent a 200-grain lead bullet barreling at a thousand feet per second in a direct line to the left side of the man's chest. The bullet was not slowed by the man's vest or shirt, punctured his hide, and was deflected by a rib and then ripped through his left lung before it lost momentum in his aorta.

Lorraine was sobbing as she lay beside him. He reached for her and held her tight.

It had been a long day for the sheriff. He had transported a prisoner to another town and was looking forward to sleeping on a cot in a cell. He was too tired to go home. He was nearly asleep when someone burst through the door and said a fight had broken out in Montana Betsy's. By the time he got to the saloon, the fighters had vented their anger on each other, and all was quiet. With no damage, he scolded them, and headed back for the office.

The sheriff had nearly reached the office when three shots rang out from an alley. The sound of shots overcame his fatigue. He turned and ran toward an alley, while holding the handle of his pistol to keep it from falling from his holster. Once he entered the alley, he held the pistol toward four figures on the ground. Closer, he saw two men lying, both bleeding, and a couple in an embrace.

"What happened here?" he asked with his gun at the ready.

"He shot me for no reason," pleaded Jake, while holding his hand on a bleeding leg.

Adam helped Lorraine up and answered the sheriff, "His partner shot him. They were attempting to molest this girl. And I shot the other man on the ground after he shot me."

The sheriff had seen the girl around the saloon and surmised what she likely was doing in the alley at that time of night. He knew Adam had a herd outside of town, but two men were shot, and Adam showed no signs of being shot. "Where did he hit you?"

"In the chest."

"I see no blood."

"Girl, what's your name?"

"It is Lorraine," Adam answered.

"Let her answer."

She looked at the sheriff and knew he was asking her a question but a combination of shock and the noise impact of Adam's gun firing close, rendered her unable to hear.

"Isn't your name Adam Duval?" asked the sheriff.

"Yes."

"You've quite a reputation around town as a handyman with a gun given what you did with wolves. You'd better come with me."

A crowd was gathering. The sheriff crouched over Dirk who was breathing but in bad shape and he asked someone to get the doctor.

"You can't be arresting me for protecting the girl," Adam stated.

"I'm not arresting you, but you can spend the night in jail until we get this sorted out."

Before the sheriff could get him locked up, Adam pulled his shirt off and showed him a bruise the size of a watch, then showed him the pocket watch he had purchased from Emily distorted by a bullet.

"There, see he shot me first."

"Maybe so, but I'm tired, we'll deal with it in the morning."

It was a busy night at Montana Betsy's. Both Betsy and Martha were tending bar. Some patrons left to investigate shots, but most soon returned.

"What were the shots about?" asked Betsy.

"Looks like some guy was monkeying with a girl and shot two guys who tried to stop him," one answered.

"Who was the guy and girl?" Betsy asked.

"Don't know but haven't been in town that long."

"What did the girl look like?" asked Martha.

"She wore a smock and had big red hair."

Martha tossed her apron on the bar and scurried to the back door.

She found Lorraine trembling hutched in a corner of the lean-to. Her smock was covered in blood from the man's leg wound.

A quick inspection from her mother found no wounds on Lorraine.

"What happened?"

Lorraine aggressively shook her head, then pointed to her ear.

The sheriff took the cot in the adjacent cell and snored hard all night. But it was not the snoring that prevented Adam from sleeping. After a cup of coffee, the next morning the sheriff needed breakfast, but he knew he was obligated to bring a prisoner a meal if he remained jailed. The till was low for such expenses.

"Here's the deal. I'm letting you out, but do not leave town, no going back to your herd until I talk to the county prosecutor and determine what we are to do."

The sheriff had reached for the jail keys when the town doctor came in. "I just thought I should notify you the shooting victim died this morning. I did all I could. He just bled out. The other guy, Jake, will be okay with a minor leg wound but he had a gash on his head also."

Adam heard the conversation and felt the severity of his predicament with the sheriff's hard look as he hung the keys back on a peg.

After eating breakfast, the sheriff called on one of the two older attorneys in town who served as the county prosecutor and filled him in on what he knew.

"I'll interview the guy with the leg wound and the girl at the scene and get back with you," the prosecutor said.

Adam didn't touch the cold breakfast he was brought.

It was late afternoon when the prosecutor entered the jail. "What did you learn?"

"Jake, the man he shot in the leg, says Dirk and him were riding out of town when they heard a girl scream. He said they tried to help, but Adam was too quick for them and shot them both. It seems the girl is so traumatized by the event she can't hear or talk."

"Adam does show evidence of a bruise from a bullet damaged watch," the sheriff said.

"We don't have any choice. I'm temporarily charging him with murder. The judge can sort it all out at an inquest hearing when he gets back into town."

"You can't do that without hearing what really happened from me," Adam hollered from the cell.

"You'll get your chance. We can't let a gun fighter back on the street. Anyone who can drop six running wolves with a handgun is dangerous and apt to also be a people killer," answered the prosecutor.

"I only shot four and only one was running," Adam replied.

"When will the judge be back in town?" asked the sheriff.

"Two weeks, I reckon."

"I'll need the city council to authorize funds for jail feeding then."

"It'll be done," replied the prosecutor as he left, feeling somewhat avenged for losing a lucrative potential client to the new lawyer in town.

*"Nothing travels faster than the speed of light, with the possible exception of bad news, which obeys its own special laws."*

Douglas Adams

# ★ CHAPTER 14 ★

It was late in the day when he heard the sheriff say, "You have a visitor."

Nate was escorted to Adam's cell. "Are you to be his attorney?" the sheriff asked.

"Yes, if he'll have me."

The sheriff left the cell block and closed the door to his office. "I'm sorry I didn't get here earlier. I'd been in the office all day until I took a walk and heard the talk the town is obsessed with."

"Can you get me out of here?"

"Only the judge can set bail, and if the charges stick at the inquest, he won't allow bail on a murder charge. Our focus must be on the inquest. Tell me exactly what happened and don't leave out any details."

Nate pulled out a notebook as Adam started to describe what he saw and did in the alley. Adam had gone over it many times in his head and started when he heard Lorraine scream.

"No, back up, start with what you were doing two hours before you heard a scream from the alley and don't leave out any details."

"After Emily and I got back from the picnic we played carrom with Elmer..." he started his recollection of events and ended with the sheriff taking him to jail.

Nate reviewed his notes and said, "Okay, now I want you to start over and go through it all again, add any details you forgot the first time."

Nate checked off his notes as Adam retold the story. It matched. He knew Adam well enough that he believed him, but he learned in law school that concocted testimony often varied. It was difficult to keep all details exactly the same if they were inventions. It was easier to remember the truth than a lie you told. And any inconsistencies should come out now instead of in the court room.

"So, I'm doomed here for two weeks?" Adam lamented.

"Most likely, but I'll start to work immediately."

"Has word got to Hank and the cowboys?"

"I have no idea. It's all everyone is talking about in town, but if they have no contact here, they haven't heard."

"I don't know who else to ask. Can you ride out and inform the crew that I'll be here for a while?"

"Where are they?"

"We're in winter quarters," Adam caught himself. "At least they are. You know the properties I homesteaded and purchased. You rode there to see the chute work."

"I remember, but..."

"It's about a six-hour ride north-northeast, an eight-hour ride for you."

"When I get back, I'll talk to Lorraine, hopefully she'll have her hearing back and be able to talk. And I'll get some background on Jake and Dirk. Oh, and make sure you save that pocket watch."

Nate left early the next morning and rode with only one stop for eight hours. He could hardly walk when he dismounted at what he thought was his destination but with no herd in site. It would be dark in an hour. All he could think about was wolves. He had no gun. Even if he did, he had only shot his grandfather's shotgun once.

He was desperate. At a distance, he saw a wisp of smoke or was it a low cloud, Indians or not, he had no choice and rode toward it.

Over the next rise, relief came when he not only saw it was smoke, but it came from the edge of a large herd of cattle. He saw no cabin, which told him he had stumbled onto another herd. Nevertheless, wolves would not tear him apart.

"I've seen you around town. What are doing here?" Chance asked as Nate dismounted at the Barnhouse herd camp.

"I'm looking for the Duval herd and quite frankly, I got lost."

"They're about two hours ride that-a-way," he pointed west. Best you stay with us and head there in the morning. We've food left, help yourself."

"I don't know what I'd have done if I hadn't stumbled on you."

"You'd probably have made wolf feed unless a mountain lion beat them to it. Only a fool would travel out here by himself without being armed."

Nate ignored the remark though he knew it contained some truth.

"I suppose you'll be representing Adam since you've done work for him. They gonta hang him?"

"He's innocent, I have no doubt. Jake isn't with this herd, is he?"

"Ya, he's on watch on the other side until midnight."

"I'd like to ask him a few questions since I'm here."

"Suit yourself, but I'd not put much stock in anything he'd tell you."

"Why is that?"

"If I'd not been disparate for hands, I wouldn't have put those two on. The few times I've met Adam, he doesn't seem like the kind to...you know. He could buy it, why do that? But if they hang him, it'll make gettin his herd easier since he refuses to sell."

"No doubt we'd like to have his herd, but there are limits, even for scalawag cowboys like me."

Nate had brought a blanket. Chance loaned him another and he half slept close to the fire. He heard the exchange of herd scouts in the middle of the night but would question Jake in the morning.

In the morning, he introduced himself to Jake and asked about the alley episode.

"Why are you so interested?" Jake asked.

Having no ethical choice, he told Jake he was representing Adam.

"Ain't talk'in. Told sheriff and proceyator, whatever you call him, all, enough talkin," Jake said and hurriedly left camp.

"Well?" Chance asked.

"A guy telling the truth usually doesn't have a problem repeating it," Nate answered.

"I won't disagree," Chance added.

Nate arrived mid-morning at the Duval winter quarters cabin. The cowboys were leaving from a late breakfast. They were shocked by the news.

"Adam wouldn't do such a thing," Hank said. "I don't believe it."

"Neither do I, but he wanted me to ride out here and inform you."

"If'in he did, a hangin would be the proper thing," remarked Herman.

"Shut up, Herman. When Adam returns, I'll tell him what you said. You'll ride night shifts for a month," warned Fancy.

"I'd appreciate it if one of you would ride back with me and talk to him," Nate said, thinking about the danger of getting lost again as much as company for Adam.

"I'll go," said Hank.

Half in jest, Fancy said, "Maybe we should all go and break him out. They sell dynamite at the general store and Emily being his squeeze in'all, she'd supply us."

Adam had not seen anyone for two days except the sheriff as he pushed a plate of food under the cell door. He had thought and re-thought all that had happened. What he could have done differently, he did not know. The more he thought, the scarier his thoughts became.

*What if Lorraine never recovered her hearing? What if Nate got lost and was eaten by wolves or bought off by Barnhouse to protect his cowboys? He should have been back by now. Emily had never come to see him. She had to know. Was she dumping her boyfriend killer?*

It was ten days until they said the judge would arrive. *Would he still have his sanity?*

"You have a visitor," the sheriff startled Adam. It was preacher Ken.

"I've seen you in church occasionally and consider you part of my flock. How are you?"

"I only shot the man after he shot at me and got involved to protect a girl. Is that a sin, preacher?"

"Only God can determine that, son. I am not to judge."

"But if they convict me, they'll hang me."

"Death is not the end for the righteous, son, only the beginning. Let me say a prayer for you."

> Lord, protect this man here. Let the truth come out, whatever it is. We know that forgiveness is your and only your purview, and we know our trials here on Earth are cast upon us for a reason. We trust in your ways. Amen.

The preacher continued, "If you did commit sin in the alley, whatever it may have been, a confession now the Lord would look kindly upon."

"I will swear on a Bible that I did no wrong and have no regrets," Adam said so firmly that the preacher was convinced of his innocence.

Later that day Hank arrived at the jail. "What can I do?" he asked.

"Nothing, unless you can prove Jake is lying."

"Perhaps I can find him, and we can come to an understanding."

"I suggest not. That could easily backfire, and you'd be in here with me. Who'd run the herd then?"

"What if he just disappeared before the inquest?"

"Again, too dangerous. I might have considered such given the mood I was in before the preacher paid me a visit. You know how to handle the herd better than I do. Just take care of it. Dad will be here next spring, and I'd hate to tell him we neglected the herd just because I got into a little trouble."

The two visitors had improved Adam's mood. When the sheriff delivered his supper, Adam asked if there was any new information about the alley fiasco. The sheriff said there was not, but the prosecutor and Adam's lawyer did not confide in him. Still, Adam slept better, perhaps because of sleepless prior nights.

It was still dark outside when Adam was awakened by conversation in the office. "Do you have anything in that basket but food?"

"There are two books in there. Do you want to see them?" Adam recognized Emily's voice immediately.

"No, go on back, but please don't come in this early again and wake me."

Emily walked back to his cell. She wore a black duster, the kind a cowboy would wear. It was oversized with a hood that she had pulled up high over her head. Once the office door was closed, she dropped the hood. Below the duster all that could be seen were boots. On the sidewalk she would have passed as a small man.

"I didn't know it was snowing outside," Adam said, glancing at the duster.

"It isn't, but I have my dad's business to protect."

Her tone did not set well with Adam. "Rumor of having visited a killer might hurt your family business. I get it. I assume the duster and early morning hour is an attempt to conceal this visit. Why did you bother coming?"

"I have an investment in you I'm not willing to discard."

"Oh, I'm glad to know I have value."

"You took that wrong."

"How should I take it?" Adam asked.

"I have a great deal of affection for you. I know you as a person, and I don't believe that you committed the horrendous crime of which you are accused."

"I killed a man."

"Why did you do that?"

"I was protecting an innocent girl, and he shot at me first."

"There you have it. It's not murder, it's self-defense. Among much we learned at Miss Wolcott's finishing school, we learned that the Christian translation of Moses's tablets incorrectly says, 'thou shall not kill' when the proper translation is 'thou shall not murder.'

"Thank you."

"Do you have any regrets?" Emily asked.

"Yes, I regret that I'm locked up here. I do not regret what I did. Let me show you something." Adam handed her the bullet-damaged pocket watch.

As she inspected it, he added, "The watch I purchased from you the first day we met saved my life. In some respect, I owe my life to meeting you."

"By this, it is shown that providence says we have a future together."

She lifted the napkin from her basket, slid two books and a plate of brownies under the door and said, "You likely need something to occupy your time and avoid depression. Now I must go before people occupy the streets."

Emily reached between the bars, clasped his hand, pulled him to the door, and quickly touched her lips with his through the gap between bars. She then secured her hood tightly over her head and left.

Adam struggled with what he had learned from her visit. An analysis of the visit produced various assessments in Adam's mind. *Was he but an investment, like a new item stocked in the store with hopes of selling it? She admitted she had affection for him. Did she make him feel better arguing that what he had done was not sinful only to protect her investment. Concealing herself walking to visit him indicated store business was more important than publicly supporting him. But she did not dump him and risked coming, still believing they had a future together.*

After overanalyzing her visit, he picked up Mark Twain's The Adventures of Huckleberry Finn that had come out recently which she left. In the end she had brought him what he needed most, something to distract his mind. He was blessed to have her as a girlfriend.

Judging by the angle the sun was shining through the narrow window high in his cell, it was early afternoon that Nate came. He asked Adam to repeat the sequence of events in the alley for the third time. Adam did, remembering no more that he had earlier.

"Well?" Adam asked the big question.

Nate looked to the closed door separating the cells from the sheriff's office, nodded his head toward the door, raised his index finger to his lips, and gave a thumbs up with his other hand. The message was clear: Nate was confident but wished to conceal his confidence from the sheriff.

After Nate left, Adam heard schoolboys laughing as they walked in the alley behind the jail. Their presence told him school was out and it was after four. Other than the sun, they were one of the few ways he could tell the time of day.

"Here is where it will be built," he heard one say.

"Will it have thirteen steps?" another asked.

"They always do, just like the rope has thirteen loops. Dad says the sheriff already ordered the wood at the lumber yard."

"Mom says they'll let school out on the day, so we'll learn not to be killin people."

"Think he'll cry before they put the rope around his neck?"

"Yeah, they may have to drag him up the stairs."

"I wonder whether he'll soil his pants when he hits the end of the rope."

Adam pulled his cot under the window, climbed up on it, and peered out the window. As he expected, he did not see kids standing in a circle discussing the details of a hanging, but they were all lined up looking up at the window.

When they saw Adam looking out the window at them, they all tore down the alley as if being chased by the devil.

If it had not been for the reality of the possibility, he might have found humor in the childhood prank. He did not.

*"Cherish each hour of this day for it can never return."*

Og Mandino

# ★ CHAPTER 15 ★

Nate Clements stepped into a waiting room outside the long-time attorney, city council member, and part-time prosecutor's office. "I would like a few minutes of the prosecutor's time," he said to Eloise Johnson. Eloise had served as the prosecutor's secretary for twenty years. She was also the sheriff's wife.

The prosecutor's wife had been confined to a wheelchair for as long as most people in town knew her. Eloise spent more time with the prosecutor than she did with her husband, the sheriff who worked long and varied hours. Not unusual in a small town was rampant speculation about the secretary and lawyer's relationship.

Eloise opened the door to the lawyer's office, leaned in and whispered to the prosecutor. "You may go in," she told Nate.

"What brings you to my office? Does your client wish to plead guilty and beg for leniency?"

"Not at all—he is innocent. I came here as a courtesy. Drop the charges before we waist the court's time and you embarrass yourself."

"And why might that be?"

"I came because I seek to establish a working relationship with you based on trust."

"That might be the lamest argument I've ever heard. When your

119

client hangs, you'll have less clients than you do now, which is nearly none. Coming into town, you should have taken my offer and become my assistant."

"Have it as you will," Nate said, picking up his hat and leaving the room.

"That was short," Eloise observed as Nate walked through the reception area on his way out.

"Unfortunately, for him, it was," Nate replied.

That evening a buggy sat near the Barnhouse cowboy bunkhouse as the crew rode in. Chance rode to the buggy and was told, "Send Jake over here. We need to talk."

Earlier in the day the prosecutor paid the town doctor a visit. He asked about the condition of the saloon-cleaning woman's daughter. He learned that the combination of attempted molestation and the trauma of watching a rescuer killed added to a gun burst within inches of her ear could cause long-lasting damage. It had been two days since the doctor examined her, but she showed no signs of improvement.

The prosecutor was convinced Nate's ploy was out of desperation. But he had to admit, it was something he would have tried in the same predicament. Nevertheless, he would double check his witness.

Jake reluctantly walked up to the buggy. "Dinner getting served," he motioned the kitchen shack. "I don't want to miss it."

"Take a seat up here with me. I won't be long. Start from the beginning and tell me what happened."

"Dirk and I each had one whiskey and one beer at the saloon and decided we'd socialized enough with a big workday ahead. We headed back to the bunk house when Dirk heard the girl scream in the alley…

"Whoa, you told me earlier that it was you who first heard the girl scream."

"Maybe so, what difference?"

"Just go on."

The prosecutor found two other discrepancies in Jake's recollection. "I want you in my office at nine in the morning. We're going to go through your testimony until you have it right, as it happened."

"But I've work here to do."

"I'll speak to Chance and take care of it."

"I don't know, been thinking about movin on. Heard cowboy pay better in Wyoming."

"You can't do that. I'll issue an order, called a subpoena, requiring you to stay and testify."

"Yeah, might have a hard time a findin me," Jake said as he started to leave the buggy.

"Hold on here." The prosecutor reached into his pocket and pulled out a five-dollar Liberty Head gold coin. "Take this and come to my office in the morning. After the inquest I'll have another for you."

"Sure thing—I'll say anything you wish."

"No, this is not to alter your story—just get it straight, understand?"

"Yes, sir."

After hours with Jake, helping him refine his recollection of events, the prosecutor was becoming less convinced of Adam's guilt, but his priority was to win the trial. Losing would be bad for his law practice. It was Nate's job to defend his client; his job was to convict him. He would do what he needed to do, but he decided once Adam was found guilty at a trial, he would recommend a life sentence rather than hanging. He would not give God cause to strike him with a bolt of lightning.

Twice more Emily had visited Adam in jail, once early in the morning, once late evening. She still came in disguise for which he could not blame her. Her family had the general store long before Adam had arrived from wherever he did not know. Once the competing general store closed, some in town sought another store to compete with her family store. Fraternizing with a killer would only energize the search for another general store.

"How are you holding up?" Emily asked.

"As well as can be expected. I finished the two books you brought and have started the first one again."

"Any other visitors?"

"Only Nate and Hank. Nate won't really say anything," Adam said as he nodded his head toward the sheriff's office door.

"I stopped at his office yesterday and offered to testify as a character witness as a last resort, if needed. He said I wouldn't be needed."

"I thank you for that."

"Is there anyone you expected to visit you who hasn't?"

"Yes, there is. I hoped Mildred would visit. Seems to me she would be interested in my side of the story about what happened to her daughter. Her absence tells me she believes otherwise. Lorraine, I understand, is still in shock. Nate refuses to discuss her."

"You know what they say—hard times will separate your friends from others," Emily answered.

School was cancelled for the day. The schoolhouse served other purposes in the town as did the church. The preacher Ken would not allow trials to take place in the church; that left the school.

The judge sat at the schoolmarm's desk. Tables were placed for the prosecutor and defense attorney. School desks were lined up behind the attorneys for spectators.

"It's time," the sheriff said as he unlocked Adam's cell door. In his office he picked up a set of handcuffs, thought about it, then laid them down. "I don't think we'll need these."

What in later years came to be known as the Stockholm Syndrome also worked in the opposite manner. After the sheriff had spent two weeks with Adam, he had come to know him. No offensive or aggressive mannerisms did he ever detect. He was convinced Adam was not a flight risk.

Adam hesitated after a few steps outdoors. The direct sun and light breeze he had missed. It was a welcome although a nearly forgotten experience.

Upon entering the school door, all heads turned. Adam was escorted to a table with Nate. The sheriff sat with his wife behind the prosecutor's table. Adam turned and saw Mildred, Lorraine, and Betsy sitting directly behind him. Mildred and Lorraine were smiling at him. It immediately struck him that Mildred would not be smiling at him if she believed Jake's story. Sitting near the back were Emily and Elmer. Their eyes momentarily met until Emily diverted hers.

"All stand," said a man Adam did not recognize. The judge walked in and took the schoolmarm's seat. "This is not a trial. This is an inquest to ascertain whether enough evidence is present to warrant a trial. Prosecutor, call your witness."

Jake took the stand and gave his testimony. Nate made note that Jake avoided eye contact with Adam throughout the testimony. The prosecutor and judge also noticed, and all remembered tell-tales signs discussed in law school Witness Testimony 101.

"Defense, do you have any questions for this witness?"

"Have you met often with the prosecutor to go over your testimony?" asked Nate.

"A few times."

"How many times?"

"I don't know."

"Do know the penalty for perjury?"

"Objection," the prosecutor hollered, rising from his seat. "He isn't allowed to badger the witness."

"Sustained. You'll restrain yourself," the judge scolded Nate.

"You and Dirk had been friends and together how long?"

"Years, many years."

"Where did you meet and learn ranching?"

"Texas."

"When did you come to Montana?"

"This year."

"Why did you come here?"

"Objection, your honor. What is the point of this?" the prosecutor asked.

"I can assure you, your honor, there is a point to this," Nate answered.

"Okay, but don't waste our time on a goose hunt. Answer the question, witness."

"We heard wages were higher here."

Nate picked up a letter and telegram from his desk and approached the judge. "Judge, I have here a Texas arrest warrant for Dirk on the charge of molestation of a woman issued earlier this year. Also, I have a telegram saying that charges may be brought against Jake as an accomplice. The defense is finished with this witness."

An outbreak of whispering and side talk among the spectators caused the judge to slam a hammer on the desk. "There will be quiet in this hall. Call your next witness, prosecutor."

"I call the proprietor of Montana Betsy's to the stand."

"Do you know the defendant?"

"Yes, he occasionally visits my establishment."

"Does he ever inquire about Lorraine?"

"Yes."

"How often?"

"Most every time he's there."

"Given your experience with men, is it safe to assume a man who frequently asks about a woman harbors an infatuation with the woman?"

Nate stood to protest, but the prosecutor said, "No, you don't have to answer that question. I'm finished with this witness."

"No questions now, your honor, but I reserve the right to recall this witness," stated Nate.

"Next witness," the judge said.

"The prosecution, having shown just cause for a trial, does not want to waste this inquest's time. Other witnesses will be saved for the trial."

"How about the defense?" the judge asked.

"The defense calls the purported victim of this crime to the stand," stated Nate.

"Your honor, I object. This witness was alleged to be deaf and dumb from the tragic ordeal and I was not allowed an interview."

"The prosecutor is right, your honor. She was for days, but she recovered. And the prosecutor did not follow up with a request for an interview," argued Nate.

"Enough, enough." The judge looked at Lorraine. "Just tell us in your own words what happened to you that night and start with why you were in the alley."

"My brother and I were out of water. Although Mom told me not to leave the lean-to, I went for water. At the well, Dirk and that man," she pointed at Jake, "rode by and gave me, you know, an uncomfortable eye, and…"

When she finished, Nate said, "That tells the story, I'm finished with her, your honor."

"I'm not," said the prosecutor as he jumped up.

"Were you not lying on the ground in tight embrace with the defendant when the sheriff arrived?"

"Yes, he was hugging and consoling me, he wasn't trying to put his hands under my smock like that guy did," she pointed at Jake.

"Are you, your mother and brother into debt with the defendant?"

"No, he's never given us money."

"Did he"—the prosecutor pointed at Adam— "not prevent your mother from being lynched for cattle thief? If she had been hanged, would you and your brother not have been alone on your own in the wilderness?

"I told the truth."

Jake got up and headed toward the door. The sheriff followed and stopped him. "You may be called back, you better stay."

"Nature calls."

The sheriff nodded to his deputy at the door. "Make sure he returns."

The prosecutor continued, "It seems to me that you owe this man much. Would not preventing him from being hanged be a payback for saving your mother from the noose?"

"No, I'm telling the truth," Lorraine hollered back at him.

"We're supposed to take the word of a cattle rustler's daughter who works in a saloon, lives in a lean-to, and does who-knows-what on the side?" finished the prosecutor.

"That remark was entirely uncalled for," the judge reprimanded the prosecutor as Lorraine burst out in tears.

"My next witness is Sally Milford," Nate stated.

"Miss Milford, where do you work?"

"I work at Montana Betsy's."

"What do you do there?"

"I help serve drinks and socialize with the patrons."

"Does this socialization ever take place on the second floor?"

An unusual quiet came over the room, before she answered, "Sometimes we go upstairs and read Shakespeare."

The school room erupted in laughter. Again, the judge brought down his hammer on the teacher's desk, "No more outbursts like that.

"Were Dirk and Jake patrons on the evening in question?"

"Yes."

"What was their state of intoxication?"

"Don't know how many whiskeys they'd had but it was many—you could tell by their slurred words."

"And what words do you recall?"

"They wanted to go upstairs; you know…for a reading, but they only had six bits between them."

"So, you told them no?"

"Yes sir, but they weren't happy with it. Dirk tried to grab me to prevent me from leaving his table, while Jake more than laid his hand on my backside. I slapped his hand away and thought for a moment he was going to hit me. Then Jake said they'd do better on their own and left."

"Prosecutor, do you wish to cross examine this witness?"

"No, your honor."

"I would like to recall Betsy, the owner of the saloon, to the stand, your honor," Nate said.

The prosecutor stood. "Your honor a point of privilege if you will."

The senior lawyer and prosecutor in town had not lost many cases. In those he lost, he had learned to avoid embarrassing himself and cut his losses. Looking back later, he realized signs of doubt had been apparent, but his desire to teach an up-and-coming attorney his place masked them.

"Your honor, given testimony that I was unaware of, possibly due to the misconduct of the defense attorney, I wish to drop all charges against the defendant."

"It's about time, prosecutor. The defendant is hereby released. Now is that all, prosecutor?"

"I instruct the sheriff to arrest Jake on charges of attempted molestation and perjury."

Both the deputy and sheriff blocked Jake's fruitless escape attempt.

Mildred and Lorraine jumped up and cheered as the judge left the room. Hank stepped forward and shook Adam's hand. Emily left the schoolhouse as she saw Adam, Mildred, and Lorraine in an embrace.

*"Words are, of course, the most powerful drug used by mankind."*

Rudyard Kipling

# ★ CHAPTER 16 ★

After hugging Mildred and Lorraine and thanking Nate, Adam couldn't wait to get out of the temporary courtroom. He turned to the door and saw Chance leaving with a stately sized man well-dressed beyond what was seen in Great Falls. Adam assumed the man was the Lord Barnhouse he had yet to meet and wondered what his interest was in the trial.

Hank insisted that they celebrate at Montana Betsy's. Half of the herd's crew was on hand to participate. After Hank bought Adam his first regular non-alcoholic drink, it was Adam who bought the drinks.

Nate joined Adam and Betsy at the bar. "Glad to see there is justice in this town," Betsy told them.

"I hate to admit it, but I suspect part of the prosecutor's focus was on me. He sees me as a threat to his business. Embarrassing me in court would have left me with much idle time," Nate admitted.

Adam added, "I suspect losing won't do his business any good, particularly given the shallowness of the evidence. You'll soon be too busy for me."

"I don't think so; stop by in the morning. We've chute business to discuss."

With several people now congregating around them, Adam said,

"One of the disadvantages of being out of jail, I'll have to pay for my room tonight," bringing laughter at the bar. People he hardly knew congratulated him saying they always knew he was innocent; whether they actually did or not, Adam was too happy to contemplate whether they were truthful.

Later in the evening, Adam saw Fancy walking up the stairs with Sally and his other cowboys at the poker tables. Betsy went to the back room, Nate left, and Mildred was tending the bar.

"I was concerned that I never heard from you while in jail," he commented as Mildred got him another watered-down sarsaparilla.

"Sorry, I wanted to visit, but Nate insisted that Lorraine and I stay away. He said it would provide too much information to the prosecutor through the sheriff and his wife."

"You, Lorraine, and Sally sure made a presence in the court room. Lorraine's dress conveyed the aura of an innocent schoolgirl. No one would ever know that Sally usually dresses, shall we say more provocatively. And I noticed the judge's eyes on you a few times."

"Thank you."

"You didn't make all those dresses, did you?"

"I had to do something to keep away from the jail and my mind off the worst."

"That's amazing," Adam said. Then it struck him. "Betsy and the other girls in here have upped their wardrobe by you, right?"

"I enjoy doing it."

Adam asked, "Could you do more seamstress business if you had a better place to work?"

"Yes, non-saloon women aren't apt to have their dresses made in a lean-to at the back of the saloon."

"I guess you are right. What is your plan to prevent anything like this happening to Lorraine again?"

"I think she's learned her lesson to stay in the lean-to after dark."

"She's sixteen going on seventeen, don't you think it is abnormal to expect her to stay in those small quarters for hours?"

"I don't know what else to do. I'm putting away money with seamstress work and other on the side but can't afford a proper place right now."

"What do you mean by other. Betsy only gives you meals and a place to say, such as it is?" he asked.

After a good deal of hesitation, she answered, "I was a proper lady with a good husband. He was killed by a man who took advantage of me in untold, unspeakable ways. I had to become accustomed to the fact that my life would be different. It was turned upside down in several ways. Now I make some money on the side in a way that can't tarnish my morals further. Please don't judge me."

"I don't know what to say about that, but what about Lorraine. How can you protect her?"

"As you said, Lorraine will turn seventeen soon. I understand the danger living close to an establishment where men often drink too much. She will soon be of the age things happen to girls. If such were to happen in safer quarters under more scrutiny and control, it would be for the better. You must understand where we are in the social strata at present.

"Are you suggesting she work with Sally and others in here?" he glanced at the stairs.

"She would be much safer here. The girls here do what they have to do. They look out for each other. In time, we could move out of town and start a new life, perhaps in Helena."

"Promise me this: you won't change anything with Lorraine until she turns seventeen."

"You've been good to us; you have my word."

After breakfast at the hotel, Adam entered Nate's office at nine. "Okay, hit me with it. What's your fee for keeping my head out of a noose?"

"Forty-two hours I worked on your defense. You can figure it," Nate said.

"Guess I didn't have much of a choice."

"You can very well afford it." Nate showed Adam the bank statement detailing fees deposited from his share of the chute patent that had accumulated while Adam was in jail. "You can imagine how much more your share was."

"What did you say about my share? I can't hear you with all the pounding. What's going on upstairs?"

"I told you before you got yourself locked up; I'm having the second floor remodeled. I want to make some money from my inheritance which purchased this building. When its finished, I'll have two two-room apartments, plus a studio to rent out, in addition to the one I'm living in now."

"Can you show me what you're having done?"

There was another burst of pounding. "Sure, let's go have a look."

The second floor had stairs outside from the alley and indoor stairs from the lobby. On one side of the hall were Nate's living quarters and another two-room apartment. The other side of the hallway was being turned into a two-room apartment and a studio apartment.

Adam asked, "Any thoughts about making one three-room apartment on one side of the hall instead of a two-room and a studio?"

"I thought I could get more rent this way."

"How much rent are you seeking?"

"I know I can't get near hotel rates long term. I was thinking eight dollars a month for the two-room apartments and six for the studio."

Adam walked around the construction, thought, and said, "I suppose if you turned the two-room and studio into a three-room apartment, you'd take twelve dollars a month and save yourself hassling with two renters."

"Yes, but someone with a family seeking a rental could be harder to find. And since I'm living and working here, I don't want rambunctious kids running around disturbing me."

"I'll relieve you of that worry and take both the two and three-room apartments for twenty dollars a month."

"What would you do with them?"

"As much as I stay at the hotel, it makes sense for me to get a place. The two-room apartment will do fine. And I know of a family who could use better accommodations in the three-room apartment."

"I suspect I know who the family is."

"I suspect you do and, of course, it's contingent on Mildred's approval. Now let's go downstairs. I want to discuss something else."

The building had two street-side windows on either side of the entrance door. The door opened into a small foyer with an office on both sides. "Have you had any luck finding another attorney?"

"Don't be silly, I'm hardly busy myself, although your trial might bring me more business.

"Glad I could be of help."

"You know what I meant. I suppose I'll rent that office out, but you never know in the future I may need it if the practice expands."

"It'd make a great place for a seamstress business, don't you think?"

Adam entered the general store to find no one. He could hear Elmer out back with a customer. A quick scan of the store brought his eyes to spools of material, linen, cotton, and wool. He stepped closer, realizing how little he knew about fabric.

"Thinking about a new shirt?" Emily asked, startling him.

"Just looking around, but it's a new watch I need."

"Glad to see you on this side of the bars. How about a watch like you have without the bullet damage?"

"I'll take it," Adam said, reaching for her hand. She let him take it but didn't step closer.

"You should know that I am older and not inclined to rolling around in alley dirt with a guy."

He wasn't sure whether her remark was in jest or a jealous snip at him, but he chose to be wary. "It wasn't rolling. We both fell when I was shot, and I felt obligated to sooth her sobbing."

"Yeh, that's what Dad said, but some of the looks I got at church last Sunday...."

"You are reading too much into looks. You are my steady. It is nearly noon. Let's go to dinner."

"Okay, but I'm not taking an alley shortcut with you."

He laughed, pulled her hand toward the door, and said, "May I have the pleasure of escorting you to dinner?"

All the eyes at the noon-time diner drifted to them as they walked in. Adam noticed a familiar face sitting alone.

Emily and Adam had finished their meal when the man Adam now recognized stepped up to their table. "I'm glad to hear you got that alley ordeal straightened out. And congratulations are in order for your cattle contraption patent."

"Thank you, Emily, this is Thomas. He works for the federal land department. He has checked on my homestead at our winter quarters. Thomas meet Emily."

"I just wanted to make you aware that, twice I've been unable to find you on the property. Once you were in jail, and the other time I don't know where you were. The rules say you are supposed to inhabit the homestead. I can work it out, but maybe another game of cards would be in order."

Adam was taken back momentarily before answering, "Sure, how about my hotel room at nine this evening?"

"Will work fine, see you there," Thomas said as he left.

"Dad told me you had no proclivity toward poker. Has that changed?" Emily asked.

"No, I don't," he answered then explained the inspector's ruse to attain a bribe.

"I can't believe it. If government employees are allowed to do such, where will it end in the future?" she prophetically commented.

"You're right. He'll bleed me for as much as the quarter section is worth eventually."

"We've eaten dinner at the diner, once is enough for the day, join

Dad and me for supper," Emily offered.

After walking Emily to the general store, Adam stopped at the sheriff's office, then he went back to Nate's office.

"Back already?" Nate asked.

"I see you're not busy."

"More activity than normal—two potential clients stopped by after you left. Hopefully, you haven't found more trouble."

"Could be, but I plan on nipping it in the bud. The property I'm homesteading, can I scuddle the homesteading thing, purchase it, and get a deed this afternoon?"

It was four o'clock at the land office when Adam folded the new deed and put it in his vest pocket.

Mildred was in the lean-to taking a break before her evening bartending shift. Adam knocked on the thin tin siding beside the door. "Adam, glad to see you," Mildred said. "What brings you here?"

Although it was Mildred who had asked him a question, he caught his eyes unconsciously drawn to Lorraine. To cover the embarrassment, he asked, "Where's Gerald?"

"He's sweeping the floor over there before the crowd comes."

"If the two of you have a few minutes, I'd like to show you something over at Nate's office."

Adam considered taking them through the alley to avoid Emily seeing them, but they had no reason to sneak. Mildred got the message as he glanced at both.

"You go on. Lorraine and I will quickly change and meet you there."

Emily was not outside the general store as they passed, although she saw them from the upstairs kitchen window. Elmer was sitting on a rocker. He tipped his hat at Mildred and said, "Good day."

Adam greeted them on the sidewalk and led them up the outside stairs at Nate's building. "My lawyer friend, Nate, bought this building with an inheritance from Iowa. He is making his home in one apartment here and is renting out the other two and three-room apartments."

"Look, Mom, this room has a window overlooking main street. Isn't it neat?" commented Lorraine.

"Yes, it's a fine setup, but why are you showing us this?" Mildred asked. "You know I can't afford it."

"Well, the thing about it is, I was looking for an apartment. I'm tired of staying at the hotel and made Nate an offer. He said he would be so pleased to have me as a neighbor he'd throw in the other apartment."

"You aren't?"

"Yes, I am. Gerald, Lorraine, and you should move in here. Come downstairs. There's something else I want to show you."

They walked down the inside stairs into the empty office opposite Nate's. "With the patent and ranch work, I need an office but not this much space. I was thinking I'd start a business the town needs."

"What business would that be?" asked Lorraine.

"A seamstress business. If I could find a partner, we'd go in together 50/50. I'd supply the materials, sewing tools, and space. She'd supply the labor."

Mildred stepped toward him and hugged him. With his other arm, Adam reached out and pulled Lorraine into the hug.

Emily had fixed rosemary-marinated roast beef for dinner. Elmer said it was her best dish. Adam only knew of her chicken dishes, but this was a step above.

"As delicious as this meal is, you must have worked on it most of the day," Adam said.

"Yes, she was up here in the kitchen most of the afternoon, while I worked the store."

"Anything unusual at the store today?" Adam tried to keep the conversation going.

"I saw Lori and Mildred walk by. Mildred is a good-looking woman. If Mildred didn't work at the saloon, I'd ask her out," Elmer replied.

"Dad, how could you say such a thing? Goodness only knows what all she does at the saloon."

"Your mother has been gone eight years now. If you think I plan on living alone the rest of my life, you're mistaken, girl."

"I think you could do much better than a woman with two brats."

Adam reeled at her remark and couldn't let it stand. "I wouldn't necessarily call them brats. The family was just put in a bad situation and are trying to make the best of it. I heard a rumor that they may soon be out of that place they're in by the saloon."

"I guess 'brats' was a poor choice of words. Where'd you hear that rumor? Saloon, I suppose?"

Elmer scolded his daughter. "Emily, watch your tone. Men socialize at the saloon as women have your tea parties. Most everyone knows that, although Adam has an occasional beer, he usually drinks those watered-down sarsaparillas Betsy makes."

"People know it isn't whiskey?" a surprised Adam asked.

"Of course. Now let's get the carrom table out while Emily does the dishes."

"May I help?" Adam asked Emily.

"No, dad wants you to play with him."

After a few games, Emily walked Adam to the door. "I'm sorry if I was short tempered tonight. Will you forgive me?"

"I'll have to think about it," he answered with a smirk.

"Will two kisses tonight instead of one help?"

Elmer was waiting for her when she came back upstairs. "Emily, I think you need to focus on your couple situation rather than speculating on mine. You'll be twenty-six soon. Displaying an uppity attitude toward men is not becoming."

"Yes, father," she said, heading toward her bedroom.

*"It is impossible to live without failing at something unless you live so cautiously that you might as well not have lived at all, in which case you have failed by default."*

J.K. Rowling

# ★ CHAPTER 17 ★

Double doors separated Adam's hotel room from an adjacent room. They could be opened when a guest required two rooms for a family. Adam pulled the door on his side ajar a few inches. The door on the other side was open.

Adam moved a wash basin and the crocheted doily on a table to the bed, pulled the table to the center of the room, and put two chairs around it. He tossed a deck of cards on the table. His new pocket watch showed five minutes of nine o'clock. He was ready.

Thomas's wife had her hand in his coat pocket when he unexpectedly walked into the bedroom.

"What are you doing?" he demanded. He jerked the coat from her with one hand and sent his open hand slamming hard on her face. The impact sent her reeling across the bed and the sound of the impact caused their seven-year-old son to hunker in a corner of the living room.

"You're to never snoop in my pockets."

His wife's hand covered the side of her face, soothing but too late to protect it from the blow.

"You had fifty dollars in your pocket yesterday, now there is none. Jimmy needs new shoes for school. His old ones are blistering his feet. Where did the money go?"

"None of your business."

"Your government pay is forty dollars a month. Where did the other ten come from? You gambled it all away, didn't you?"

"None of your business.

"Must I wire my brother in Helena for money again? He says we should leave you."

"You know what your problem is? You talk too much. A good wife minds her business and serves her husband decent meals. I'm working tonight. Maybe I'll earn enough for his shoes," he said as he put his coat on.

"Meals might be better if you allowed me money. You're going out again. What are you going to gamble with tonight? You have no money."

He grabbed her by the shoulder and pushed her to the wall. "I'll deal with your mouthiness when I get home."

Thomas stepped to the hotel desk. "I have a meeting with Adam Duval. In what room would I find him?"

"214."

At exactly nine, Adam heard a knock on his door. For whatever Thomas was, he was prompt.

"Ah, looks like you're ready for business," Thomas said looking at the table and cards. "I think tonight we should up the ante to five dollars a hand. I can't be too long; I've got some unfinished business at home."

Adam sat down, shuffled the cards then placed them on the table instead of dealing them. "Why play this game? We're both adults. I purposely lost four dollars to you last time."

"The rules say to qualify for a homestead deed you must reside on the property. If I report your continued absence, you will lose the property."

"I know that. How do you suggest I rectify that?" Adam asked.

"I think ten dollars now, and five dollars a month for the next year will take care of the situation. You can afford it. It'll be less than the two hundred dollars it would take to buy the property at a dollar and a quarter an acre."

"Will it end in a year?"

"You have my word," Thomas replied, requiring Adam to control his expression.

"Let's make sure we understand each other. If I pay you ten now and five a month, a total of sixty-five dollars, you will certify in the required government forms that I am living full time on the property, correct?"

"That's the gist of it."

Adam reached into his pocket, pulled, unfolded, and handed Thomas a document.

"What is this?"

"It is a deed to the property I was homesteading and now own outright."

Thomas saw what the document was and paused while he contemplated its meaning, then said, "Perhaps we can come to another understanding."

"I don't know what kind of leverage you have for any understanding."

"If you think you set me up, it won't work. You have no evidence and …."

He was interrupted by the sheriff walking in from the adjoining room. "You are under arrest for soliciting a bribe as a government official."

As the sheriff led Thomas from the room, Thomas glared at Andrew. "You'll pay for this, I swear."

The next morning Adam was at the general store as it opened. "You're early. You going to take me to breakfast? That would make three meals together in a row," Emily asked.

"No, although I'd like to." His flirtatious smile told her he had forgotten about her previous night's behavior. "I want to order furniture."

"You can't get much in that crowded range cabin."

"I've rented a place in town. Is it okay with you if I spend more time around town?"

She pleasantly accepted his question, avoided an answer, and pulled out the furniture catalog. He picked out a modest settee, table and two chairs. Then she showed him a bed in the stock room.

"I know it isn't much, but it is a start. I'm headed for the winter quarters now, and probably won't be back for a couple weeks. I've got some concerns about the herd getting through the winter I must work out."

"Where do you want the delivery made?"

"The apartment is above Nate's new office."

As he started to leave, she approached him and said, "I'm glad that you are going to spend more time here. It is a step in the right direction for us."

The hot, dry summer had limited the growth of bunch grass in the winter valley. It was the bunch grass that sustained the herd when heavy snow came which could come any day.

Adam and Hank rode around the valley assessing what they knew would be a shortage of grass before the winter was over.

"Seems to me we have two choices. We can either plan on hauling hay from the stockyards near the train station or we can cut the herd back," stated Hank.

"The hay will be expensive and take most of our time hauling hay. But I don't want to cut the herd back. With Dad coming back in the spring, what would he say with the herd reduced? He'd think we were bad managers."

Before they headed back to the cabin, Adam saw a contraption on wheels he'd never seen before and a man on horseback riding toward them from a distance. Hank waved three times toward July, who was on horseback near the cabin. Three waves were a sign for all hands to come immediately. It usually meant danger. All six cowboys joined Hank and Adam as the wagon contraption pulled up.

It was the fanciest buggy rig Adam had ever seen. The buggy sat spring mounted on a large-wheeled cargo wagon. A driver wearing a tall black hat sat on a wagon seat forward of the buggy. The buggy had two seats facing each other with a black canopy over both. Side curtains were rolled up which were obviously meant to be rolled down in bad weather. The large wheels on the wagon allowed the contraption to move over terrain the normal buggy carriage could not.

Adam recognized the man on horseback as Chance, the Barnhouse spread foreman. The well-dressed portly man sitting in the black leather buggy seat Adam had seen at the trial. They had never been introduced. Neither Chance nor Lord Barnhouse seemed intimidated by eight cowboys lined up facing them all carrying handguns.

"Lord Barnhouse, this is Adam Duval, son of the owner of this herd," Chance introduced while pointing to Adam. Adam didn't feel slighted at the time by the lack of a reciprocal introduction.

"Your little escapade in a saloon alley cost me two cowboys," stated the Lord in a raspy English-accented voice.

"If they would have behaved themselves, you would still have them," Adam responded.

"What difference should it make to you if they took advantage of the future whore daughter of a whore?"

Adam nudged his horse forward as he felt his blood pressure rise. "You will not talk that way on my property."

"My apologies," Barnhouse answered, then turned to Chance. "I like the boy's nerve."

Looking back at Adam, he said, "Let's get to business. Whatever happened in the alley ordeal, it cost me two cowboys which I must replace." He looked over at the cowboys facing him and addressed them, "Whatever you are getting paid here, I'll double it if you come with me."

They all exchanged looks without responding until Hairy rode forward. "Sorry, Hank but that's a lot of money." He refused to look at Adam.

"Hank, that's what you call yourself, right?" Barnhouse looked at Hank.

"I'll also double what you make as foreman to be assistant foreman for me."

"Thank you, but NO. One boss is enough."

"Well now this leaves you with another problem Adam. Short grass, shorthanded, you just as well sell your herd to me and stay in town. It would give you more time to chase the general store owner's daughter."

Adam was so angered he couldn't address Barnhouse. He rode aside the wagon driver and said, "Get that thing out of here now."

The driver looked at Barnhouse for direction. The Lord replied, "Let's go; we've been as neighborly as we can."

As they watched the wagon roll, and Chance and Hairy ride away, Hank said, "We can't replace him. We'll be workin twenty-hour days haulin hay."

Adam didn't respond as they sat and watched the wagon disappear. With the other cowboys gone, Adam said, "The first of the week we'll cut out a quarter of the herd and drive them to the railroad pens."

"You could have sold them to Barnhouse and saved us the hassle."

"I wouldn't sell that man a cow pile no matter what he offered."

Well on their way back to what the town was calling the limestone mansion, Barnhouse motioned Chance to join him. Chance tied his horse back of the wagon and took a seat opposite the lord.

"See to it that that Hairy fellow is soon less hairy. My outfit will not convey an image of ruffians."

"What if he...?"

"Just get it done."

"Should I see what it would cost to get Jake out of jail?"

"We will pay no bail for him. He can suffer the consequences of his actions. It'll send a message to the rest of the crew. And forget our plans to harass Adam's outfit with night riders. I've got to respect the young guy. He'll come around but only with neighborliness, not antagonism."

The jail in Great Falls had four cells. With Thomas's entry, three were filled. Beside Jake awaiting trial for perjury, assault, and attempted rape, the sheriff had locked Harris-Bear up for pulling a knife in a bar room brawl. It was the second time Harris-Bear had pulled a knife on someone.

Harris-Bear was half Indian and named accordingly. He was a big man who often behind his back was called Hairless Bear. Knowing the judge wouldn't be back in town for three weeks and busy when he arrived, the sheriff planned to let Harris-Bear out in another day.

The prior day Thomas asked his attorney to check on his wife and son and let them know that he would be out soon. The attorney thought it unlikely but planned to convey his message.

"Well?" Thomas asked as his attorney entered the cell hallway.

"Your place is empty, and this envelope carrying your name was tacked to the door." Thomas opened it and found the message short:

Enough, Gone to safety.

Thomas kicked the door twice, ripped the note into pieces, and said, "Curses to Adam. I'll get him for this."

Jake, who had been listening to it all, said, "You'll have to stand in line after me. I've first shot at him."

The attorney stepped to his other client's cell. "Jake, not good news. The prosecutor is standing firm on the charges and not inclined

143

to negotiate. I suspect his embarrassment over your false testimony has made him unpliable."

Hearing only a sigh from Jake for response, the attorney lifted his brief case and left.

"Given that we're both going after him, his life isn't worth a plug nickel," Thomas stated.

"What are you looking out the window for," Jake asked Harris-Bear who was standing on his cot surveying a slight gap between buildings on the street from the window alley view.

"Sheriff gone. Talk now. You two want some'an real bad. How bad? I'm getin outta here tomorrow," Harris-Bear asked.

"What are you proposing?" Thomas asked.

"For the right price, I slide my knife betweenst his ribs and give turn."

"What are you asking?"

"Twenty of your green money."

"I'd pay it, but I don't have any money in here," said Jake.

"Neither do I," added Thomas.

"Too bad—job for one of you two then."

"Do you have any money on the outside?" Thomas asked Jake.

"Yes, hidden under my mattress at the bunkhouse," Jake lied.

Thomas knew that the chances of him being convicted were halved with Adam gone as a witness. It would be a good investment.

"Harris, you heard my attorney say my wife has moved. When you get out tomorrow, go to my house and you'll find a loose stone above the upper left corner of the fireplace. Behind it is twenty-five dollars. The extra five will be for you keeping your mouth shut. Jake, I assume you'll reimburse me half when you get out."

"Sure will," Jake answered.

"Deal," said Harris-Bear, "but it's Harris-Bear, not Harris and pect you to remember."

What the three inmates didn't know was that the deputy was in the office with the sheriff before he left.

Emily was good with paperwork and numbers. The order for January's delivery of goods had to be in by the tenth of December, constricting her to the office for the day. The few rush orders she had placed included Adam's order which incurred an extra fee.

With business slow, Elmer was sitting in his rocking chair on the sidewalk with a blanket wrapped around him. He would not let cold weather change his routine. Down the sidewalk came Mildred carrying a chair and Lorraine and Gerald each carrying a box.

Mildred had few things to move from the lean-to. They had brought nearly nothing from the wilderness. Most of what they had people had given them. Without a horse or wagon, a few trips on foot would complete their move.

"Looks like you are moving," Elmer said discarding the blanket, then regretting his presumptuous remark.

"Yes, we have a place now," Mildred answered.

Elmer stood and reached for the leg of the chair Mildred was struggling with. "Let me help. Business is slow today."

Elmer's help made what would have been three trips to their new place two. And with a man helping them, they felt safe taking a short cut through the alley.

Emily ignored the ring from the bell hanging on the front door. Her dad would take care of the customer. Then an insistent ringing of the bell on the counter caused her to leave the office and help the customer.

"Sorry for the delay. My dad must have left without telling me," Emily told the customer.

When Elmer returned, she asked, "Where'd you go? You should have told me you were leaving."

"I just went for a walk," he answered, not wanting to open a discussion from which no good could come.

*"The things you really need are few and easy to come by; but the things you can imagine you need are infinite, and you will never be satisfied."*

Epicurus

# ★ CHAPTER 18 ★

The price he received for a quarter of the herd was above Adam's expectations. With little choice in the matter of the herd, he was satisfied with the explanation he would give his father upon his return. A bank draft from the Armour Meat Packing Company in Chicago in hand, Adam headed for the bank.

Harris-Bear had been watching the cattleman's activities from around the corner of an alley. He ducked back when he saw Adam walking on the sidewalk toward him. At the last minute, Adam decided to take a shortcut to the bank through an alley. He rounded the corner from the sidewalk to the alley closely, just as Harris-Bear decided to look out and see where Adam was.

Both were startled as they collided, and Adam's momentum sent them both to the ground. Harris-Bear reached for his ten-inch blade in the holster attached to his belt. He lifted it to Adam's ribs. Before he drove it deep, a thought hit him. *Was money really hidden in the chimney or was Thomas a liar? He would not risk the hangman's noose for nothing. As easy as encountering Adam was, he could do the deed after he had the money.*

He replaced his knife, helped Adam up, and apologized. "Just as much my fault," said Adam.

Harris-Bear noticed a paper lying on the ground. He picked it up. "This yours," he said handing it to Adam. It was the bank draft that had fallen from Adam's pocket.

"Thank you. I must stop at the bank. Meet me later at Betsy's and I'll buy you a drink."

Harris-Bear briefly considered it but thought it better to not fraternize with a man he likely would need to deal with later.

Emily was sealing her January order form in an envelope when she heard the bell on the door. Although Mildred had never been in the store, Emily recognized her immediately.

"May I help you?" Emily asked as she walked to the counter by the canned goods.

Mildred scanned the store and stepped to the fabric selection. "I need some sewing supplies."

"I can help you with that," answered Emily as she reached for a couple spools of calico, the cheapest fabric in stock, and placed them on the counter.

"I may want some of that, but what do you have in Cambric linen, wool, Duck cotton and Calamanco?"

Emily was taken aback. "You seem to be well-versed in fabric."

"Yes, it's always been a hobby until I started at it seriously around Betsy's and now, I'm opening my own shop."

Emily soon had an order filled out containing many spools, thread, needles, adjustable mannequins, and a foot-powered sewing machine. "You've quite an order here; let me tally it."

When Emily showed her the tally, Mildred counted out bills for payment. Shocked that she had the cash to pay, Emily observed, "Looks like the saloon has done you well."

"I have a brother in Cleveland," Mildred answered without lying, and let Emily assume he was financing her business.

"Where is your shop to be?" asked Emily.

"In the building Nate Clements has a law office."

It was after Mildred left and Emily was restacking the spools that the coincidence struck her. She had found Adam looking at the fabric last week, and now Mildred was opening a shop with ample money in the building where he had an apartment. It smelled, no it stunk.

Elmer entered the store to see Emily tossing spools on the shelf in a manner obviously irritated by something.

"What's wrong, dear?"

"Mildred from the saloon just ordered seamstress supplies and is opening a shop where Adam has an apartment."

"A shop there? It makes sense why her and family are moving there," Elmer answered before he thought.

"How do you know that?"

"I helped her carry her things over there yesterday while you were doing books."

"And you didn't tell me? I don't like it. I don't like it at all."

"Just calm down. I know what you're thinking. Mildred must be forty, too old for Adam. You may be older than Adam, but Mildred is out of the question."

"You're thinking Mildred is just right for you, aren't you?"

"She won't be at the saloon anymore. And she is…well, you know."

"Attractive, yes say it, but it is Lori. That's who I'm concerned about."

"You wouldn't have this worry about her if you'd have sealed the deal with him by now."

"Getting me out, married, and with your grandchildren on the way, that's all you think about, isn't it?"

"Not exactly," he answered.

Emily knew she had to come up with a plan to keep Adam and Lori apart. A successful plan could not be hatched from afar. She needed to get to know the family. Only then could a seed of discord with Lori be sown or their incompatibility exposed.

Hearing that Thomas was in jail and his family had vacated the property, the bank quickly foreclosed on their home. The mortgage payments were ninety days past due. The bank had secured the front door with a padlock.

The sheriff lived in a house kitty-corner across the street from the foreclosed property. Given the inmates' conversation the deputy relayed to the sheriff, they were watching the house and Harris-Bear. With only two of them, they could not keep tabs on the house around the clock. But keeping tabs on the house was easier than following Adam or Harris-Bear.

The sheriff had a rat terrier that was inclined to bark at anyone or anything out of the ordinary in the neighborhood. Because of neighbor complaints, he usually kept the dog in a fenced area in the back yard. He could not monitor the abandoned property all night. He drove a stake in the front yard and tied the dog with ten feet of rope. The neighbors might complain, but his alarm system was installed.

In the middle of the second night the dog was tied, the sheriff's wife shook him from a deep sleep. "Can't you hear that?" It was the first thing she'd said to him all evening.

"You've got to shush that dog, or the neighbors will no longer speak to us. You may sleep through it, but I can't."

He pulled a robe over his underwear, wrapped his gun belt around it, and walked outdoors holding an unlit lantern. The dog immediately quit barking in hopes of being fed or pet. The sheriff saw a hint of light from a window in the abandoned house. He was unsure it was anything but a reflection of the moon in the window but would check it out.

Harris-Bear used his knife to pry the hasp which the padlock was attached to from the wooden door. Working his way around the room he tripped on a broken chair that had been left. It was the middle of the night; he felt safe lighting a candle to find the right stone on the chimney. At the upper left corner as Thomas described he found a loose stone. Behind it in a pouch were three five-dollar gold coins and five silver dollars. He searched the hole for the other five dollars that Thomas promised but found no more. Twenty was what he had asked for; he would accept it.

The sheriff saw the hasp had been torn from the door and carefully opened the door to see a man reaching in a chimney space. As Harris-Bear put the money in his pocket and turned toward the door, he heard someone ask, "What are you doing in here?"

Even with the candle all Harris-Bear could see was someone standing in the doorway wearing what appeared to be a long dress. He could not tell it wasn't a woman but a robe wearing man holding a gun on him. He let out a yell, pulled out his knife and charged the unknown.

The sheriff was uncertain who it was, but reflection of light off the shiny knife the creature held while howling and charging him, left him no choice. He squeezed the trigger on his 45. The bullet hit Harris-Bear squarely in the chest, but his momentum and proximity to the sheriff slammed the sheriff to the ground.

Both lay confined in the doorway; it took some effort for the sheriff to roll the heavy attacker off him. He lit the lantern he had sat outside the doorway and saw it was Harris-Bear.

"What are you doing here?" the sheriff asked him.

Harris-Bear didn't answer but moved his hand to his chest. The burning sensation was intense. He felt moisture, looked at his hand, and saw it saturated with blood. He knew it was soon time to join the spirits.

Again, the sheriff asked the question.

Twenty dollars was all that was in the nook. Thomas had lied to him. The extra five were to be for his silence. He felt numbness working up his legs and arms.

His eyes met the sheriff's. "Paid to use knife on Adam."

"Who paid you?"

"Thomas and Jake," he whispered before his eyes froze open, directed toward another dimension and life was gone.

Thomas's wife had known for some time about the nook behind

the chimney stone. She kept tabs on the contents, but never had taken money from it. She would have been the only suspect if the money were missing. Another beating she would not encourage.

As she had packed to leave with her son, she had taken a five-dollar gold piece from the nook. It paid for stagecoach fare. She hadn't taken more, suspecting that taking more would have given Thomas incentive to find her.

Although the door was closed, extra commotion in the sheriff's office the next morning could not be missed by Jake and Thomas. Conversation between the prosecutor, sheriff, and their attorney could be heard, but not the words.

They knew something had happened; it was the demise of Adam they expected.

Thomas speculated, "Without Adam's testimony in either of our cases, they likely are discussing dropping the charges. I'll expect reimbursement of ten of the twenty I supplied Harris. The other five was on my own."

"I'll get it to you as soon as I get to the bunk house," Jake replied, while knowing that once he mounted his horse he would immediately be bound for California.

The disappointment came when their attorney entered the cell block. "Did you get a deal struck?" Jake asked.

"No, but you both have charges added."

"What? How?" Thomas asked.

"You've both been charged with soliciting an attempted murder. It seems that your former cellmate was killed threatening the sheriff while picking up payment for a murder."

"What could that have to do with us?" asked Thomas.

"He gave a near-death testimony to the sheriff that you both hired him to kill Adam Duval."

"That means nothing. He was out to get us. He flew off the handle when I omitted part of his name," responded Thomas.

Jake added, "He is half...you know...you can't trust em. No one will believe."

"According to the sheriff, a jury may believe his deputy's testimony about the conversation the three of you had before Harris-Bear was released. I want you to recall anything that may have caused the deputy to have misinterpreted the conversation. I'll be back tomorrow."

The sheriff found Adam in the bank and filled him in on what had happened. It was five o'clock. He had an hour before his date, time enough to check his apartment. When he reached the top of the stairs above Nate's office, Lorraine was standing at the end of the hall.

She scampered toward him and embraced him, "Thank God you are alright."

"How did you know?"

"The whole town knows. A rattlesnake avoiding me, wolves meeting their end attacking you, you keeping Mom from a noose, a bullet missing you and you keeping a man from...you know...to me. Someone is looking out for us, don't you think?"

"Yes, a lot to think about what you mentioned." His repeated pats on her back indicated the hug should end. "I better check my apartment." Nevertheless, he couldn't help smiling at her as he left her in the hallway.

Only the bed had been delivered to Adam's apartment. The few pieces of ordered furniture had not arrived, but he would stay the night.

The speed at which knowledge spread around town of Harris-Bear's plight meant that Adam's date likely also knew much about the tenant arrangements in Nate's building. No need existed for a newspaper as fast as news traveled in the town.

Emily would want an explanation for the living arrangements and what he hadn't told her. It was naivety that caused him to think he could avoid it. Emily was good for him. She had taught him much about the time and culture in which he found himself. A time that part of him still felt alien to. He would make amends with her whatever it took.

Elmer was at the counter in the store busying himself as Adam entered. "She is running a little late. Bookwork has her frustrated tonight. Come on upstairs. We can talk while you wait. I want to hear everything about this Harris-Bear thing."

*Bookwork frustration, that was a good sign*, Adam thought. It might lessen any frustration from knowledge of the apartment arrangement.

Emily was in her bedroom putting finishing touches on her hair. She had rolled her mid-back length brunette hair into a tight bun. She checked her clock. It was five minutes after six. She would wait another ten minutes and be fashionably and tormentingly late. Her lateness would exasperate Adam's trepidation of knowing an explanation for his and Mildred's living arrangements would be expected.

She burst into the living room with an excited smile, walked right to Adam and hugged him. "I'm so glad you're here. What we heard was so frightening."

She turned her head offering her cheek for a kiss. He didn't deny her although her dad was present.

"You look so vibrant tonight. Your hair and dress. Mr. Doyle, you have the loveliest daughter, and I am so fortunate to have her accompany me to dinner."

Elmer knew his daughter was irate. He had unsuccessfully tried to calm her and put things in perspective. Now he smiled more to himself than the others, wondering who was setting whom up for what. His bet was on his daughter.

After being seated at the hotel diner before they ordered, Emily said, "Sorry I was late, but I was frustrated this afternoon."

*Ah*, Adam thought, *here it comes*. But he didn't take the bait and waited until she continued.

"The company I order flour, sugar, and salt from has overcharged me, more than the stated price in the catalog."

"You should make a copy of the catalog page and send it to them," Adam suggested.

"How would I do that? They would say my handwriting changed the price?"

Adam couldn't understand where his crazy remark about copying had come from and suggested, "I think you should see Nate for legal advice on the problem," before realizing that directing her to Nate's building was another stupid mistake.

"Good idea," she responded but was interrupted by the waitress as they ordered their meals.

When the waitress left, Emily said, "I just want you to know I think what you did helping Mildred and her family out of that nasty predicament was so admirable. And helping Mildred start a seamstress business, which this town needs desperately, was not only a good investment, but charitable. I will be among the first to be fitted for a new dress. If I had any doubt about your goodness and my choice in a partner, it is gone."

It was as if Adam had fallen into a pit of rattlesnakes and not been bitten. He was speechless.

*"Life shouldn't be a journey to the grave with the intention of arriving safely in a pretty and well-preserved body, but rather to skid in broadside, thoroughly used up, totally worn out and loudly shouting Wow!* **What a ride! Thank You, God!**"

Author Unknown

# ★ CHAPTER 19 ★

The first week in December brought snow to the valley. It was clean and cold, and it brought a beauty to the valley that seemed to wash away all the bad happenings of the year. Christmas would soon be celebrated. Maybe the snow was like Christmas—put upon the Earth to wash away sins.

A cold gust of wind whipped snow from the valley ridge and caused Adam to secure the top button of his sheepskin coat. His horse never felt it. If the buckskin gelding did, he did not show it. If only things could roll off Adam as easily. He enjoyed the tranquility of the winter camp. Sure, he had to break up an occasional fight among the cowboys, but there was a steadiness to living here, unlike the highs and lows of being in town.

*Was a flatline between highs and lows something to seek? Were we put here for the purpose of minimizing all risk? Yes, there were dangers away from the relative solitude of the cabin and valley, but where would one be without a special relationship with Emily, or dare he think Lorraine?*

*What would he learn about who he was from his father next spring? Did he have a mother? Of course, he did, but where was she? There were so many questions, but if life was but checking off boxes laid before you in an orderly fashion with known answers, why be here? Why go through monotony?*

"What are ya thinking about?" Hank startled Adam riding up to him.

"You name it, Hank. I'm thinking about it," Adam answered getting a bewildered look from Hank as they rode to the cabin's warm fire.

Emily had seen Nate Clements in the courtroom from the back row and in church but had not officially met him. She entered the foyer of Nate's building. On the left was a door with *Clements at Law* painted in black on the walnut door. On the door to the right the door sign said *Great Falls Custom Dresses* painted in purple. She tapped on the left door.

Nate had learned from his older brother in Iowa that the first step in profiling a potential client was the nature of their knock on the door. A bold solid pounding marked a man of means who felt a need for an attorney to avoid being cheated. A rhythmic knock signaled someone with no great legal need who was prone to much talking. A soft knock normally meant someone who was guilty of the crime they were charged with or had been served divorce papers for cheating on their spouse—they were timid about taking a step other than ignoring it. A knock of medium strength and rapidity with fewer than four strikes usually indicated a woman.

Emily knocked with medium rapidity and strength four times. "Come in, it's open," Nate responded from his desk seat. Given the four knocks, he placed her in the category of a strong-willed woman.

"I'm Emily Doyle. You do work for my friend Adam Duval. Clements, isn't it?"

"Yes, I've seen you. Please have a seat," he said as he stood. "Just call me Nate."

"Would that be short for Nathaniel?"

Nate had an opinion of Emily established before his knock profile of her. He had advised Adam that a girlfriend and her father sitting in the front row at his inquest would have painted a better picture of his character to the judge. Adam would not advise her where to sit. He had suggested at last resort to call Emily to the stand as a character witness. A girlfriend testifying to the gentlemanly behavior of a man could move the needle in such a case. Again, Adam demanded that he scratch the thought.

He found Emily attractive, more so, sitting across the desk from him. She seemed older than Adam, perhaps a good match as Adam acted beyond his stated age of eighteen. Her movements all seemed calculated and purposeful. Before sitting she stroked the back of her dress so as to not encourage a wrinkle to develop while she sat. No doubt she was a handful for any man. Only a man seeking direction or one supremely confident in himself would be comfortable with her.

"Yes, it is. What brings you here?"

"Adam suggested you might help me with a problem. I have a supplier overcharging for a product. They supplied me with this wholesale catalog stating a price, then billed me a higher price which I will not pay," she stated before handing Nate the catalog and billing statement.

Nate noticed Emily's impatience as he studied the document. Finished, he handed it back to her and said, "I will write a letter to the company and make them aware that this business practice is unethical at the least."

"Very well, what do I owe you?"

"Adam is a very good client and friend. There is no charge for this visit. It is my pleasure."

"Very well. Good day to you." She stood, smoothed her dress to the length of her arms, picked up her purse, and nodded at him.

Nate, who was inclined to over-evaluate everything, appraised her last movement. *Was the iron-like hand movement down over her dress an attempt to keep it wrinkle free, a protective gesture to discard any germs that she might have picked up in an unclean office, or a subtle effort to display her body shape?*

If it was intended to be a tease, it would have worked had it not been that she was his best client's girlfriend.

In the foyer between the marked doors, Emily momentarily took stock of Nate. He was articulate and well-organized as evidenced at the inquest hearing, handsome enough, and older than Adam. Town scuttlebutt indicated he didn't have to have a suitress. If not for her major investment in Adam, Nate would be a prospect.

Emily's knock on the seamstress door was solider than the law office. She did not wait for an answer, opened the door, and said, "Are you open?"

"Of course, come in."

"My, my, you are set up well," Emily remarked surveying the room.

"Thank you, and I'm glad you sent our order over in haste as we already have customers."

"I believe you need another and as you patronize me, I will you."

"What can I do for you?"

"I shall need a new dress for the Christmas dance in which Adam has asked me and one to bring in spring next year."

"You know what fabric I have in stock."

"Yes, and I have ordered special fabric for the dresses which should arrive tomorrow. I wish to…you know…not see my fabric on others."

"I understand. I should get your measurements now and have the mannequin adjusted to your size when you bring the material."

While Emily stood erect, Mildred measured her and recorded the measurements, Emily asked, "Where are Lori, and your son? I'm sorry I forgot his name?"

"It's Gerald. They're in school. They started last week."

"It must be a challenge for them starting at their ages with no learning," Emily inquired.

"No, they are enjoying it. I have schooled them at home or wherever we found ourselves for years. Lori is reading above her grade, and Gerald, well, he'll always have issues, but he's a good kid."

"Oh, that's wonderful. I'm sure you've been a good mother," she replied, although skeptical of the mother-tinted analysis.

At the time school was dismissed, Emily found the sidewalk needed to be swept and windows cleaned in front of the general store. As she anticipated, Lorraine and Gerald were walking to their new home from school.

"Good afternoon, children. I'm Emily. How was school today?"

"It was okay, Lorraine answered.

"You don't sound so happy about it. Come inside. We just received fresh licorice sticks."

Gerald could not wait to get a stick in his mouth. Lorraine said, "I'm not fond of licorice," finding herself ill at ease in the presence of Adam's girlfriend.

"I was with your mother earlier today. She is to make me dresses," Emily said, hoping to start a conversation.

Gerald was too busy with the licorice to respond. Lorraine's eyes were exploring the store.

With no response, Emily continued her effort to spur a conversation. "Lorie you're carrying two big books. May I see them?"

The books Lorraine was carrying validated her mother's assessment of her reading skills. Emily was handing them back to Lorraine when Adam unexpectedly walked in.

"This is a pleasant surprise," Emily said. Taking advantage of Adam's sudden arrival, she wrapped her arms around him, turned her head presenting her cheek for a kiss in a greeting he never received in the presence of others.

After planting a quick peck on Emily's cheek, Adam turned his attention to Lorraine. "Are you enjoying school?"

Her eyes had left Adam since the kiss was planted. To Gerald, she said, "We should be getting home now."

Emily did not miss Adam's eyes following Lorraine as the pair left the store.

"I didn't expect you in town until tomorrow."

"I decided to send Dad a telegram to get a better handle on when he's coming."

"As you saw, I'm trying to reach out to Lori and Gerald. It's the right thing to do. They've a big adjustment, but Lori no doubt exhibits social awkwardness."

"She'll get past it, and she prefers to be called *Lorraine*."

"My experience is that even in an adolescent as young as her remnants of gracelessness can never be fully extinguished."

Emily's comment did not sit well with Adam, but he had no comeback. *What would he say? What would it lead to? Perhaps she was right.*

"How about escorting you to the diner this evening."

"Why, I haven't had a better invitation all day."

"I'll be back at six."

Adam sent a telegram to the address he had received from his dad a few months earlier, then went to his apartment to change clothes for dinner. In the hallway to his apartment, he met Lorraine. She had spent an hour looking out her apartment window for Adam.

"Can I ask you a favor?"

"You always can," she replied.

"I'm at the cabin much more than I'm here. Could you take this spare key and check on my apartment every few days that I'm gone?"

"Sure, you want me to clean?"

"No more than I'm here, I don't think that'll be necessary, but thanks. Now tell me what do you think of school? You evaded the question at the store."

"I hate it. Everyone either picks on me or ignores me. And I can read and do numbers better than anyone."

"How do they pick on you?"

"They call me names that I won't repeat."

"What do the names pertain to?"

"Things that happen in the saloon and you know…the alley."

"Just ignore their nasty comments. If you don't react to their name calling, the fun of it will end."

As Adam turned toward his apartment, he was startled when she asked, "Are you going to marry her?"

"I don't know, but I do know one thing."

Her look told him to continue. "I'll always have a special place for you in my heart."

He embraced her, and when he started to pull away, she looked at him and quickly stood on her toes and touched his lips with hers. Adam backed away, startled again.

"That was my first kiss. I wanted my first kiss to be with you," she said. "If you become engaged, it would be too late."

"I'm not sure that was…I'm not sure of many things," he said as he entered his apartment. He closed the door and leaned against it as if to protect himself from what he did not know, his mind heading in many directions.

Emily and Adam had ordered at the diner when they saw Nate and a woman enter. "Do you know who she is?" Adam asked Emily.

"Sure, she's the schoolmarm. I believe her name is Jane. Let's ask them to join us."

After the introductions were made, Emily asked whether the couple were going to the Christmas dance.

Nate asked Jane, "Do you want to go?"

"Sure, it sounds like fun. It will be in my schoolhouse."

After an appropriate amount of small talk, Emily asked Jane, "How is your new student, Lorraine, adjusting to school?"

"Her schoolwork is phenomenal. She's already ahead of most who graduate from the school, but she is having adjustment problems."

"What are the problems?" Emily followed up. Adam was surprised at Emily's interest in Lorraine. She was asking the questions he had intended to ask.

"She often stays at her desk during recess. I suspect the other children are jealous about her performance."

Adam jumped in with a question, "Do the other students call her names?"

"I haven't heard of it. I don't allow teasing in the classroom. But on the playground, they usually do. I can't monitor it all."

Later as Adam walked Emily home, he asked, "I'm surprised you are so interested in Lorraine. Frankly, at one time I suspected some jealousy about me helping the family."

"I know the family is important to you. And helping them is the right thing to do. She seems like such a nice girl, although social clumsiness will be hard to overcome."

At the door, Adam said he would pass on a game of carrom for the evening because he had to leave at daybreak for the herd's winter quarters. Emily was disappointed and limited him to one kiss.

On the walk to his second-floor apartment, it struck Adam that he had kissed two women in the same day. The fact that he did caused sleep to evade him.

"Where's Adam?" Elmer asked as Emily entered the living quarters.

"He must leave early tomorrow."

"Does that disturb you?"

"No, not at all. He has a business to run."

"It seems to me he would be spending more time here instead of less if things were heading in the right direction."

"Dad, I have a handle on things. Mind your own business."

"I think my daughter's future is my business."

Emily answered, "Mildred is making me a burgundy muslin dress for the Christmas dance Adam is taking me to. Charolette was married after she wore a burgundy dress to last year's Christmas dance."

Elmer ignored talk of the Christmas dance and said, "I've been stocking coffee beans shipped in from San Franciso for years. People like the beans, but I'm now ordering some from New Orleans. People can always change their tastes, and one must be prepared."

As sleep did not come easily for Adam, neither did it for Emily. The purpose of her dad's talk about coffee sources was obvious. As much as she hated to admit it, he had a point. The prudent always had a backup plan.

On another front, Lorraine's social shortcomings would not lessen Adam's concerns for her, only enhance them. She was a very smart girl according to her teacher. Suddenly, an idea struck Emily.

*"The greatest tragedy of life is not unanswered prayer, but unoffered prayer."*

F.B. Meyer

# ★ CHAPTER 20 ★

The good news was that the stagecoach trip from Helena was much smoother than it would have been in the summer. A fresh coating of snow obscured the roughness of the trail. But it was cold weather that allowed the snow and caused both passengers to cover themselves with blankets to stay warm on the trip.

The man wearing a bowler hat said to the other, "I'll go to the hotel. You go to the stable and rent a horse before you check in. And stay in your room out of sight, no saloon, no walking around. You can eat jerky from your saddle bag."

It was December 20, four days before the Christmas dance. Emily was carrying a large box tucked under her arm. She was coming back from Mildred's seamstress shop with her burgundy dress for the Christmas Eve dance. It was gorgeous beyond her hopes. Mildred was the great dressmaker she was rumored to be. If the dress didn't move Adam to discuss their future, she would.

The stagecoach from Billings had arrived. Two men were stepping down from the coach as Emily approached on the sidewalk. They both tipped their hats at her as she passed. One was smartly dressed; the other wore an Irish flat cap with a poorly disguised bulge on the right side of his waist.

After she passed, she turned and saw the gentlemanly looking man reach up for a suitcase exposing white spats over black shoes. The other man reached for a saddlebag and showed shiny brown boots. Neither man was a likely customer for the new shoes and boots the store had stocked.

Their arrival made sense, thought Emily. Adam was bringing his monthly culls from the herd to town tomorrow. The pair must be a money-carrying cattle buyer and his armed guard from Chicago. She was right on one count: they were from Chicago.

After dropping the box at the store, she headed for her second errand. In route, she met Lorraine and Gerald leaving school.

"Stop by tomorrow," she told Gerald. "We've received more licorice."

Then turning to Lori, she asked, "Is school going any better?"

"No." was her only response.

Jane was grading papers at her desk when Emily entered the schoolhouse. Emily asked her to write a letter of recommendation for a student. Jane was happy to write the note and thought Emily had a great idea.

"I look forward to seeing you at the dance," said Emily as she started to leave.

"I'm also looking forward to it. I just hope I don't catch the flu some students have been coming down with."

"Oh my, I hope not," replied Emily as she rubbed her hands on her skirt and made a note to wash them as soon as she was home.

"What is your business with the prisoner?" the sheriff asked, giving the bowler, and spat-dressed man a going over in the sheriff's office.

"I'm western district director of the federal land office. Thomas was under my employment."

The sheriff escorted the man to the cells, left and closed the door. The man, who Thomas recognized from an agency conference in

Chicago, motioned for Thomas to move close to the cell bars. Their conversation was carefully whispered.

"Your conviction on extortion would cause a congressional investigation of the agency. We cannot have that. It would place many in jeopardy. Who is their witness?"

"Adam Duval," Thomas answered. "He brings cattle to town monthly. Should be in tomorrow."

Adam was sitting on the top railing of a pen holding the monthly twenty head of culls when he saw an apparent buyer walking toward him. He hoped to get a top price without sitting in the chilling wind most of the day.

"Offer me your top price now and let's leave the bickering to a nicer day," Adam suggested.

"I'd love to, but I got a telegram from Chicago this morning. The plant is full up for the week and they shut me off," he lied.

"Why are you out here in the cold then?"

"Habit, I guess, checking out the place for next month. Are you Adam Duval?"

"Yes, why would you ask?"

"Heard you are a regular, maybe I'll buy your cattle next month," he said as he raised his bowler and ran his fingers through his hair. The Irish man standing as inconspicuously as possible a few pens over saw the signal. His target had been identified.

"You have a good day now," the man said and left.

After a real cattle buyer soon purchased Adam's pen, he headed for the bank discreetly followed by an Irish man. From the bank Adam went to the general store. Emily was getting ready to go to the post office when Adam walked into the store.

"I didn't expect you before this evening," Emily said. Alone in the store with no one to impress, she did not greet him with a hug and cheek to kiss.

"You were expecting a new shipment of boots. I should buy a pair and wear them back here for dinner tonight."

"Great idea," she said as she slid an envelope under the counter out of sight.

"What are you fixing for dinner tonight?" he asked as he tried on a brown pair.

"Fried chicken and green beans."

"Sound great. I'll go clean up and be back at six. Let me take that letter you were holding and drop it off at the post office. It's on my way to the apartment."

"Thank you, but I need to ask the postmaster a question."

Once Adam was out of sight, Emily went to the post office and mailed an envelope containing a letter from Emily and a note from a schoolteacher to an address in Denver.

As usual, Adam took a shortcut through an alley on his walk to his apartment in Nate's building. Shortly before six, cleaned up and wearing new boots, Adam was ready for fried chicken at Emily's. In his room he left his gun and holster, which Emily preferred he not wear to dinner at her place.

Lorraine had been helping her mother in the seamstress shop after school and was on her way to fix dinner when she ran into Adam in the hallway.

"I swept the floor in your apartment while you were gone," she said.

"Thank you, but it isn't necessary."

"I like your new boots," she added.

"Thanks again. Now you have a good evening," Adam said as he started down the stairs. He had decided it was not sensible to give Lorraine any ideas about them.

Emily's fried chicken was good, as always. Most conversation centered around Christmas and the upcoming dance. Emily did not reveal she had a special dress made. She would surprise Adam. During carrom, Elmer admitted that curiosity would cause him to attend the dance this year.

At the door as he left, Emily said, "I think this Christmas season is the time for us to make plans for the future, do you?"

"I agree. I've been thinking the same thing," he answered.

She let his goodnight kiss linger longer than she normally did.

Gerald dropped off some of Mildred's seamstress work before he started sweeping at Betsy's saloon. He was putting away cleaning tools in the lean-to which had been his home when he heard men talking. Their conversation volume was such that it was intended to be private. Gerald would not interrupt them but listened while peering between tin siding on the lean-to.

"That guy you identified as Adam takes alley path to his place, be a perfect place to drop him."

"Okay, make sure he is dead and have your horse ready to get out of town. With snow coming tonight you'll never be tracked. I'll leave here first; you wait a few minutes before you leave this alley."

Gerald held his breath as the remaining man looked toward the lean-to. A noise on the other side of the alley caused him to pull his gun and turn. A cat scamped from behind a garbage can. Shortly, the man followed the cat out of the alley.

Gerald waited another few minutes then ran down the alley in the other direction toward the second-floor apartment. He burst into the apartment out of breath.

"What's going on you look like you've seen a ghost," Lorraine asked him.

"It's what I heard…. about Adam."

"Tell me," Lorraine demanded.

Once Lorraine heard and processed what her brother had told her, it was she who ran toward the sheriff's office.

Adam was in the alley taking his normal shortcut home thinking about the lingering kiss, a Christmas dance, and how Emily and his relationship would change when he heard someone behind him.

He turned to see a man reach for his gun. Instinctively, Adam reached for his to find none. Adam dove for cover behind a storage box. In his dive, he felt something strike his shoulder, then saw a flash from the man's gun followed by sound.

Lorraine was running by the door to Betsy's saloon when Hank stepped out. Her momentum nearly knocked him over. "What's the hurry girl?"

"Adam alley…man to shoot him…hurry."

Hank started toward the alley. Lorraine continued to the sheriff's office. A few feet from the alley Hank heard a gunshot. Lorraine was telling the sheriff what she knew when they heard the gunshot.

"NO! NO!" cried Lorraine. The sheriff told his deputy to stay with Lorraine and the prisoners and he left in haste.

Adam was lying on the ground gripping his shoulder that felt as if it was struck by a branding iron. A man wearing an Irish flat cap approached him. "Why?" Adam asked.

"It's a job," the man answered and pointed his gun at Adam's head. Adam closed his eyes, waiting for the inevitable.

Hank was twenty feet away when he made out a man standing over Adam with a gun drawn down on him in the dark alley. He pulled the hammer back on his single action before it was out of the holster, and squeezed the trigger before he'd pulled it high enough to aim properly. Unlike the future reputation gunmen acquired, shooting from the hip was a hope and a prayer.

Adam heard the shot and felt nothing but a burning shoulder. *Was this how it was? Did one enter the hereafter, so alert? Would his mind soon fade?*

He felt something fall on his legs. It was heavy. He opened his eyes to see Hank over him and the Irish looking man laying across his legs. The sheriff joined Hank and asked what happened.

"He shot me," Adam answered, nodding to the man on him.

The alley became a flurry of activity which Adam did not remember well. The saloon had emptied into the alley, a doctor arrived and stuffed cloth at Adam's wound. The sheriff was asking everyone questions. The dead man was pulled off him. He was lifted by men and taken down the alley.

The deputy finally gave up keeping Lorraine detained. "Okay, but you go straight home."

She ignored him. When she approached the alley, men were leaving the alley carrying a body covered by a blanket on a stretcher. The blanket was not long enough. Bright new brown boots pointed up below the blanket. They were headed toward the undertaker.

The men nearly dropped the stretcher when they heard a girl screech in terror and run away.

With a part-time deputy watching the jail, the regular deputy was assigned to notify the surviving victim's commonly known woman companion of the incident. It took an ample amount of pounding before Elmer cracked the general store door. He woke Emily. In short order Emily was at Adam's side as Elmer waited outside the room. The doctor was gathering instruments to retrieve the bullet and tie off the bleeding arteries. He was preparing a bottle of ether and told Emily it was time to leave.

Adam handed Emily a key to his apartment and told her to fetch some other clothes.

As the doctor escorted her out of the room, she asked, "Will he?"

"I believe he has a decent chance."

Emily was glad Adam had given her an errand, waiting outside the room Adam was in would be too unnerving. She had never been to Adam's apartment. Going there, given their relationship, would not be proper and a cause for town gossip. Walking up the outside stairway, it struck her that she knew not which would be his apartment.

In the hallway, Mildred was standing outside a door trying to talk through it. "Let me in or come out, Lori. You can't stay in there like this. Talk to me." She kept trying to turn the doorknob, but it was locked.

Emily stood for a moment wondering why Lorraine had locked her mother out of their apartment. Realizing she couldn't help and desiring to get back to Adam with what he wanted, she asked while holding a key, "Excuse me, could you tell me which apartment is Adam's?"

"This is his apartment and she's locked herself in."

"How did she get in?"

"Adam gave her a key. What is going on here?"

It was the evening's second blow for Emily. Her expectant fiancé was shot and now she discovered another woman had a key to his apartment.

Reluctantly, she unlocked the door and answered, "Adam has been shot."

Lorraine lay on Adam's bed with a bedspread over her head sopping. Mildred sat beside her and pulled the bedspread down. "Quit crying, honey. Emily says Adam is going to be okay."

"No, he's not. I saw him dead, his boots."

As much as Emily now despised Lorraine rather than fearing her, she couldn't let the girl continue such misery.

"I just left the doctor's office. I assure you—he's alive. He's having an operation as we speak.

Mildred consoled Lorraine as Emily found the clothes Adam requested.

"I'm leaving now and will let you know as soon as I have news," Emily said as she started to leave.

"I'm going too," Lorraine said.

Emily knew the girl wouldn't be stopped.

Emily sat in the waiting room with her father. Lorraine sat across from them with her mother. Hank sat in a lone chair between the families. Emily glanced at Lorraine every few minutes. *Was there another explanation for Lorraine having keys to her future fiancé's apartment or was it the most obvious?*

It was an hour later the pastor arrived. He sat between the families opposite Hank and reached for Emily's and Lorraine's hands. All hands were soon joined in a circle as the pastor prayed for Adam's survival.

Pastor Ken struck up a conversation to take minds off what was happening in the other room. He said to Emily, "I know Adam and you have been seeing each other often and I see you sitting together in church."

He looked at Hank. Hank answered, "I'm his herd foreman."

Turning to Lorraine and Mildred, he said, "I've also seen you in church, but how do you know Adam?"

Mildred explained that Adam got them a job at the saloon when they were desperate, leaving out the cattle rustling. She said that Adam and she were partners in the seamstress business, and he was a good friend.

Lorraine added, "He saved me from a rattlesnake and two-legged ones. Then gave me his room key to keep tabs on his place while he is out of town with his herd."

Suddenly, it struck Pastor Ken that Lorraine was the girl that Adam had saved from the drunkards.

"We should remember that God has brought us all together for a variety of reasons. His will shall be done. We just pray that he decides to leave Adam with us."

Emily could feel the rage she had for Lorraine start to dissipate. They all needed Adam in their own way.

It was another hour before the doctor entered the room. No one asked a question, but all eyes were on him. "He survived the surgery. It's touch and go. We should know by mid-morning."

*"Life is a storm, my young friend. You will bask in the sunlight one moment, be shattered on the rocks the next. What makes you a man is what you do when that storm comes."*

Alexandre Dumas

# ★ CHAPTER 21 ★

The land office agent had been purposely sitting in Montana Betsy's to be seen by many when the first alley shot was heard. He finished his whiskey as a solidary toast to a job done and was preparing to leave when he heard the second shot. A second shot could mean many things—none were good.

He followed the crowd to the alley where he saw the Irishman lying crossways across Adam. "Only one is dead," he heard someone say.

Earlier from his hotel window, he had seen the Irishman tie a rented horse across the street, packed with enough provisions to survive a cold night. Although he had ridden a horse seldom, if the Irishman were alive, he had no choice but to take the horse and get out of town fast. He could not rely on the Irishman's silence.

He breathed a sigh of relief when he heard someone yell, "Adam is alive." The failure of what was his goal a short time ago was now a relief.

The sun had broken the horizon when the doctor walked through the waiting room into the room where Adam lay. The motion was enough to stir three women who had stayed the night. Hank had left for a hotel room. Lorraine was adamant she was staying. Emily would not leave Adam while Lorraine stayed. Elmer volunteered to walk Mildred home. He walked her to the apartment to check on Gerald, then back to the doctor's office to stay with Lorraine before he went home.

Three anxious women awaited the doctor's words when he came out of Adam's room. "He is still unconscious."

"We'd hoped for better news," Emily said.

"That is good news. He is still alive."

It was nine when the sheriff entered to check on Adam, but more importantly to question Lorraine.

"How did you discover someone was out to kill Adam?"

"My brother, Gerald, overheard two men discussing killing Adam from the lean-to back of Betsy's."

"Can he describe the men?"

"I didn't ask him. I just ran to your office and bumped into Hank on the way."

"Where is Gerald now?"

"He's in our apartment," answered Mildred.

"Would you come with me while I question him?" the sheriff asked Mildred.

They were walking the sidewalk to question Gerald as the 9:30 stage was boarding for Helena. The sheriff noticed the federal land office official boarding.

After hearing Gerald's description of the two guys discussing killing Adam, the sheriff telegrammed the Helena sheriff to pick up the bowler-hat-wearing man when the stagecoach came into Helena.

The federal land official was a cautious man. It had enabled him to rise in the agency. He left the stage at a horse-changing stagecoach station and waited on a stagecoach going in a different direction. It delayed his return to Chicago a few days, but safety was worth the delay.

Another attempt on Adam would be too dangerous, but there was another way to achieve his goal of dampening concern about agency extortion and prevent a congressional investigation. The agent would work on a different solution.

It was like a marathon between Emily and Lorraine. Lorraine wouldn't leave because she felt a mystical connection to Adam. Emily stayed because Lorraine wouldn't leave. At noon, Mildred came back and sat with Lorraine, encouraging her to leave and volunteering to stay herself. Lorraine refused.

Early afternoon Elmer came carrying a sandwich for each of the ladies. Both parents urged their daughters to go home and get rest. Neither would budge.

Mid-afternoon the doctor came from Adam's room and said, "He's awake. I believe the worst is over and he will make it. Lorraine hugged Mildred as Emily hugged Elmer.

"He said he wished to see Emily."

Emily jumped up and followed the doctor into Adam's room. Lorraine was relieved. She didn't expect him to ask for her. He would live; that was all that counted.

The doctor checked his vitals again and left the room. Adam reached his hand out and whispered, "Emily, hold my hand. I wish to discuss our future. I believe we would make a good couple. I'm talking permanently. What do you think?"

"Is this a proposal?"

"I guess most would call it that," he replied. She answered him with a kiss.

Her smile was radiant as she entered the waiting room. "From the look on your face I gather he is going to be okay," Elmer said.

Emily could not have assembled a better group in which to make an announcement, "Dad, I want you to know I am now engaged to be married."

Mildred stood and congratulated her. To Emily's surprise, Lorraine also congratulated her and wished them the best.

"You should step in and see Adam before you leave," Emily said to Lorraine.

"I was so worried about you," Lorraine said to him with Emily standing nearby.

"I understand you missed school today."

"That's the only good that came out of you getting shot," she answered bringing a laugh from all.

Once Lorraine was gone, Adam asked, "Can you check the telegram office to see if I have anything from dad?"

"Sure," she said. "You need your rest. I'll be back in the morning." She found no telegram and no return mail from Denver.

With promises that someone would check on him regularly, Adam was released to his apartment on the second day. The doctor said he would visit twice daily. Emily checked on him regularly, brought him more books to read, and stayed with him in the evening until Elmer came to walk her home. Both men insisted that she not walk alone after dark. Given his condition and their engagement, she would ignore any rumors of her time spent at his apartment.

On the morning of Christmas Eve, Nate stopped to check on Adam. "Are you looking forward to the dance tonight?" Adam asked.

"Yes, I was, but Jane has come down with the flu and can't attend."

"That's a shame," Adam replied as Emily entered his apartment. After a kiss, she asked, "What is a shame?"

"Jane is sick, and Nate now has no one to take to the dance."

"Too bad, Nate. Don't feel alone missing the dance," Emily replied.

"I'm sorry you won't get to show off the special dress Mildred made for the dance," Adam remarked.

"How did you know about that dress? It was supposed to be a surprise. Wait till I talk to Mildred."

"Nate, why don't you take Emily to the dance? You both want to go. I'm not the jealous type, and after all, Emily and I are engaged."

"We couldn't do that," Emily answered.

"Why not, it's just a dance?"

"Are you sure?" asked Nate.

"Yes, under one condition. You bring Emily here before you take her to the dance so I can see her in that special dress."

The doctor had told Adam that in a week he could resume normal activities, but until then he was to remain in bed or on a chair. Although he didn't plan to adhere to the advice, he was in a chair and smelled Emily's fried chicken before she and Elmer entered. Emily's burgundy dress looked so exquisite on her Adam soon forgot the chicken.

"Elmer, you have a gorgeous daughter, and I'm lucky to have her as my bride someday."

He then noticed Elmer wearing a grey jacket over a black vest and tie.

"Are you going to the dance also?" Adam asked.

Mildred and Nate entered the room. "Elmer is taking me to the dance," Mildred answered as she reached for his arm. Adam thought he caught Emily's eyes rolling at the gesture. Nate kept an obvious proper separation between him and Emily as they started to leave.

"Have a good time, everyone. I wish I could join you," Adam told them as they left.

Although Adam would have preferred to attend the party, finishing a book Emily had given him he looked forward to. *A Country Doctor* by Sarah Jewett had come out earlier in the year. *It could have been written by Emily*, thought Adam. In the book, Nan, the doctor's daughter, encounters much strife when she decides to challenge conventional values and become a doctor.

"Come in," he responded to a knock on the door.

"I don't mean to bother you if you are into a book," Lorraine said.

She was wearing a dress he had never seen on her. It was periwinkle with white lace around the neck and sleeves. It may have been a spring color at Christmas time, but it looked great on her, making her look older. *Older?* it struck him. She was only one year younger than he, not the three that he'd almost convinced himself of.

In February, she would be seventeen and he eighteen. Anyone in town who cared to know thought Adam would soon be twenty, including Lorraine, Nate, and Emily. Once he stretched his age to gain credibility with Hank, he couldn't take the lie back. Emily would turn twenty-seven next year. *If she knew his true age, what would she think?*

"I'm sorry. I didn't mean to interrupt you," Lorraine said and started to turn toward the door.

"No, Lorraine, you never bother me. Don't leave. You look beautiful in that dress," he said then thought better of his choice of words.

"Lorraine, you are an attractive young lady. The dress just really brings out your natural beauty. Pull that chair up beside me."

She was now blushing. "What is the book you are reading about?"

"It's about how times are changing. More fields are opening to women. Maybe someday in the future women will earn as much as men."

"That'll be the day. I just wish I was a boy."

"Why? Is school still not going well?"

"I hate it. I don't learn anything. Mom taught me all that I hear there. Sometimes I wish I was dumb, then the boys wouldn't be jealous of me."

"Do they still tease you about your work at the saloon?"

"Yes, but don't ask me to repeat the words."

Adam thought, then said, "Maybe I should have a talk with Jane, your teacher."

"Wouldn't do any good, Mom's met with her, and Emily even talked to her."

*Emily seeking to help; he had made the right decision proposing to her,* he thought, then asked, "Have you tried ignoring them?"

"Yes, but how can you ignore them when they put a garter snake in your handbag? Mom said we may think about leaving Great Falls next year."

"Leaving? You can't do that. I'd miss you," he said, then added, "and your mother and Gerald."

"Mother said it would be a new start for us."

On the dance floor, it was the fourth time Emily twisted her head to check on her dad when Nate finally said to her. "Perhaps we should leave if seeing your dad having fun upsets you so much."

"I'm sorry. It's just that I'm not accustomed to seeing him like that. I guess after my mother left, I thought he would never have an interest in women again. And her having worked in a saloon and all that could entail."

"I think she's a great lady who has had much thrown at her and has done a great job of raising her children in a difficult situation, and now she has her own successful business."

"I know you're right; I'll forget about it. And by the way you are a great dancer."

"Thank you," he said as he startled her with an unexpected dance move.

"All are looking at us now," Emily said as his move brought the attention of others.

"I think it is you in the gorgeous burgundy dress they are gawking at."

Suddenly it struck Emily her friend Charolette married her escort to the dance last year after wearing a burgundy dress. It was the reason Emily picked the color. She was now engaged but with another man.

"Enough dancing, I need to sit," Emily said.

Sitting watching others dance, Nate broke the silence saying that next year would be busy for him with new clients and the building.

"How can the office and apartments take much of your time?" she asked.

"I'm having a house built at the edge of town. With my share of the chute patent royalties and leftover inheritance, I thought it would be a good investment."

"How big, how many bedrooms?"

"It'll be two stories with three bedrooms, a den, living room, and office."

"What will you need all that space for?"

"I don't plan on always being single without children."

Lorraine stayed at Adam's until she heard her mother in the hallway. Both had found their conversation easy and comfortable, often with stories to make the other laugh. She and Adam talked about almost everything.

The only subject that was not addressed was their propensity to inadvertently protect each other from danger. But as she stepped toward his chair and wished him good night, it was on both of their minds. Adam was in bed when he heard Nate walking down the hall and into his apartment.

On Christmas morning Adam had risen and dressed when Elmer tapped on his door. "Thank you for getting your buggy for me," Adam said.

"Merry Christmas, and you're welcome. She isn't expecting you and will be thrilled when you show up and show her the property."

Elmer found Adam needed little help walking down the stairs from his apartment and up the stairs to the Doyle residence.

"Emily, we have company," Elmer called toward the kitchen where she was preparing Christmas breakfast.

"Who would be here at this hour?" she said as she stepped through the door wearing a robe over what Adam assumed was her sleepwear.

"Merry Christmas," Adam said.

"Oh, my you mustn't. What I must look like."

"I think you look fine."

"If you have breakfast fixed, we'll eat, then Adam wants to take you for a buggy ride," announced Elmer.

"The Christmas church service starts at noon with dinner

afterwards. We won't have time for a long buggy ride, and it is too cold anyway," she argued.

"We won't be gone long," Adam said.

Emily hurriedly took a few bites and left to dress. In a longer time than Adam expected, she finally made her appearance wearing the burgundy dress from the dance.

"I hope it is proper to wear the same dress today."

"I think it is, who cares if someone thinks otherwise. You look great."

She carried a blanket to toss over them in the buggy. "What are you taking me to see?" she asked.

"You'll see. How was the dance last night?"

"It was fine. I had a good time with Nate. And you should know that he was a proper gentleman with an engaged woman."

"I expected no less," Adam replied.

At the edge of town, Adam turned the buggy from the trail and stopped it on a slight rise. "Isn't it a great view from here?" he asked her.

"It's a fantastic view. Maybe we should picnic here next spring, but it's too cold to stay here today and appreciate the view."

"We will enjoy the view many times. I purchased this property, and builders will start on our house in the spring. Consider it your Christmas present."

They snuggled under the blanket until church time approached. Elmer was leaving when they entered the residence. "Where are you going, Dad? Aren't you coming to church with Adam and me?"

"I'm going to walk Mildred and her children to church."

After the Christmas meal at church, Adam asked Emily, "You seem agitated. You should be happy today."

"I am happy, but the vision of Mildred and family living with my dad and taking my place is a little unsettling."

"You, my dear, are jumping to unwarranted speculation that is not likely."

"You're right. Here's your Christmas present."

He opened it to find a spool of fabric and looked somewhat puzzled.

"It's the best mohair wool. I've hired Mildred to make you a suit from it. My husband will only wear the finest."

*"There are so many unpleasant things in the world already that there is no use in imagining anymore."*

Lucy Maud Montgomery

# ★ CHAPTER 22 ★

It was the day after Christmas when Nate and Adam were in Nate's office going over patent royalty deposits.

"The money just keeps on coming. It's unbelievable. Maybe I'll build a bigger house than I planned," said Adam.

"Yes, and you'll notice the monthly deposits are continuing to grow," added Nate.

"Anything I tell you is confidential, right?" Adam cautiously asked.

"Yes, anything unless it involves a crime you are planning."

"Confidential to not only the law but also our friends and acquaintances?"

"Absolutely."

"How old do you think I am?"

"What kind of question is that?"

"I've told everyone. No, I told a few who were interested and let others assume I was nineteen to be twenty next year. Truth of the matter, I'll only be eighteen in February."

"So, you are seventeen today?"

"That's right."

"That's amazing. Think of what you've accomplished at your age:

managed a successful herd, invented a contraption that is changing the cattle industry, and caused the catch of the town to almost plead for your proposal."

Adam ignored him. "You've come to know Emily to some degree. She will be twenty-seven next year. She thinks she is seven years older than I am, but she is nine years older. What do you think her reaction will be if she discovers the truth?"

"She knows you are younger. I don't think two years will cause her to run. When do you anticipate getting married?"

"Probably late next year after the house is built."

Their conversation was interrupted by a knock on the door. "Come in," Nate said.

It was a boy not over twelve carrying a satchel with a strap over his shoulder. He was wearing long socks and knee breeches tight at the knee to hold his socks up, unlike the common country boy attire in Great Falls.

"What can I do for you?" asked Nate.

"My father is Lord Barnhouse. Are you Mr. Nathaniel Cements?"

"Yes, I am."

He reached into this satchel and withdrew a letter. "This is for you. Do you have an idea where I might find a Mr. Duval?"

"That would be me," answered Adam.

The boy withdrew another letter and handed it to Adam. "Have a grand day, gentlemen," he said as he spun and left.

They opened the letters and found an invitation addressed to each and one guest to an adult New Year's celebration at the Barnhouse estate.

"Wow, I expect that to be quite a party, but I'm not an adult."

"Yes," Nate said, "but back to our conversation, you are getting married next year could prove to be a problem unless you can prove you are eighteen at the time."

Adam's look caused Nate to continue, "Montana is not a state, it's a territory so it falls under federal law. If the judge does not perceive you to be thirty years old or more, he will require either a birth certificate or an affidavit from a parent verifying that you are of age, which is eighteen."

"My dad is coming back this spring according to a telegram I received this summer."

"Then it shouldn't be a problem."

Emily and her dad were in front of the general store—Elmer in a chair with a blanket drawn over him, Emily sweeping a skift of snow from the sidewalk—when the Barnhouse boy handed Elmer a sealed envelope.

"Would you like a licorice stick?" Emily asked the boy.

"No thank you, Mame. My father, the Lord, says candy dilutes one's character."

"What is it, Dad?" she asked as Elmer read the invitation. He handed it to her. The message was in glossy print on thick cardstock.

*You are invited to the*
### *First Annual Lord Barnhouse New Year Eve party*
*At the Barnhouse Estate*
*From eight to midnight December 31.*
You may bring one adult guest with this invitation.

Emily expected her dad's guest to be her. As she handed the invitation back to her dad, she heard the driver of the afternoon stagecoach from Helena holler "Whoa." The driver was leaning back pulling the reins tight as it slowed to a stop a block away. The afternoon stage from Helena carried the day's mail. She stepped inside to wrap her heavy shawl around her and made her way to the post office.

Four passengers exited the stagecoach: a married couple, and two men of opposite looks and demeanor. One was a short, slight man who wore a Reinsman felt derby hat and spectacles. His chatter on the stage was continuous and aggravating to the other passengers. The other passengers were glad to be of leave from him.

The other man was as quiet as the other man talkative. He wore tattered black boots, a Staker hat in the style of the time, and a worn duster. Although the cowboy-dressed man was from Cheyenne, he was not a cowboy. He had been hired by a firm in Chicago to do a job.

The spectacled man, carrying a briefcase, said his goodbyes to all, including the drivers, and greeted people on the street.

The cowboy-attired man drew no attention as the bespectacled man usurped it all. He reached for a blanket securely wrapped with a long rope from atop the coach while the slight man asked Emily for directions to the hotel as she passed. Emily obliged, thinking nothing of it, and continued to the post office.

Without words, the cowboy-appearing man tipped his hat to Emily as she passed. He followed the other man at a distance, then waited outside the hotel until the spectacled man had checked in and started up the stairs.

"Room, sir?" the clerk asked.

Seeing the cowboy nod his head, he asked, "How many nights?"

"One."

"Do you have a preference for rooms?"

"Yes, as far from that guy as possible," he answered, nodding toward the stairs, then added, "and without a street view. Noise disturbs me."

After placing the blanket roll in his hotel room, the man took a quick walking tour of the town, then ate in the dining room before retiring to his room early.

At the post office, Emily found no telegrams for Adam but received mail she had sought from Denver. Back at the general store, she fixed supper for her dad and sandwiches to take to Adam, telling her dad she'd be home early because she needed to discuss a matter with him.

"I can't believe you're going to the winter cabin this soon after being shot," Emily hounded Adam while they ate.

"I need to check on things at the camp and sitting around here is driving me nuts."

"Better than being shot again, next time by someone with better aim. The sheriff instructed you to be careful. Whoever came after you may again."

"I know. That's why I'm not riding out alone. Hank is bringing the wagon in for supplies, and I'll ride back with him. He's as good an armed escort as one could have. I'll be back Thursday evening for Thomas's trial on Friday. That reminds me. I'm invited to the Barnhouse New Year's Eve party Saturday evening. I assume you'll accompany me as my betrothed."

He was still feeling amusement from the irony that Barnhouse had instructed all invitees to bring only an adult guest but had not considered that an invitee might not be an adult.

Emily was hoping that she would be her father's guest had not Adam been invited. If she wasn't, she feared who her father would ask, but she would not decline her future husband. "Of course I'll go with you. I'm dying of curiosity to see if the place is as plush as rumored."

"It will be interesting," Adam noted.

"I must leave early tonight, paperwork awaits me. I want you to come early for breakfast in the morning. I have an idea that would stop the torment to the girl next door."

The man in room 217 had unrolled his blanket and attached the double barrel to the stock of the shotgun. Into both barrels he inserted a 10-gauge buckshot load. After a nap, he rose at one a.m., put on his duster, and slid the shotgun into an inside pocket sewn for the purpose.

He opened the window facing the alley, tied one end of a rope on a bed leg, and tossed the other end out the window. Once he had shimmied down the rope, he turned left at an alley intersection and saw a couple walking toward him. They were more interested in each other than who they might encounter in the alley and never noticed him slinking in a doorway.

He crossed the street, turned at another alley intersection, and pulled a large freight box under a small window with crossbars. Although he stood on the box, the cells were too dark to see anything inside as he expected. He pulled the shotgun from the duster, leaned it between him and the wall, reached into his pocket, and pulled a small flare.

The flare lit the cells well enough for him to see a man sleeping on a cot in the cell beneath him and another in an adjacent cell. Thomas was in the near cell and Jake in the other, but the man on the box knew not who was where, and it would have exposed himself to have asked.

The first barrel of buckshot struck the head of the man in the adjacent cell. The next barrel decimated the nearby man's chest. He pushed the empty shotgun through the window into the cell. He would not be caught with the gun. Guns were expendable. Hurriedly, he pulled the freight box back to its original location and didn't run but walked to the rope entry into his room.

Both Elmer and Emily were sound asleep and didn't hear the shotgun blasts although they hadn't gotten to bed early. Emily outlined to her father what might be done to help Lorraine. Elmer listened and agreed with her solution. The solution would be good for Lori while it would also alleviate a potential problem for both Emily and him. It would be a win, win, win. He was proud of his resourceful daughter.

It was the deputy's turn to spend the night on the jail office cot. He was asleep when the shotgun boomed out. It had a lower pitch than a handgun or rifle. In the dim of waking, the deputy didn't recognize the sound or from where it came. His first move was to the cell block. He saw that both prisoners were dead before he opened the cell doors. In one of their cells, he saw a shotgun on the floor. He went outside and saw no commotion on the street. In the dark of the alley no evidence showed anyone had been up to the window eight feet above the alley.

He pondered what to do. If someone had been on the street, he would have sent them after the sheriff. There was no one. He locked the door and ran three blocks to the sheriff's home. After much pounding, the sheriff came to the door.

"What's up?"

"Shooting."

The sheriff's squinting eyes signaled he wanted more information.

"The prisoners, they're both dead."

"How? Where were you?"

"Sleeping."

Once the sheriff was dressed, they walked toward the jail. "Tell me more," the sheriff said.

"I was sleeping. There is a shotgun on the floor in Thomas's cell. I suspect someone tossed the gun in through the window. Thomas shot Jake in the head and then leaned the gun to his chest."

"Thomas did not seem to be the type of man with the courage to kill himself," the sheriff observed.

A lantern-lit inspection of the jail and alley by the sheriff did not reveal any evidence to counter the deputy's theory, but daylight would. The sheriff walked the street and saw nothing unusual. At the saloon, he pounded the door until weary-looking Betsy appeared in a robe.

"What's so important that you must wake me at this hour?" she asked.

"Two dead prisoners. Anything unusual last night?'

"No, normal night, no fights but some pushing and verbal exchanges."

"Anyone new?"

"Yeah, a short bespeckled guy was talking to many. I saw him taking notes."

With sunup, the sheriff and deputy rechecked the cell block. "What's this?" the deputy asked.

"It's a burned flare. How did this get in here?" He looked at the deputy thinking maybe he'd used it for more light on his first inspection.

"It's not mine," answered the deputy.

With closer inspection, the sheriff saw pellet scratches on the cell bars far above the trajectory the pellets would have taken if Thomas had shot the gun. An alley inspection showed trail marks in the dirt from below the cell window to a freight box.

"They were both shot from out here," said the sheriff.

"Someone could have moved the box to toss the gun inside," countered the deputy.

"Doesn't explain the pellet marks. They were shot from out here. The question is, why? Go fetch the doctor and undertaker."

The sheriff rang the counter bell numerous times before the hotel clerk arrived. "I'm here, I'm here. What's the emergency?"

"Do you have a smallish man staying here who wears glasses?"

"Yes, he checked in room 202 yesterday afternoon."

The sheriff started up the stairs before the clerk said, "He's not here; he left a few minutes ago."

"Do you have any idea where he went?"

"He was asking all kinds of questions about the attempted murder charge on Thomas, but he seemed to have no interest in the extortion thing."

"I didn't ask that. Do you know where he went?"

"He wanted to interview that girl who was abused in the alley."

"Answer the question."

"I told him she lived with her mother in the Clements building."

The sheriff burst out of the hotel and headed for Nate's office. Enroute, he saw the town was bustling. Word had not gotten out about the jail shooting. A cowboy was boarding the 9:30 Helena stagecoach. Adam was heading out of town on a wagon with Hank. The sheriff waved. Hank waved back but not Adam—he seemed to have a perplexed look about him. *Good,* the sheriff thought, *Adam is taking safety precautions.*

Nate told him which room held Mildred's family. The sheriff pulled his gun and turned the doorknob expecting to kick it in if it was locked. It was not.

Mildred, Lorraine and the bespeckled man were sitting at a table. Seeing the sheriff burst in with gun drawn, the man flinched in shock as if he had been shot.

"What are you doing here?" the sheriff asked.

Nervously, the man answered, "I'm working on a story for the Chicago Herald newspaper," and nodded at the notebook that lay in front of him.

"Stand up," the sheriff demanded. A quick check showed no weapons. "Where were you at one a.m. this morning?"

"I was at the hotel. I was in the saloon until nearly midnight interviewing people."

"What information are you looking for?"

"Information on the attempted murder charge against Thomas."

"How about the extortion charge?"

"My publisher told me to leave that alone."

"How long do you plan on staying in town?" asked the sheriff.

"Until the trial Friday is over."

"There won't be a trial. Thomas is dead. Now come with me."

*"Until you make the unconscious conscious, it will direct your life and you will call it fate."*

C.G. Jung

# ★ CHAPTER 23 ★

Before Hank picked Adam up in the wagon to leave town, Adam had breakfast with Elmer and Emily. Emily had said she had an idea to help Lorraine.

Emily started the conversation by saying how terrible it was that Lori was subject to such nasty abuse at school.

"I know the hurt that nasty abuse can cause. I've spent time pondering what could be done to help Lori. I've talked to Jane about disciplining boys who taunt her, but she says she can't catch them, and Lori needs to learn to take boy torment. I thought back to my childhood and what it was that made me the subject of verbal abuse. My mother had run away with another man which devastated me. While I was down, I was easy prey. Lori's experience is similar, her dad killed and mother the subject of abuse and now her. My savior was dad sending me to Miss Wolcott's School for Girls. It is a finishing school in Denver. They taught me grace, how to act like a lady and allowed me to escape the teasing boys who harassed me about my mother leaving."

"How long were you there?" Adam asked.

"I was there two years. And we can take advantage of that now for Lori. As an alumnus, I wrote to the school and explained Lori's situation and included a letter from Jane documenting that Lori was very well learned in reading and arithmetic. I received a reply yesterday. Given her situation and a discount I was promised as an alumnus, they offered a ten-percent discount on her tuition."

"Why didn't you tell me about this?"

"I didn't know if they would accept her, and I didn't want to disappoint you."

"What's the fee?"

"It's five hundred dollars for a year. With the discount, it will only be 450."

"Wow, Mildred can't afford that."

Elmer spoke up for the first time. "Adam, I know from experience it's just what she needs. The community has been good to me. I'm prepared to return to it by giving fifty dollars to help someone in need. There is a fund administered by the church to help needy children. I'm sure we can secure a contribution from them.

The hint was obvious to Adam. They expected Adam to contribute to sending Lorraine away. Away from Emily and him, and away from Mildred and Elmer.

It was also obvious to Emily that her dad's sudden benevolence might have something to do with being able to spend more time with Mildred.

"Have you discussed this with Mildred and Lorraine?" asked Adam.

"No, because you have been so keen on helping her, we thought we should run it by you first."

"I think Hank is probably waiting on me. I'll think about it, and I suggest you discuss it with Mildred and Lorraine. Lorraine should have a say. You know she is hardly a child."

"You're unusually quiet today. What are you pondering?" asked Hank as Adam sat beside him on the buckboard seat in route to the winter camp.

"Be careful on the frozen ground. Each bump hurts my shoulder," Adam said. "And in two days I must make this trip again back Thursday afternoon for the trial on Friday."

The buckboard seat sat on springs in the front bed of the freight wagon. The springs helped dampen the bumps, but not enough to eliminate all the pain in Adam's shoulder. But the condition of his shoulder was not all that was bothering him.

To date, it had been an average winter temperature-wise, but little snow had fallen. Given the short grass in the valley because of the hot, dry summer, little snow cover was good as it saved the bunchgrass from overgrazing.

They heard shots before they passed over the ridge into the winter valley. "Hurry," Adam said, "There must be trouble."

"But you said not to shake you much account of your shoulder."

More shots rang out. "Forget my shoulder, just get there," Adam said.

Hank started laughing, "What's funny?"

"The guys are just plinkin for the New Year's Day shooting match. Just had a little fun with ya. Get you mind off what's bugging you."

"How many of you are going to participate?"

"With Hairy gone and not counting Sky, our cook who doesn't shoot, that only leaves Herman, Clint, July, and Fancy. I told them two must remain with the herd so only two could go."

"What about you?"

"They know I could outshoot them, so I gave myself a pass. How about you?"

Adam thought for some time, then said, "Shooting the wolves gave me a reputation whether deserved or not. I think I'll just hang on to that and pass."

The cowboys were putting guns away when Hank and Adam pulled up. "Well, which two of you won?" Hank asked.

July answered, "Herman and Fancy, I can't believe Herman won. I'd never seen him shoot."

"Reading the Bible pays dividends," Herman replied.

"A couple years ago, I'd have won this," lamented Clint. "Wait to you tenderfoots get to be my age."

"Other than becoming the talk of Great Falls, why are you guys so into this?" asked Adam.

"This year it's one hundred dollars for the winner, and the fee is only a dollar," Fancy answered.

"Where's the money coming from?" queried Adam.

"Merchant collection to promote town. Betsy gave five," Hank said.

Adam found cutting the herd by a quarter had more than cut the workload by that amount. They had made sure most of the more rambunctious and troublesome cow brutes were among those culled. Even without Hairy, and Adam gone much of the time, the others had more free time, which was not necessarily a good thing.

"Looks like your shoulder mended well. Are you staying with us for some time?" July asked Adam.

"I've got to leave Thursday afternoon. I'm to testify at Thomas's trial Friday. Then I'll just stay in town through Sunday, New Year's Day, and see who wins the money."

"Who will you be rooting for?" asked Clint.

"The winner," he answered, drawing laughs.

At eight in the evening, Emily and Elmer expected to find Lorraine and Mildred in the apartment, but saw the shop was lantern lit. They tapped on the door before entering.

"Working late, we see," Elmer said to Mildred as he walked to her and put his arm around her shoulder, sending a shiver up his daughter's shoulder.

Emily ignored the shiver and said to Lorraine, "We want to talk about a great opportunity for you. Jane says you are a great student and stand above others in the school. It would be a shame if your talents were not fully developed. I was fortunate to be sent to a finishing school while dealing with the distress of my mother's unexpected departure. I was enduring the taunting of schoolboys as you are. It was making my life a nightmare. In many respects Miss Wolcott's school saved me and molded me into who I am today. My father and I cannot stand idly by and not assist you in having the same experience."

"What would this school cost?" asked Mildred.

"The yearly tuition is five hundred dollars of which dad and me will each donate fifty dollars. *That her "donation" was a discount Emily didn't mention.*

"No way can I afford the balance," stated Mildred.

"I think through the community and other sources we can raise the balance. What do you think, Lori?"

"Would they teach me to talk and walk like you?"

"They will mold you into a real lady. When and if you return to Great Falls, you will be the envy of all the young women and desire of all the young men. What do you say?"

"Is the school in Helena?"

"No, it's in Denver."

"Where is that? Isn't that far?" asked Lorraine.

"It's just a stagecoach ride to Helena, then a train ride to Denver, not far," Emily answered, although she could have said the same thing about Chicago.

"I think Lori and I should spend time thinking about it. But whatever we decide, it is so wonderful to have friends who offer help," said Mildred.

"Adam's helped me so much. I want his opinion," added Lorraine.

"Well, I know what Adam will say," Emily answered knowing she could influence a favorable opinion from her fiancé.

The next evening was the end-of-the-month meeting for the church's charitable fund board. Emily, Pastor Ken, schoolteacher Jane, the county prosecutor, and Amanda, wife of the church founder, were board members.

After the minutes from the last month and the treasure's report were read, Emily made the case for donating money to sponsor Lorraine at the girl's school in Denver. She drew parallels between her situation and Lorraine's and how the school turned her life around.

"I don't deny it would be good for her, but I can't see how we can spend that amount of money. It would nearly deplete our present funds," the county prosecutor said.

"Then we need to put together another fundraising drive," answered Emily.

"We had one in September," Amanda reminded the others.

"Jane, tell the board about the harassment Lorraine is getting from undisciplined boys who would rather toss profanities at a helpless girl than do their homework," Emily said.

Jane took offense at the use of *undisciplined* as that fell under her purview. "I'm not denying that boys will be boys and it is happening, but I have not heard such talk myself. I have a special chair and a bar of soap ready for any utterances of profanity in my school."

Amanda spoke up, "I can relate to the mean-spirited teasing Emily experienced and Lorraine is now. I move we finance half of Lorraine's Denver school tuition for one year."

After hearing the arguments, Pastor Ken spoke. As pastor, he was presumed to have a better understanding of how God's word would apply, hence his opinion carried more weight than the others.

"I can understand the need. But we have many needy people in our community. If Lorraine and family still lived in a saloon lean-to, I would look at it differently. But now they have an apartment, and Mildred has a business. We must be frugal with our funds and see to it the money we raise goes to those in the direst situations.

Maybe we should talk to the city council and see if funds can be found to hire someone to help Jane monitor activities on the school grounds."

"I believe more and better books would be a better expenditure of money," Jane quickly stated.

"Pushing it from the playground would just incentivize the boys to up the scale of harassment off the school grounds," Emily argued.

"I call for the vote," the prosecutor declared.

The prosecutor, Jane, and Pastor Ken voted against the measure. Amanda and Emily voted for it. Emily huffed and abruptly left the meeting.

Pastor Ken rode out of town the next afternoon. Those who saw him assumed he was off to visit someone in the congregation in need of spiritual help. He was dressed as usual in black attire wearing a wide-brimmed black padre hat although he was Protestant.

At a distance he saw a wagon with two men on the buckboard approaching. The pastor reached under his jacket and pulled the Colt from underneath his belt and placed it in a saddle bag. Although he had no intentions of doing anything unbefitting a pastor with the gun, there was no need to spark unwarranted speculation.

"Pastor, what brings you out to the countryside today?" asked Adam.

"Sometimes the solitude of nature inspires my Sunday morning message. Will you still be in town on Sunday for services?

"Yes, I plan to be. Hank here and two other cowboys from our outfit are entering the shooting match in the afternoon. I wouldn't miss it. Will you attend?"

"Oh, I'll have to think about that. What brings you to town on a Thursday?"

"I'm a witness in the trial tomorrow."

"When did you leave town?"

"Tuesday morning."

"You didn't hear? There will be no trial. Someone killed Thomas and Jake right inside our jail. The evil in the world stretches our imagination."

"Savin the hangman work might not be all evil," Hank added. Pastor Ken didn't reply.

Adam was within three miles of town; it was a much longer ride back to the winter quarters, and Emily had made arrangements for them to join Jane and Nate for supper at the diner.

Adam could smell food cooking before he entered the Doyle residence. After a quick peck on Emily's cheek, he stated, then asked, "The pork chops smell wonderful, but I thought we were meeting Nate and Jane."

"Jane and I aren't on the best terms at the moment."

"Okay."

"She got all defensive about allowing boys to torment Lorraine and voted against helping fund Lori's proper schooling."

Elmer changed the subject and relayed all he knew about the jail shooting including the gossip around town.

"You left early Tuesday. How did you hear about the shooting?" Emily asked.

"I didn't know until this afternoon when Hank and I ran into Pastor Ken leaving town."

"He is another on my bad list. He also voted against funding for Lori. I've of a mind to not attend services Sunday."

After supper, Elmer excused himself saying he was going for a walk. Emily looked out the window as Adam helped her with the dishes. "Just what I thought," she said.

"What?" asked Adam.

"He is walking in the direction of Mildred's apartment."

"Do you have a problem with that?"

"I guess I better get used to it."

Since Emily was avoiding it, Adam asked, "Tell me about Mildred and Lorraine's reaction to the prospect of her attending the finishing school."

"Mildred could see the merit in it. Lori seemed to have mixed feelings. And she wanted your opinion on it. What is your opinion?"

"I don't know. The school likely would be good for her, but she's never been away from her mother. You are totally invested in getting her to that school. I understand you can relate to her torment, but is there another reason?"

"We are to be married. You have helped the family many times. I share your desire to do what is best for them. Your charitable desires are mine. Unfortunately, you helping them may have been cause for rejection of the funding."

"What are you talking about?" he asked. She relayed the pastor's explanation in voting against the funding.

*"The finest souls are those that have the most variety and suppleness."*

Michel De Montaigne

# ★ CHAPTER 24 ★

At six in the evening, Adam was considering what to wear to the Barnhouse New Year Eve party. His selection was slim. The outfit he wore to church was his only appropriate outfit.

He answered the knock on his door. It was Mildred. She looked gorgeous in a dress he had never seen. He couldn't help wondering whether Lorraine would be as attractive when she turned her mother's age. If so, the man who married Lorraine would be very fortunate. After taking her in, he noticed she was carrying a suit on a hanger.

"Emily had me put this on a rush order for you from the material she gave you for a Christmas present. I hope it fits. I'm sure she is expecting you to wear it tonight."

"Thank you so much. You look lovely. Is it too much to assume you are going to the Barnhouse party with Elmer?"

"It would not."

"I hope Lorraine isn't too disappointed she's not going to Denver in February."

"She's a little disappointed but coming to terms with it."

"What is she doing this evening?"

"She'll be at the party also, but in a different capacity. The Barnhouses took on extra help tonight to serve the guests."

Emily said she'd come to his place before the party. Adam didn't understand the reason but was ready when she opened his door without knocking.

"You look like the gentleman I hoped to marry in that exquisite suit," she greeted him.

"Thank you. It could serve as my wedding suit also."

"I think not. I've another design in mind for that," she answered. Twice in a month was enough for her burgundy dress. She wore a mauve purple outfit trimmed in a darker boysenberry purple with a matching hat.

"And you look like a woman a guy might dream about," he said as he hugged her.

"Are you ready?" They heard Elmer ask from the hallway. He was with Mildred. The men helped the women into the double-seated buggy Elmer had rented for the night.

The couples expected the party to be formal, but it was beyond their expectations. A formally dressed butler answered the door, asked for their name, checked it with the guest list, then motioned another butler to escort them to the receiving line.

Mildred and Elmer were first to be greeted by Lord Barnhouse and his wife. "Ah, a local merchant," he said to Elmer, then turned to Mildred, "and you have a seamstress business, I'm told," surprising them with his familiarity of the town.

When Emily and Adam stepped up, the lord said, "Congratulations on your engagement." Looking at Emily, he said, "Perhaps you can keep his time filled such that he has no time to manage the herd."

Then he looked at Adam, "You will sell me the herd and that parcel of range soon."

Adam ignored the remark and said, "Thank you for inviting us to your party."

The main hall of the mansion was more opulent than they expected. White and black tile covered the floor in a checkered pattern, a fabric which appeared to be silk served as wallpaper and white crown molding a foot wide lined the ceiling. A five-piece band played in the corner. A twenty-foot-long table was filled with food in smorgasbord style. And in the opposite corner was a bar.

A line had formed at the food table and bar. The band struck up a dance song and Emily reached for Adam's hand and said, "We can eat and drink later."

While dancing, Adam noticed most men stood a few inches above the women they were with. Emily and he were the same height. A strange feeling came over him that at another time short men would have difficulty finding women. He passed it off. Wherever he came from, he was at the right place or time.

Adam found himself gazing over Emily's shoulder. He was still checking the place out, seeing who he recognized; then he realized he was more focused on finding Lorraine. She wasn't to be seen. On the dance floor, he also saw Mildred looking around.

They bumped into Nate and Jane. "Sorry about that," Adam said.

"It's quite okay," Nate replied, then turned to Emily, who was still peeved at Jane's vote against funding Lorraine to the Denver school and wouldn't look at Jane. "May I have a dance with your future?" Nate asked Adam. Adam stepped back and reached for Jane.

Jane said to Adam, "I know Emily is upset with me. I'm doing the best I can in school. If I ever catch boys saying naughty words to Lori, it'll be a bad day for them."

"I understand you're a little upset at Jane," Nate said to Emily.

"Yes, I am. I would have hoped we women would stick together."

"Lorraine is one of my tenants and I'd hate to lose her, but would a donation from me help?"

Emily stopped dancing and looked at Nate.

"I was thinking fifty dollars," he answered the unasked question.

Emily leaned forward and hugged him. He hugged her back. The hug lasted longer than either intended or realized.

Adam and Jane stopped dancing, curious about their partner's embrace.

"Let's eat," Emily said as she reached for Adam's hand.

In line he asked, "What was that about?"

"Nate has agreed to give generously to Lori's school. It would be nice if others also did."

Emily led him to a table other than Jane and Nate's. The remark slapped Adam hard. He had decided he would give if the shortfall was one hundred dollars or less, but even with Nate's promise they were 350 dollars short. But the real elephant, which he fought to not admit to himself, was that he would miss Lorraine if she moved away.

Lorraine caught Adam's eye as she entered the room. She approached from the kitchen wearing an apron that matched all the kitchen staff. He saw her pick up empty plates and carry them to the kitchen. Emily saw him watching her.

"If you really care about her, you'd see to it she gets what she needs," Emily said in a challenging tone.

Adam stood. "I'm going to talk to her and see how badly she wants to go to that school." He headed for the kitchen. More than a few people noticed him leave, embarrassing Emily.

Not seeing her in the kitchen, he asked, "Where did the girl go carrying empty plates?"

"She took trash out," someone answered.

He went out the kitchen door and heard a commotion. At a distance, he could see three boys confronting Lorraine as she carried an empty bucket. The boys' backs were to Adam, making them unaware of Adam's presence.

"Come on, little Lori, we know you like to make guys happy."

"Yeah, it won't be the first time for you," another said.

"You're just like your old lady, aren't you?" the third taunted.

Adam recognized the voices from when he was in jail. It was the boys who tormented him from the alley about the prospect of being hanged.

Emily, embarrassed that Adam had followed Lorraine into the kitchen, had stepped outside. She saw Lorraine and heard the last two taunts. She also saw Adam grab the first boy he came to by the shoulder, turn and deck him with a left-hand swing.

Unbeknownst to most, Adam only had a couple years on the boys and not much in terms of size, but he was angered with pumped adrenaline and the two boys seeing their friend hit the deck from Adam's fist were scared. They were teasers, not fighters. This time they had miscalculated. They turned and started away but not quickly enough. Adam pounded the second boy and caught the third before he was far.

Emily restrained Adam before he hit the third boy the second time. "Enough, Adam. Surely this is enough to show you how much she needs to get away from this?"

Lorraine had dropped her bucket and was crying. Emily went to her and hugged her. "It's going to be alright. You will not be subject to this any longer."

Hearing about the outside commotion, some of the guests stepped outside and saw two party goers and a maid hugging while three boys scampered away.

"What happened here?" the sheriff asked.

Adam said nothing while Emily explained what had happened.

"I guess from the way they're moving you didn't hurt them too bad. Perhaps it taught them a good lesson," the sheriff said as he turned and walked back to the party.

Nate and Jane had come out and overheard Emily's explanation to the sheriff. Jane seemed in shock.

Emily said to Jane as Adam and her passed, "If the schoolteacher had done her job in maintaining discipline or funds were available to get Lori away from harassment, this incident wouldn't have happened."

Jane didn't reply, feeling guilty without any support from Nate. Pastor Ken, who had been invited to the party, saw Jane was taking undo blame and consoled her. "You mustn't blame yourself. Remember God has a plan, and all will work out."

Sunday morning Elmer, Mildred, Adam, Emily, Lorraine, and Gerald took up one pew of the church. The pew drew attention from throughout the church as most everyone had heard about the incident at the Barnhouse party and were speculating how that could affect the engagement between Emily and Adam. Those concerns were allayed as the six sat together as one big family.

Many of the people who attended the Barnhouse party and who were regularly in church were missing. Pastor Ken made a note of the church regulars who were absent. He surmised they may have included too much liquor in the party reveling. *Perhaps, next Sunday's sermon would be about moderation,* he thought. But this New Year's Day he preached on new beginnings.

After church, Elmer was invited to dinner at Mildred's place. Grudgingly, Emily had accepted the budding relationship. Her father was becoming easier to live and work together with in the store. And her impending marriage had eliminated his nagging her about finding a husband.

Adam and Emily had dinner alone in the second-floor residence above the general store.

"Do you have any regrets about last night?" Emily asked.

"None."

"You know the three boys may be more cautious in their torment, but there will be others. I know you did the right thing. But because boys will be boys, it could become a status symbol of courage to badger her and flaunt adults like you."

"I know, I know."

"What do you think should be done?" She pushed him.

"When do tuition funds need to be secured for her to enroll?"

"The term starts the first day of February, and tuition is due the middle of this month," Emily answered.

"I'll see to it that the tuition is paid, but I must ask you something. I know you endured similar torment, but is the primary reason you want her in Denver is to have her away from Great Falls?"

Emily took a deep breath and let it out slowly before answering. "You asked a question about an honest concern you have, so I will answer honestly also. I do feel sorry for Lori and wish the best for her, which I believe would be finishing school. However, I sense a deep attachment between you and her. I'm focused on making our marriage work. I understand you feel obligation to her, but whatever feeling you have for her makes me feel somewhat insecure even though she is so much younger than you."

Now it was Adam who needed to compile his thoughts before answering. Lorraine was much closer to his age than Emily. Someday he must tell Emily the truth about his age, but it wouldn't be today.

"Thank you for your honesty. I do have deep feelings for her. But it is you whom I have chosen to take as my wife and start a family. Doesn't that say it all?"

He got up from his end of the table, walked to her and kissed her. "Now let's get the dishes done. We don't want to be late for the shooting match."

The prior year's annual shooting match had been canceled because of snow and zero-degree temperatures. This year it was in the twenties, cold but tolerable for Montanans. A gallery of sort was set up at the edge of town. Baskets of bottles were placed beside a hay wagon. Each participant would be given ten seconds to hit six bottles placed on a shelf above the wagon.

Vendors had set up around the crowd selling hot apple cider, coffee, biscuits, and a new craze sweeping the country, ice cream. Although iced cream had been invented in China before Christ, it was becoming popular. For many in the crowd it was their first experience tasting it. Adam was buying a cup of ice cream for Emily when a man approached him.

"I want to apologize for my son's behavior last night. What you did was appropriate. When I found out the reason for you smacking him, I added my belt to his hide. Hopefully, he has learned his lesson."

Emily and Adam had both decided that ice cream would be more fitting served in the summer as another man approached him.

"I want you to know that disciplining my boy is my responsibility, not yours. Maybe you'd like to pick on someone closer to your age. If so, I'd be happy to meet you at a place of your choosing."

Adam answered, "If you'd have done an adequate job of teaching your son manners and proper behavior, there would have been no need for my action."

The man bristled and stepped closer to Adam. "Let's settle this right now," he said and pushed Adam into Emily, nearly knocking them both down. Adam dropped his empty dish of ice cream and charged at the man. Fortunately, the sheriff was close and interceded.

"I'll not allow fighting here. Where's your son now, Frank? Or do you care?" The sheriff said causing the man to huff and leave.

The mayor stood on the hay rack, welcomed all, and announced the winner of the match would get one hundred dollars collected voluntarily by our upstanding elected council members and himself. He said the shooting match would start following a few remarks from him.

As he started on the second page of his notes, someone in the crowd yelled, "Are they going to shoot or are you just going to talk us to death."

"Yakety-yak-yak," someone the crowd yelled.

After laughter died down, the embarrassed mayor put his remaining notes in a pocket and proceeded to introduce ten contestants who had paid the dollar entry fee. "Are there any others among us who wish to participate?" he asked.

"I do," someone standing behind Adam yelled. The crowd turned and saw Pastor Ken hand his overcoat to his wife, Ginger, exposing a colt stuffed in his pants, and walk to the front.

*"Ask and it will be given to you; seek and you will find; knock and the door will be opened to you.*

Matthew 7:7

# ★ CHAPTER 25 ★

"Do we have anyone else here who would like to join the contest?" pleaded the mayor standing before the crowd. "How about our sheriff and the wolf killer?" He shifted his gaze from the sheriff to Adam.

Both had a reputation to maintain. Neither saw it prudent to chance diminishing their stature.

Other than Hank, Fancy, Herman, Pastor Ken, and Chance, the Barnhouse foreman, Adam knew none of the contestants other than a couple he had seen in Betsy's. His crew was over-represented.

The ten-second time limit allowed the shooters to pull their gun up for eyesight aiming rather than shooting from the hip. Even though all used single action revolvers, which required the hammer to be pulled back between shots, it was ample time to aim properly.

The first two shooters only hit three bottles of the six bottles lined up, a few only hit two. Hank, Fancy, Herman, Chance, and Pastor Ken each took down five of the six bottles. With half the contestants eliminated, the mayor called for another round for the five remaining. They drew cards for the order they would shoot in. The one drawing the lowest card went first. Fancy drew a six of hearts. Pastor Ken drew a king.

Fancy hit four bottles, Hank hit six, Chance and Herman each hit five. Pastor Ken was last. He needed to hit all six or he would lose. To the amazement of all in attendance, he shattered all six bottles.

After conferring with men setting up the target bottles, the mayor said, "Since another runoff is in order and we are running short on bottles, we are going to double the distance the contestants will shoot from." The board they were required to stand behind was moved sixty feet from the targets.

Hank held his hand up to keep the clock from starting as he practiced aiming at the greater distance. "We can't allow you more time," said the mayor.

Hank's bullets struck three of the six bottles at the extended distance.

Pastor Ken stepped to the board, looked up for a moment, then nodded to start the clock. When his gun was empty only one bottle remained.

Sensing Pastor Ken was out of his element, he had been considered an underdog. Consequently, the crowd cheered when he was announced the winner. The banker handed the mayor a one-hundred-dollar greenback.

Betting surrounding the match caused many to unwittingly make contributions to the church. Unbeknownst to all, the pastor's wife, Ginger, had recruited a deacon to place bets on behalf of the pastor. The winnings went into the church building fund.

"Hoodlums better not monkey with our preacher man," someone in the crowd hollered.

The local photographer, who had set up his wooden box camera, asked the mayor and Pastor Ken to step in view for a picture as the pastor was awarded a crisp, new one-hundred-dollar bill.

"Who would have guessed our pastor would win the contest?" Emily said to Adam as they started walking away.

"Yeah, a bet on him would have won a lot of money," he replied.

They stopped when they heard someone yell for them to wait. Turning, they saw Pastor Ken heading toward them.

"I voted against financing Lorraine's Denver schooling because money was given to the fund for charity to the neediest. But after what I saw last night, she needs to get away from the evil talk of boys. Take this bill and apply it to her school."

"Thank you. No one knew you could shoot like that," said Adam.

"Remember the day you met me leaving town. I was heading out to practice. Remember what Mathew wrote: 'ask and it will be given to you; seek and you will find.' The chairman of the church building committee just told me we have reached our fundraising goal."

After thanking the pastor again and walking away, Adam said, "That was so generous of him."

Emily answered curtly, "Yeah, it sure saved you some money."

Adam ignored her and said, "I saw Mildred and your dad leave before us. You suppose they're at her apartment?"

"I'm sure he's walking her home."

"Let's go and tell Lorraine and Mildred we've collected enough money to send Lorraine to the Denver school. We can tell them Pastor Ken donated his winnings. And Elmer and Nate each donated fifty, but we don't need to reveal where it all came from. I'd rather the amount of my contribution remain anonymous."

"Understood," answered Emily.

"We have good news," Emily said as Mildred opened their door.

"Come in," Mildred invited. Lorraine was sitting in a corner using light from a window to read.

"Lori, we've collected enough money for you to attend my alma mater, Miss Walcott's school for girls."

"Really?" She jumped up. "I'm really going, mother?"

"Yes, if you wish. I must ask, where all the money come from?"

"Pastor Ken donated his shooting match winnings. Nate, Dad, Adam, and others all contributed to the fund." Adam was relieved when Emily followed his wishes and didn't reveal his amount of contribution.

Lorraine hugged Elmer, then gave Adam a longer hug and

whispered in his ear, "I'll miss you."

Emily heard the whisper but ignored it. Lorraine would soon be gone. She and Adam would be married and all would be well, including Lorraine's education. It was all good.

Before traveling to the winter camp, Adam checked for telegrams — still nothing from his father in Texas. Since the winter had been less cold than normal, he crossed the Missouri River northeast of town where it was broad and shallow, there the current kept it from freezing. In normal winters, the ice was thick enough to cross upstream. Danger lay in assuming the ice was thicker than it was. Adam often imagined while crossing the river what the Missouri was like hundreds of miles downstream.

All was well on the ranch. The cowboy banter was uplifting. Fancy was teased about his performance in the shooting contest. Hank talked about what he had planned to do with the hundred dollars he didn't win.

"Just as well, I'll stay away from town since I have no money, while Herman and Fancy go next weekend," lamented Hank.

"Herman and Fancy went last weekend. It will be their turn to stay with the herd," Adam corrected him.

"They must go to town — I lost the bet," observed Hank.

"What are you talking about? Someone fill me in," pleaded Adam.

"That preacher fella bet Fancy and Herman he'd whip them shootin. Ifn they lost, they promised to attend his church Sunday."

July tormented, "I suppose Herman thinks he knows more about the Bible than the pastor. He'll discover otherwise in church. Maybe we won't be subject to as much Bible talk from Herman in the future."

"I think I know my Bible well enough," countered Herman.

"How about you, Fancy?" asked Clint. "Are you afraid while you're in church a bolt of lightning will rain down from above and fix you for your sinin with that little blonde lady of the night?"

Fancy answered, "Just because you're an old man you think I'll ignore your insults. Someday you'll go too far, and I'll whoop you."

"I must ask, what did the pastor promise to pay if he lost?" Adam inquired.

"Him being a preacher an all, we just assumed that'd not happen and didn't ask," Fancy admitted.

"Maybe next spring I better look for smarter cowboys," stated Adam, causing general mayhem in the cabin.

In his cot that night, Adam mused about how he lived in two different environments, the town and the ranch. Traveling from one to the other allowed a break from the other. But as always somewhere in his mind he knew that he came from a culture most in Montana could not fathom. It was not that he had a desire to travel to his previous existence. His gut told him it was toxic. But curiosity sometimes ate at him.

It wasn't only the lumpy cabin cot that kept him awake. *Would his dad's arrival answer questions for him? What if his dad didn't recognize him or disowned him? Would the arrival of his dad send him back to the place from where he came? He was already missing Lorraine. Would he be able to forget her?*

Saturday evening, the twenty-first of the month, Adam sat at Elmer and Emily's walnut dinner table in his usual spot near the end where Emily sat. The other end was vacant as Elmer was at Mildred's place. She had fixed beef stew. It warmed his insides as the ride sapped heat from him.

"Do you like this table?" she asked.

"Yeh, I guess, why?"

"It came from my mother's family. She left it when she hastily took off. Dad said he'd rather I took it because it reminds him of her. It doesn't bother me, and you don't think that little flimsy thing you eat from will do, do you?"

"It's fine with me."

"Good. Nate took me on a ride to his future home while you were at the ranch. It's been framed. It will be a wonderful house. He hopes to move in late this summer. You told me our home will have three bedrooms, but you've never shown me the blueprints."

"That's because I don't have any."

"Do you expect builders to just toss wood together at their will?"

"I'll be using the same builders as Nate is using. We'll make some variations to his design when they start."

Emily added, "Nate took me by the plot our home is to be built upon. Nothing has happened. The sod hasn't even been scratched."

"The ground is frozen. As soon as it thaws, the foundation crew will start."

"If we're using the same construction crew as Nate and they don't finish his until late summer, that means ours won't be started until then."

"The foundation will be complete then," Adam tried to reassure her.

"If we are to be married next fall, where will we live then without a house built?"

"We may need to stay in my apartment for some time."

Emily huffed and started picking up dishes. "You seem adrift tonight. What's on your mind?"

"Herd issues mainly," he lied.

"If your dad doesn't take control of the herd when he returns, I think it's time for you to turn herd management over to Hank. At some point one must move on."

"I still enjoy being out there with the cowboys."

"Well, you should know that I will not dally around there. And I expect my husband to be with me."

Adam came up behind her at the sink and wrapped his arms around her. "Don't worry so much; all is going to turn out."

She turned in his arms, enabling him to kiss her. All would be alright, she knew. She had the will and constitution to mold her future husband.

Sunday at church Pastor Ken spoke on new beginnings, how past sins would be forgiven for the truly repentant. Because Adam invited Fancy and Herman to sit with Emily and him, Elmer, Mildred, Lorraine, and Gerald sat in another pew.

Emily had not been comfortable sitting with a family that had done God only knew what at a saloon. Now she was more uncomfortable sitting at a pew with two raggedy dressed cowboys who thought wintertime bathing wasn't necessary.

Pastor Ken batted .500 with the new attendees. Herman was touched discovering that the pastor knew the Bible as well as he did and told him upon leaving that he would become a regular part of the congregation.

Fancy breathed a deep sigh of relief as he exited the church avoiding lightning striking him for his sins. He saw the respite as an okay on his activities. Within a few minutes, he was at Betsy's with a whiskey in one hand and Sally in the other.

Although the general store was closed on Sunday, they had received a shipment of goods Saturday afternoon. Elmer and Emily needed to stock the goods before opening Monday morning. After dinner, Adam helped them until all that was left to do was paperwork. He excused himself and was at his apartment shortly after dark.

Lorraine would be leaving on the 9:30 stage for Helena in the morning. From there, she would take the train to Denver. Adam, among others, would see her off on the stage. He wanted to tell her goodbye in his own way, but that had a downside. What would he say? When she returned, if she did, he would be married and live on the outskirts of town. Her mother and Elmer—who knew where that was headed? She would be changed. *Would he recognize her? Perhaps it was better to hold his memories of her as she was now.*

His thoughts were interrupted by a knock on his door. It was Lorraine.

"I thought you'd want to see me off," she said standing in the doorway.

She was not in nightclothes, but her red hair was streaming down both sides of her face past where her collar bone would be. It had obviously been brushed but still had a mind of its own and did not lie straight. He guessed she now stood at five two to five three. A girl of nearly seventeen years, she'd likely reached her full height.

"I will tomorrow."

"Would you rather I leave you alone now?" she asked.

"Of course not, have a seat."

The period of silence began to make both nervous until she said, "I'm going to miss you."

"And I you. But you're going to that school is for the best."

"If you wish me to stay, say so and I will."

"Often in life we must do what we must because it is the right thing to do. This is the right thing. Do you have spending money to take with you?"

"Mom gave me three dollars."

Adam reached into his pocket and pulled out five ten-dollar gold coins. "Take this; call it your birthday present. It's next week, the sixth, right?

"Yeah, you remembered."

"Yes, but don't tell anyone where the coins came from, promise?"

"I promise, but you already paid most of my tuition."

"How do you know that?"

"I just know. I'm not stupid."

"You certainly are not."

Lorraine stood and said, "I want you to know I wish Emily and you the best. But I won't come back for your wedding."

As she started for the door, from impulse he turned her around, and kissed her deeply, before catching himself. "I'm sorry, I shouldn't have done that."

"I'm glad you did. Now I'll have two kisses to remember you by," she said as she left.

Although his apartment bed was three steps above his lumpy

cabin cot, sleep didn't come easily for Adam as he was torn between guilt having kissed her and another emotion he could not identify.

At 9:30 the next morning a small crowd surrounded the stage-coach: Lorraine's family, Elmer, Emily, Pastor Ken and Ginger, and Adam. With Lorraine's luggage loaded, she started to spread her goodbyes and hugs.

Adam thought it better to avoid another goodbye. Before she reached Adam and Emily, Adam said to Emily, "You need to get back to the general store. I'll walk you. We've done all we can here."

Emily tucked her arm under his elbow and grasped it tight as they walked away. From the stagecoach window, Lorraine saw the couple disappear from her view as the stage headed out. Adam reached deep inside himself to muster discipline to avoid turning to see her leave.

*"We must always change, renew, rejuvenate ourselves; otherwise, we harden."*

Johann Wolfgang Von Goethe

# ★ CHAPTER 26 ★

After Adam's eighteenth birthday in late February, he sent another telegram to his dad in Forney, Texas, where last summer's telegram had come from. Before he left the combination post office and telegram office, the clerk said he had a letter.

Finally, a response from his dad, so he thought. But the return address was Denver. Inside was a folded paper; the message was short.

*Happy Birthday*
*Congratulations on turning twenty!*
*Your very close friend,*
*~ Lorraine*

It bothered Adam that Lorraine, a close friend as she described herself, did not know his true age. He had just turned eighteen although no one knew his real age but Nate. Had he not proven himself—herd manager, inventor, engaged to an older lady who some said was the catch of the town? So, what did age matter other than a number? The bigger question was how he knew he was eighteen instead of twenty or twenty-one. He did not know how he knew, but he knew. It was something he needed to get past, but how?

It was early morning the first day of April. The sun had yet to poke above the horizon when Fancy rushed into the cabin, exclaiming, "Wolves! A pack of ten molesting the herd, hurry!" then left abruptly.

The crew flew from their cots, and reached for their pants, while hearing gunshots at a distance. A quick saddling of their horses and they galloped over a ridge from where they heard the shots only to see Clint and Fancy dismounted, bending over in laughter.

"April Fools," they said together.

April Fools' jokes had become a common ploy on the range among cowboys. Attempted midday they seldom worked, but in the dim of morning sleep this one worked.

Realizing no harm was done, Adam said, "Okay, you got us. Now let's go back and have an early breakfast."

Breakfast was ready when the crew returned to the cabin. "How did you know we'd be back soon?" Adam asked Sky.

"I'm not gullible as some."

"Yeh, he probably overheard Clint and I talking last night," offered Fancy.

What little snow that had accumulated for the winter had melted. With little snow, heavy spring rains would be required to produce enough summer grass to feed more cattle every year as Lord Barnhouse continued to expand his herd and other herds grew.

Making that case to Lord Barnhouse was one of the reasons Adam headed to town. Another reason was to see if he had received a telegram from his dad. Spring roundup and processing cattle would start in two weeks. In the only telegram he had received, his dad had said he would be back for the spring roundup. *What if his dad was in town? How would he recognize him?* he wondered. Seeing his fiancé was also on his to do list, but he hoped she would not hassle him more about getting the house built sooner.

At the post office, he found no telegrams from his father, but five letters, all from Denver. He put them in his saddlebag before heading to Emily's. He saw no upside to making her aware of Lorraine's letters.

Emily greeted him at the door. She was properly dressed as always but not in a party dress. Her dark brown hair was uncovered but tied up in a bun as always unless she was outdoors with a hat. He noticed a line of white pearls along the tight bun of her hair.

She noticed his attention to her hair and asked, "Do you like my new barrette with white pearls?"

"I think it is lovely. Why don't you let your hair down? We are engaged, you know."

"You answered your own question. We are engaged, not married."

She then changed the subject. "I have seen no activity on the house site, and the frost is now out of the ground."

"I'll check with the foundation foreman before I leave town. I'm sure they'll be starting their digging shortly. Any news in town?"

"Nate and Jane are no longer seeing each other."

"What happened?"

"I think she was much too plain for him. You'll be in town tomorrow evening, I presume."

"Yes, what do you have in mind?"

"You haven't been to that saloon lately; maybe it would be a chance for you to go. Nate has asked me out to dinner."

"I hope the two of you have a good time."

"You have no problem with your betrothed going out with another man?"

"I might, but I'm not gullible enough to fall for your April Fools ploy."

When he started laughing, she tossed a chunk of fried apple at him and huffed in frustration. "Well part of it was true. Nate and Jane broke up."

"Really, why do you think that happened?"

"I told you. She's not sophisticated enough for him. He deserves a finer woman."

He left Emily's earlier than he normally would. The letters from Lorraine were on his mind.

At his apartment he found each of the five letters from Lorraine was longer than the previous one. She liked the school a lot, said everyone at the school was very nice and she was learning a lot. She also said she missed much of Great Falls, and she thanked him for the two letters he had sent her.

The last sentence in the last letter struck him the most.

> I don't miss the teasing in Great Falls, but I do miss my mother and brother, but especially you. It is my hope to see you again, the sooner the better. And I wish you the best with Emily.

The next morning Adam met Nate at his office. They went over the chute royalties collected. Money was still coming in above their expectations. Given the accumulation of royalties, he would not need to borrow money to build the house, nor would he need to touch any money from cull sales of the herd. The herd money he kept in a separate bank account in addition to what was buried in the black box.

If his dad did not recognize him or claim him as a son, the herd earnings would belong to the man he thought was his dad. Adam would not even make a claim for wages. He would not put himself in a position to be called an interloper or cattle thief.

Adam told Nate, "I still haven't heard confirmation from my dad about his arrival. None of my telegrams have been answered. I guess he shows up when he desires."

"Not much else you can do. If he doesn't show up for your round-up as he promised, you might contact authorities in that Texas town. What is it?"

"Forney. By the way, Emily tried to pull an April Fools on me yesterday by saying you were taking her to dinner tonight."

"Did you fall for it?"

"No, I think I know you better than that," answered Adam.

"I'm sure you do, but do you know her that well?"

Nate's question vibrated in Adam's head causing his mind to wonder. *How well did he know her? She was well crafted in playing people, no doubt. She knew what she wanted. She would not be a wife he could lead around, but he had no desire for a subservient wife. But would she attempt to lead him where he might not be comfortable?*

"Did I lose you? Are you awake?" Nate asked, bringing Adam back to reality. "Are you ready to take a ride to what is starting to look like my future home?"

The builders were in the process of placing windows in the framework and boards on the roof. Adam visited with the foreman and made plans to meet with him and go over blueprints for his home after Adam was back from the herd roundup and processing.

On the ride to the plot for Adam's home, Nate said, "I've added amenities to the house plan given my share of the royalties: more dorm windows, and a wraparound porch. But the builder says it will not delay them starting on your house more than a few weeks."

They found the foundation crew starting to dig the basement for Adam's house. His house would have a full basement. Building a basement added little to the cost as the footing needed to be deep in the Montana climate regardless of whether it had a basement. The extra cost was in moving a lot of dirt by hand.

Next on Adam's agenda was the limestone mansion. A butler answered the door, asked for Adam's name, and said he would inform Lord Barnhouse of his presence. He was asked to sit in the marble foyer. During his wait he inspected the place more than he had at the New Year's Eve party. The house he intended to build was nothing compared to this mansion. After a few minutes he checked his pocket watch. It was twenty minutes before he was escorted into the lord's study.

One wall was covered with walnut book shelving, and it was full. He had no idea how many books there were, and it would have been awkward to start counting them. Lord Barnhouse was sitting at an ornate mahogany desk.

"Have a seat." He gestured toward a chair.

"You have a magnificent library, sir."

"Thank you. I understand you are building a house."

"They are starting on the foundation." Barnhouse's knowledge of what was happening in the town continued to amaze Adam.

"I can recommend builders I used from Helena, if you have a need."

"I have made arrangements with local builders."

"You did not come here to discuss house building. Have you decided to sell your herd?"

"No, but to discuss the range situation. Also, for your information, my father owns the herd, and I am managing it. He will be arriving shortly, and I will make him aware of your interest. Selling it would be his decision."

Adam took a deep breath and spoke his piece, "Your herd keeps expanding. More herds are moving into the area. Soon there will not be enough grass unless we move further away for grazing. Moving too far will put us in Indian territory, which could bring trouble. We should think about the long-term effects of continued expansion."

"Very perceptive young man, you are. On the other side of the equation, the demand for beef keeps growing as the country grows. If we don't meet the demand, others will. About the Indians, modern times are coming, more railroads, more people. Those who choose to live as nomads in a hunt-and-gather mode are doomed. Times change, you either adapt or die. Be assured I have no desire to squeeze your herd out of grass because I believe eventually you will sell it to me. Why? Because you are building a house in town and your wife-to-be desires a businessman rather than a cowboy."

"I should point out for the second time that my father owns the herd, not me," Adam replied.

"Then I recommend that if he doesn't show up for roundup as he promised, you should go to Texas and find him."

"It's getting late. Miss Doyle is expecting me for dinner, and I have another stop to make. Thank you for meeting me."

"It was a pleasure. You stop back anytime," the lord answered as he walked Adam to the door.

On the way out to Emily's, he stopped at the post office and mailed a letter to Lorraine. Still no telegram from his dad.

After dinner, he asked Emily, "Why do you think we are a good match?"

"What a silly question. You are an up-and-coming businessman, and I will inherit the only general store in town."

"Aren't there other reasons?"

"Yes, I have dresses and blouses with E.D. monogrammed in needle point. Your name is Duval, mine Doyle. Both start with D and have five letters."

"That's it?"

"Well, I think you are rather cute also. Why do you ask these silly questions?"

As was the norm, she limited him to two kisses when he left for his apartment. Over and over, he thought of Lord Barnhouse's comment, "your wife-to-be desires a businessman rather than a cowboy," and Nate's question, "Do you know her that well?".

Adam left before breakfast for the winter quarters in a supply-loaded wagon and spent the rest of the week upgrading cattle pens and reinforcing the funnel fence to the processing chute.

Processing went quicker than it had the year before. Both a smaller herd and improved chute tactics made short work of what had been the most laborious part of cowboying. He found himself looking toward the ridge toward town often for the father who never came.

"I see ya looking to the ridge toward town often. Missin the squeeze I suppose," said Hank.

"No, I was wondering what kind of horse dad would be riding," he answered.

"Knowin your dad, he probably got himself held up at a table."

"What do you mean?"

"You know how your dad likes to play poker. Sometimes he can get tied to a game for days. He's lost this herd more than once but got it back before he left a table."

Adam was shocked. He had no idea. People just assumed he knew many things about his dad. He did not. For him to ask more questions would only raise suspicion about who he really was.

He would give his father a week to arrive. Whatever the outcome would be from meeting his father, it would give him a background to his life and clarity for the future.

*"The search for truth is more precious than its possession."*

Gotthold Ephraim Lessing

# ★ CHAPTER 27 ★

It was ten days after the annual roundup and processing of cattle. Adam and Hank were taking the freight wagon into town for supplies. Adam's plans would be determined by what he found or didn't find at the post office. He found two letters from Lorraine and nothing from his father.

When Adam came out of the post office, Hank asked, "Ready to head to the general store for supplies?"

"No, we need to talk first."

Hank dropped the reins and looked at him.

"I need to find out where dad is and what he's doing."

"How ya purpose ta do that?"

"The telegram I got last spring was from Forney, Texas. I'm going there to find him and see why he hasn't come back."

"How long you spect to be gone?"

"I don't know. At least a week to ten days, I suspect. If I have difficulty finding him or he wants me to stay awhile longer, I can't say for sure.

"Are you sayin you want me to run the herd while you're gone?"

"You know how to handle the herd as well as I do. I trust you. If it becomes time for the monthly cull, bring them here and sell them.

Put the money in the black box and get money from the box if you need supplies. Go easier than normal on the poker and whiskey. If you get locked up for saloon trouble, who will bail you out? Your pay will be double while I'm gone."

"Sounds like you're a planin to be gone longer than a week."

"I don't know. Move the herd between grazing valleys as usual."

"When you get back how will you know where we at?"

"If no one in town knows, I'll have to wait until one of the crew comes to town and leads me there."

"When will you be leavein?"

"I'll take the 9:30 stage to Helena in the morning. Let's go get the supplies so you can head back to camp, but don't say anything to Emily about me leaving."

Hank pulled the wagon in the alley, and Adam walked to the front door. He held it open for a customer leaving carrying a bag, then entered. Emily was standing behind the counter with her back to the door arranging can goods and heard no bell ring alerting her to another customer. He quietly stepped behind the counter leaned over her shoulder and whispered in a disguised voice, "I'm looking for a date tonight, you available?"

She jumped, let out an *eek*, and dropped two cans of beans. When she realized who it was and got control of herself, she snapped, "How dare you. You have no right to sneak up on me. I won't tolerate such from anyone including a fiancé or husband. Sometimes you act like a schoolboy."

It was as if he'd been hit by a sledgehammer. It wasn't what she said as much as how she said it. It was a tone he'd never heard from her. He turned and headed for the door.

"Where are you going?"

"I'm going to see Nate; perhaps later you'll be more civil. Hank's around back with a list of supplies needed."

Adam notified Nate that he would be leaving town in the morning for an undetermined amount of time and explained the reason.

"How would I reach you if need arose?" asked Nate.

"When I get to Forney, I'll telegram you and let you know where to reach me."

"Is there anything you'd like for me to do while you're gone?"

"Yes, two things. Pick up my mail at the post office. Also, I would appreciate it if you would check on Emily, periodically."

"What does she think of your leaving?"

"I haven't told her I'm going to Texas yet. I will this evening. And that reminds me. Lorraine has been writing to me regularly. I'll tell the postmaster you'll be picking up my mail. If you pick up a letter from her at the post office, don't mention it to Emily. That would unnecessarily upset her."

"I get it."

"I'm going to check with your house building foreman now. He is supposed to have blueprints ready for Emily and me to look at."

"Go ahead and check, but I believe he's gone for a couple days."

"Oh boy, I hope he's back; otherwise, it will delay the start until I get back."

Adam rode to Nate's house construction site to find Nate was right. The building foreman was gone. A few blocks away at Adam's house lot, he found the foundation and basement were nearly finished. Emily would want an update and likely not be happy with the progress.

In route to his apartment, Adam stopped at the bank and picked up what he needed for the trip. In the lobby of the apartment building, he had an idea and entered Mildred's seamstress shop.

Mildred was standing in front of a fabric covered mannequin. She was wearing an apron with needles protruding from a front pouch with various colors of string on them.

"Adam, glad you stopped in. I made a record of the mannequin settings on the suit Emily had made for you. I would like to make you a suit in appreciation for all you did for Lorraine. I've already purchased the wool. Look on the second shelf, third from the right."

Adam found a grey tweed. "I like it and look forward to it. But don't hurry I'm headed to Texas tomorrow to find my father."

Mildred didn't ask any questions about his trip, then it struck Adam. She likely wondered why he hadn't asked about Lorraine. Receiving letters from Lorraine, he wouldn't mention as Mildred might tell Elmer.

"How is Lorraine doing, have you heard from her?"

"She's doing fine and has sent a couple letters. There is one on the counter over there, read it if you wish."

"I'm glad to hear she is fine. The reason I stopped is, could I borrow a needle and thread?"

"Sure, what color thread?"

"Brown will do fine."

"I'll be happy to do any patching you need done."

"It's no big deal. I'll handle it. Nice to see you."

Adam was in no hurry to meet Emily for dinner. Part of the reason was to give her time to cool down after he startled her. He reached for the leather satchel duffle bag Emily had given him for his birthday. If he had a choice, he would have taken a less status conspicuous bag on his trip, but it was all he had.

He opened the bag and with his knife he cut the cotton lining near the top of the bag. Into the gap he slid four one-hundred-dollar banknotes and other documents. With the needle and threat from Mildred, he sewed the lining closed. With time to spare, he cleaned his boots, considered polishing them, then thought better of it.

He wasn't surprised to see Elmer's buggy hitched and tied in front of the general store. Elmer would be taking Mildred for a ride.

Emily met him at the door and surprised him with a kiss. "Please forgive my nasty behavior after you startled me."

When he didn't answer, she continued, "Just know that teasing a lady in such manner is not befitting a gentleman. I have a surprise for you."

"I smell your fried chicken," he answered, "my favorite."

"We will not be eating here. Mildred is coming for dinner with dad, and we are taking dad's buggy out to the riverbank for our first picnic of the season. It's the first day of May, and accordingly I've a May basket prepared."

The Missouri River was a fraction of its normal spring size because of the short winter snowfall. Adam unrolled a blanket closer to the stream than he would normally.

Adam was on his second chicken thigh when Emily asked, "Did you get an assortment of blueprints from the builder today?"

"I stopped at Nate's house site, but the builder was gone."

"Dad stopped by our building site this week and said the foundation crew was nearly done."

"Yes, I checked today."

"Will you wait in town until the builder gets back with the blueprints?"

"No, I'm leaving in the morning."

"The ranch can do without you for a few days."

Adam took a deep breath, it was time. "I'm leaving on the stage in the morning for Texas. I still haven't heard from dad, and he didn't make it for the roundup as he promised. I must see what's going on with him. I think this is a better time than when our house is being constructed or it is closer to our wedding."

"I see, I think."

"If you hadn't seen your dad for years and wanted him at your wedding, wouldn't you want to connect with him and at least let him know you were getting married?"

"Yes, I see your point. How long will you be gone?"

"I don't know. It depends on whether I have trouble finding him. The telegram I received was from Forney. Hopefully, he's still there. But there's another reason I need to see him. Nate tells me that if a judge doesn't feel a person is thirty years old, he will require proof that the person is eighteen before he issues a marriage license. The proof can either be a birth certificate or an affidavit from a parent or relative attesting to their age. I don't have my birth certificate. You have your dad to verify you are over eighteen. I do not."

"That's ridiculous! Everyone knows you turned twenty in February."

Adam hesitated but knew he could not mislead Emily any longer. *A marriage must be based on trust*, Pastor Ken said. *How could she trust him if he didn't tell her the truth? And how could he trust her if their relationship depended upon him continuing the deception?*

"The fact is I turned eighteen in February."

"What? There is no May Fools, only April Fools."

"I know my age."

"You are not serious."

"Yes, I am. I can't prove it, but I know I'm eighteen."

"I don't believe it. You act my age, running a herd, an inventor. You must be mistaken."

"I'm not."

Emily stared out over the slow-moving Missouri River. Adam was unsure of what her response would be knowing his real age.

"What is two years? You've been accepted as twenty. Let's leave it that way."

"If you chose to think of me as twenty, fine; just know I'm eighteen. I don't want any mistruths in our marriage."

"Hmm," she said like a revelation struck her. "That means I am nine years older than you, not seven. I remember when I was ten my aunt came to visit. She and her husband were having troubles. She brought her one-year-old son. He was a baby. She taught me to take care of him—diapers, feeding and all—saying someday I'd have a baby of my own. I never had any idea the baby could have been my future husband."

"If you choose not to marry me, I will understand."

"I didn't say that. It'll just take some getting used to. How will you travel to Texas?

"I'm leaving on the Helena stage tomorrow morning. From there, I'll catch a train to Dallas where I'll rent a horse for a day's ride east to Forney." He didn't mention that he would need to change trains in Denver.

"I'm thinking while in Helena or Dallas I will pick up a wedding ring for you. Do you have an idea of what you want?"

Suddenly, all Emily's concerns were allayed. She gave Adam a detailed description of what she wanted, which she'd obviously given much thought.

On the ride back to town, Emily asked, "If I check with the builder while you are gone and he has the blueprints, may I pick out the house design we wish?"

"Sure, just remember what I budgeted for the house."

"Should I pick up your mail while you're gone?"

"Nate agreed to do that. I am expecting royalty documents."

It was late when they pulled up in front of the store. Mildred was still there, and they decided not to intrude. "You'll see me off in the morning, won't you?" he asked, thinking it better to skip breakfast with her and leave on a positive note.

"Of course," she answered, wondering why he didn't mention breakfast.

After the normal second goodnight kiss, he reached for the back of her head and pulled her to him for a third. It lasted longer than the other two. Even though she learned he was younger than she thought, he decided to show her she was marrying a man, not a boy.

After a quick breakfast at the diner, Adam packed his leather duffle and changed into clean clothes. Before he put his pants on, he put money in a money belt except for fifty dollars which he put in his pants. He wrapped the thin money belt around his thigh, pulled his pants on, grabbed his bag, and walked to the stagecoach.

He was ten minutes early. Emily was not at the station. The driver asked for bags. A thirty-something couple each had a bag which the driver put in a compartment behind the coach. Another passenger who appeared to be a businessman had no bag.

The driver looked at Adam and said, "You'll be more comfortable with the bag back here."

Adam handed him the duffle and watched him place it in the compartment and pull a canvas over it.

A man carrying a rifle came out of the station and climbed to the high seat near the top of the coach. "It's time to board," he said.

The couple had boarded when Adam looked up the street and saw Emily coming.

As he trotted toward her, the driver said, "Don't be long. We're about to leave."

"Don't worry, I'll be back soon," he told Emily.

"I know you will," she replied with a hug, but not allowing a kiss as they were in public, and it was not a proper thing to be seen doing. She was a lady after all.

Later in the day a middle-aged woman was gathering weekly supplies in the general store. She was a regular customer who Emily had known for years.

"Is your husband okay? I haven't seen him in church with you for months," Emily asked.

"He seems to always have something more important to do. He is a couple years younger than I am, and as you can see, I haven't aged well. He spends more time at Montana Betsy's than I'd like, but what can I say? He is a good provider, so I'm not going to complain."

Hearing more than she wanted to know, Emily asked no more questions.

*"All great change in America begins at the dinner table."*

Ronald Reagan

# ★ CHAPTER 28 ★

On the stagecoach the couple sat across from Adam and the business-looking man. It struck Adam as bizarre that he thought of the couple as similar age to him, although they were older, likely older than Emily.

The man who sat beside Adam boarded before Adam. As the man climbed up into the coach, his coat flared back to show his holster and side arm. Adam noticed the holster was well worn above the revolver. It obviously had been used frequently.

Adam was also wearing. He planned to put his gun and holster in his bag before he boarded the train in Helena. There had been three stagecoach robberies during the year, and the station master encouraged passengers to be armed for their own safety. Adam noticed the man sitting across from him was not armed.

A large pair of what was known as wheel horses at the rear of the six-up hitch started the coach moving. They were the largest of the six-team hitch. The swing team, or middle pair of horses were smaller. The lead team were also smaller than the wheel horses and the least well trained. They could be flighty, but the larger horses held them in check.

Adam looked out a window as the coach passed the general store.

Elmer was sitting in a rocking chair on the sidewalk. Emily was entering the door. Elmer returned his wave. Emily did not turn as the coach passed. Adam wondered how long it would be before he saw her again. He had a hunch it would be some time.

The man beside Adam struck up a conversation with the couple. He seemed interested in their reason for traveling. The wife gladly answered his questions and introduced herself as Candace and her husband as Stanley Roberts. She was from Chicago, and her husband was from Mt. Carmel, Illinois. It struck Adam as odd a town in Illinois would be named *Mount* as no mountains were in Illinois to his knowledge. Then he had to wonder how he knew that.

They lived in Denver and had traveled to see her father who lived in Chicago but was in Great Falls for a week as a cattle buyer. The man's answers to her questions were short. He was traveling on to Cheyenne was all he disclosed.

"How about you?" The man asked Adam.

"Going to see my dad in Texas."

"What do you do in Great Falls?"

The man wanted to know too much in Adam's opinion, so he answered, "I'm a ranch hand on a herd outside of Great Falls."

As stagecoach rides went, it was a long one-day trip to Helena. They weren't due before midnight. Every ten to fifteen miles was a station where fresh horses would be hitched to the coach.

When they got out to stretch their legs at the first station, Adam noticed the inside of his seat partner's boots were worn. The wear indicated he spent a good deal of time on a horse, not like what a businessman would wear. At the station, Adam took thirty dollars from his pocket and slid it into his boots.

They were halfway to the next changing station when the stagecoach slowed. A man carrying a saddle over his shoulder was on the trail.

"My horse stumbled and broke a leg back there," the man pointed. "Need a ride."

The man riding shotgun put his rifle down to help the man lift his saddle on top of the stagecoach. When he turned, the horse-less man had a gun pointed at him.

"What's this?" Adam heard the driver say, then felt his seat mate's gun poked in his ribs.

"Unbuckle your belt nice and slow."

Candace screamed and was told to shut up. Adam complied with the gunman's request. A rider approached, leading two horses behind him.

With the couple, Adam, the driver, and the formerly armed escort lined up, they were ordered to empty their pockets and pull them inside out. Adam had twenty dollars.

"Is that all you have?"

"Do you think a cowboy makes much money?" Adam replied.

The man struck Adam across the face. "I question whether you're a cowboy."

He reached for Adam's vest, pulled out his pocket watch, opened the cover, and saw the photograph of Emily she had placed inside the cover.

"Lookee here, this supposed cowboy has a girlfriend. Now ain't she cute?"

The robber put the watch in his own pocket and said, "Drop your jacket and raise your shirt over your belly."

"What?" Adam exclaimed.

He flexed his gun and said, "Just do it."

Adam complied revealing no money belt.

Stanley had ten dollars in his pocket and was ordered to raise his shirt. "It's all we've got," he pleaded, exposing a money belt. "Please leave us with some."

The robber pulled eighty dollars from the belt and tossed the belt.

The driver and escort had seven and four dollars, respectively.

The robber then stood in front of Candace. "Do you have any money hidden on you?"

"No," she answered sharply.

"Don't you dare think about it," Stanley warned.

The robber waylaid him with a pistol knocking him to the ground and said, "You are not in a position to tell us anything. We may be robbers, but we have scruples."

"Let's get out of here," the leader said.

"Not before we check that fancy bag in the back. I saw this man was reluctant to part with it when we boarded," said the man who had been on the stage.

He opened Adam's leather bag, dumped its contents in the mud and purposely ground his heel into the contents, shook the bag, then looked inside, and felt the lining. Feeling no coins, he tossed it.

Mounted, with all the firearms including Adam's, the bandits hesitated while the leader drew his rifle. Adam feared the worst. Stanley stepped in front of Candace. Two shots rang out and the large wheeler horses collapsed, rocking the stage forward.

The delaying tactic was effective. Even with Adam's help, it took a couple hours to unhitch the remaining horses, move all away from the dead ones and hitch up a four-up. They were seven miles to the next station and travel would be slower.

"What'll we do for money?" Candace asked Stanley finally in route. "How will we get train tickets to Denver or our horse and buggy from the stables without paying their keep? How will we get home?"

"I thought you kept some tucked away," Stanley answered.

"Yeh, maybe two dollars."

They both gave Adam a strange look as he pulled a boot off, reached inside, and handed them the thirty dollars he'd put inside the boot. "Take it. I'm okay without it."

"We'll pay you back," said Stanley.

"I'm Adam. I am a cowboy of sorts. I'm running my father's herd and headed to Texas to see him. I didn't talk much earlier because I was suspicious of that man."

"We live on the outskirts of Denver. I presume you are taking the same train as us to Denver, then switching trains to Dallas."

"That's right. Have you ever heard of Miss Wolcott's School for Girls?"

"Yes, we have. It's outside of town near us."

They ended up spending the night at a stage station. Adam slept on the porch. Between the remainder of the stagecoach ride and the train ride to Denver the couple learned of Adam's neighbor and friend Lorraine who was at the school and that he intended to see her before traveling on to Dallas. Adam discovered that Stanley was a manager of a leather-processing shop and a pastor.

"I assume the picture in your pocket watch was of Lorraine. Sorry you lost it," said Candace. Adam didn't correct her before Stanley spoke.

"There are no hotels close to the school. I suggest you stay with us while you're visiting your friend," Stanley offered. Adam accepted.

After arriving at the train station in Denver, they picked up Stanley's buggy at the stable. Stanley indicated he needed to stop at the shop and inform his boss why he had not made it to work that day. Adam waited in the buggy with Candace while he was gone.

When Stanley returned to the buggy, he said, "The boss gave me an advance," and attempted to hand Adam thirty dollars. "Here and thank you again for your generosity giving us money. Without it we'd have gone hungry on the trip."

"Keep your money. You offered me a place to stay, and Candace has invited me to bring Lorraine to supper tonight."

A twenty-minute ride put them at Candace and Stanley's home at four in the afternoon.

Adam was shown to a spare bedroom in the house. As he unpacked his clothes that had been thrown in the mud, he heard a conversation between the couple. While in the room he pulled fifty dollars from his leg money belt and silently thanked Nate for suggesting a leg belt rather than a waist belt.

"I can't imagine the shape your clothes are in," Candace said. "Bring them here and I shall wash them."

"And take our buggy to get Lorraine while it is still hitched."

Adam tied the buggy and walked to the main door of the school. It was a stucco building, painted beige. The carved letters on the wooden sign in the driveway identified the building as Miss Wolcott's Girls School. It made no mention of "finishing school."

In the lobby, he walked to a reception desk. "I'm looking for Lorraine Montgomery."

"Are you related to her?" the receptionist queried.

"No, I'm a neighbor, friend and business partner of her mother."

"What is your name and from what town do you reside?

"Adam Duval from Great Falls, Montana territory."

"I'm sure you understand we must be careful to protect our girls. She should be out of class in a few minutes. If she verifies the information you gave me, we'll send her out. Have a seat over there."

It seemed much longer than five minutes when the door to the classrooms burst open and Lorraine came rushing through. She was reaching for Adam before he could stand.

"I couldn't believe it was you. I've missed you so much."

"And I've missed you, even more," he replied surprising himself and unable to retrieve his words. "How do you like it here?" he quickly asked, hoping to cause her to miss his comment.

"It's great. Everyone is so nice. How is Gerald and Mom?"

"They're fine. Your mother's seamstress business is picking up, Gerald seems happy, and your mother...well," he caught himself before continuing, "is seeing a lot of Elmer."

It wasn't lost on Adam that the receptionist was intently catching every word. He turned to her. "Lorraine and I have been invited to supper at a nearby home. I assume it is okay to leave with her."

"Let me get the principal. It is not something we often allow."

While they were waiting, Adam filled Lorraine in on his trip, the robbery and meeting a couple that lived nearby.

"Where do you propose to take her?" a demure, grandmotherly looking Miss Wolcott asked.

"The Roberts'. They live only a block away. They've invited us for supper."

"How do you know them and what are their names?"

"Candace and Stanley. I met them on the trip from the Montana territory where they went to meet her father."

"I've heard of them. We usually don't make exceptions like this, but I'm leaving the school now. I'll follow you to their place and if all checks out with them, I'll allow it, but she must be back here before ten."

"I fully understand," Adam answered.

At the Roberts' home, Miss Wolcott was satisfied with the arrangement and reminded Adam to have her at the school before ten. Adam introduced Lorraine to Candace and Stanley. Candace had supper ready, and Adam followed Stanley's lead in helping Lorraine be seated. Stanley offered a prayer.

> Lord, thank you for bringing us all together for we know you have your ways of directing us. May we be mindful of your direction and know there is a reason for all that happens in this life. Now thank you for the food. Amen.

Candace said to Lorraine, "You should know we consider ourselves very fortunate that your boyfriend was on the stagecoach with us during the robbery."

The prayer and Candace's description of him struck Adam unexpectedly and hard. *Was it a misunderstanding or was reality spoken at the dinner table?*

Lorraine looked at him and smiled as if she took it as a matter of course, then said to Candace, "Adam has a way of being in the right place at the right time. He's been there so often for me."

"Tell me about it," Candace prodded.

Lorraine went through a litany of him scaring a rattlesnake away, saving her mother from a mean man, saving her from drunken saloon thugs, and financing her at the Wolcott school.

"He sounds like quite a guy," Candace said.

Adam felt himself blush, then felt a hand reaching for his under the table, "He is," Lorraine said, looking at him.

Adam considered telling how Lorraine bumping into his foreman at a saloon door and warning him of Adam's danger saved his life, but he hesitated.

After dinner, Stanley, hoping to give them privacy, suggested they use the porch swing.

Adam sat and told Lorraine to stand and turn around. "What?" she asked.

"I'm just admiring how you turned into such a beautiful lady."

Lorraine ignored him. "How is Emily?"

"Fine."

"You know I wish you the best. I don't want to interfere with your marriage. It is to be. I just want to remain your good friend," Lorraine said.

When Adam didn't answer, she continued, "How's the house coming?"

"It's slow and Emily is getting frustrated about it. I do have a confession to make."

Her gaze told him to continue. "There has been a misconception about my age. I am not twenty, but eighteen."

"You're only a year older than I am." She seemed amazed.

"Yeh, and nine years younger than Emily."

"Is that a problem for her?"

"She says not. I had my watch taken, but it must be approaching ten. Let me get you back to the school."

As they thanked Candace and Stanley for the supper, Adam found it to be just past nine.

"I hope the next time Adam is in Denver, he brings you to supper. And anytime you need to be away from the school, stop in," Stanley said to Lorraine.

"I'll be back," Adam answered to Lorraine's delight.

In the lot outside the school, they talked more, although both were ill at ease with emotions neither could understand.

"Finally, Lorraine said, "I should be going inside now. I would love to get a third kiss from you but doing so might be interpreted as interfering with your upcoming marriage, which I won't do. Thank you so much for coming, Adam, and good luck finding your father.

After a squeeze of the hand, he walked her to the door.

The next morning, Adam was on the train to Dallas.

*"When someone is in your heart, they're never truly gone.
They can come back to you, even at unlikely times."*

Mitch Albom

 ★ CHAPTER 29 ★

The Dallas train would not leave the Denver station for two hours. Adam felt he would be sitting long enough and went for a walk. The area around the train station was inundated with shops, more than he had seen since he did not know when, but he knew somewhere he had seen more.

He passed a jewelry shop, walked past it, and then thought, *why not*? He had made a promise. It would eliminate crazy ideas from his head and solidify his future.

The clerk was eager to show him an assortment of wedding bands. *Wide, bright, and shiny* was the description Emily had given him. The widest eighteen-carat was eleven dollars, most were less than eight.

He saw another he liked. It was smaller, but with a pattern of etchings on it. *More like life,* he thought, *not always simple, bright, and shiny.* Suddenly, a question struck Adam, *which would Lorraine desire a man to give her someday?*

He put the aberrant thought away and told the jeweler he would take the big, bright, and shiny. Not wanting to chance it being stolen in what rumor had it was rough Texas territory he was headed toward; he gave the clerk a dollar and told him to hold it.

Nate had set up a meeting in his office with the building foreman and Emily. He told him to bring as many blueprints as he had. Emily was excited. Adam had told her to make the choice.

"Before we look at the blueprints, what features do Adam and you desire in your house?" asked the foreman.

"I want a wraparound porch and at least four dormer windows on the second floor facing the street," Emily answered.

"That can be built on your present basement foundation. The porch would sit outside the basement. Let me find a blueprint to give you an idea."

"This blueprint only has three dormer windows," Emily answered after studying it.

"We can put four there. We'll just use smaller windows and place them closer."

"I guess we should have put a larger basement and foundation in."

"Little late for that now," answered the builder.

The builder made calculations on a pad while Emily and Nate watched him. "Given the design you desire, the cost will be twenty percent over what Adam budgeted."

"I'm sure he will be fine with it. He told me to make the decision," Emily confidently answered.

"He gave me a down payment, but not enough given what we are discussing."

Nate said, "I'm willing to add enough to the down payment to cover it. I'm sure Adam will make it right with me."

The builder ignored the offer and looked at Emily. "You are not married, correct?"

"We plan to be soon."

"Without written authorization from Adam and not being his wife, I cannot start construction on your design."

She gave Nate an inquisitive look.

"Unfortunately, I'm afraid he is right," Nate answered.

Emily jumped up, nearly upset the chair by jerking her skirt from under it, huffed, and left Nate's office.

Adam was glad to exit the train in Dallas. He had been sitting long enough. At a stable a few blocks from the train station, he sought to rent a horse and saddle.

"Where are you headed?" the stable owner asked.

"I'm headed to Forney. How far is it?"

"It's a day's ride, twenty-five miles or so. Why aren't you taking a train? The Texas & Pacific railway runs through there."

"I've been riding a train from Montana and need a change of pace."

"If you are heading there, I want double price for the rental. That place has a bad reputation for drunken ruffians and an abundance of thieves."

Forney was incorporated that year,1884. It was a frontier settlement of around five hundred residents. Despite the efforts of the town fathers to build a respectable and law-abiding town, the town was known for hard drinking, wild gambling, and tough brawling. Tales of the rough-and-tumble days there became inspiration for Hollywood Wild-West scenes in the next century.

"I could have said I was going elsewhere," Adam observed.

"Yeah, but you didn't."

"I'll pick the horse up first thing in the morning."

Halfway to Forney at midday, Adam stopped for a meal at a station called Mesquite Creek.

He asked the proprietor, "I'm heading to Forney. Is it as rough as they say?"

After looking Adam over, he replied, "I see you're not wearing, that's good; if you're wearing you need to be very handy with it."

Adam arrived in Forney an hour before sunset. He asked the first person he saw the location of the sheriff's office. With a grin, the person pointed to what appeared to be a barber shop.

"He shaves and cuts hair when he not sheriffing."

Adam entered the shop to find the sheriff finishing a shaving job. "You're next," he said.

Adam took the chair, and the barber/sheriff draped a dirty sheet over him. "You're not growin' much hair there, I see. What y'all you doing in town?"

"I'm looking for someone. Theodore or Ted Duval."

"Never heard of him, What's he to you?"

"He's my father."

"What's he look like?"

It had not struck Adam that someone would want his dad's description. All he knew from going through his dad's clothes at the cabin was his father was tall. "Over six feet and looks a little like me."

"Don't know. Best to check the saloon."

"Where's the telegraph office?" Adam asked, knowing last year's telegram came from Forney, and the promise he'd made to Emily to telegram her once he arrived.

"Didn't make it. Closed last year."

The saloon was loud. Boisterous drunks this early made Adam wonder what it would be like late. He ordered a beer at the bar and asked the bartender if he'd heard of a Ted Duval.

"Yeah, I remember him, he played cards here for a while, but moved on. I think this place was a little rowdy for the likes of him, 'specially after he fleeced many locals of money."

"Any idea of where he went?"

"No, but I'd try Terrell. Poker there probably more his style."

There were no hotels in Forney, and Adam thought it a good idea to leave anyway. It was only a half day's ride to Terrell. He stopped under a Mesquite tree, safely off the trail, an hour out of Forney for the night.

Fortunately, he used his leather bag for a pillow instead of the saddle. When he woke up the next morning, his saddle was not to be found. At least, it was the saddle gone, not his bag and he still had the horse. Stealing a horse was a hanging offense, stealing a saddle was not.

He rode bareback into Terrell. Near the town square he saw scaffolding being torn down. At first, it struck him as a strange place for scaffolding, then it hit him, it had been temporary gallows.

He stopped a man on the street. "Was that a gallows they're tearing down?"

"Yes, yesterday at noon this place was packed. They hanged a man for killing another in a poker game."

"Where is the sheriff's office?" Adam asked.

The man pointed.

"I'm looking for Theodore Duval. Have you heard of him?" Adam asked the sheriff.

"Yep, but you're too late. We buried him a few months ago up on cemetery ridge."

Adam was struck with the realization he would never see his father. He would never find the answers he sought. Adam felt only some relief that his dad was not the man hanged. "How did he die?"

"He was accused of cheating with a card up his sleeve in a poker game. No card was found there, so given no just cause for shooting him, we tried and hung the man yesterday."

"Which direction to cemetery ridge?"

The sheriff pointed. "How did you know him?"

"He was my father."

"Then before you leave town you better stop and see the judge."

"Why?"

"Duval had accumulated considerable property by cards and other means. Last I heard no one has laid claim to it."

Although he did not know his father, Adam was distraught. He had no other relatives whom he knew. The loss of worry about whether his father would claim him paled to news that his father had been murdered.

He had promised he would telegram Emily when he reached his

dad. At the telegram office his short telegram said that his dad was dead, and he would stay in Terrell a few days. A stop at the cemetery surprised him. A nice limestone headstone had been erected. The birthdate was marked *unknown*.

After replacing the saddle that was stolen and securing a room at the hotel, Adam found the judge.

"What can I do for you?"

"I'm Adam Duval, Theodore Duval's son."

"Where are you from and why are you here?" the judge asked.

"I came here from Montana to see why he never answered my telegrams. His last telegram said he would be back this spring for roundup. Can you tell me more about my dad's murder?"

"Montana, heh? That matches where others said he came back to Texas from."

"Who paid for the tombstone on his grave?"

"I did, or allowed it paid from the funds he had on him. Can you prove who you are?"

"I have papers showing Duval ranch cattle sales with my signature."

"Is that it?"

"I have a money clip of his with his initials on it."

"That might do, but here's the deal. The law says an estate cannot be distributed until notice has been given for six months. Notice was first published," he dug through some documents, "five and a half months ago. No testament of will can be found and to date you are the only relative to show up. If no one else presents a claim, assuming you produce what you said, I suppose what you describe will do."

"Can you tell me the circumstances of his death? The sheriff didn't give me many details."

"Your dad was a poker player, very good, I understand. Good enough that he won a large local herd in a game and ended up with a considerable amount of cash on him and more stashed in his hotel room. He carried a gun around town but never carried at a card table.

A traveler who had lost money to him accused him of cheating. Said he knew Ted had a card up his sleeve. When your dad refused to roll up his sleeves, the man shot him. Witnesses said they turned up Ted's sleeves and found no cards.

The combination of no evidence your dad was cheating and him being unarmed caused a jury to find the man guilty and we hanged him yesterday. If you're a card player like your dad, I suggest you be careful."

"I'm not a card player, for money anyway. What's the name of the herd he won and how much money did he have?"

"I'm not at liberty to disclose that. If no one else makes a claim, I will in fifteen days."

Adam answered, "I may or may not stay until then, but I'll bring you the documents and money clip tomorrow."

Adam stopped at the telegraph office and sent a telegram to Nate advising him that his dad had passed and there was an estate, which could cause a delay getting home.

"You are Adam Duval, right?" asked the telegram operator, looking at his signature on the pad.

"Yes."

"I just received a telegram for you. It had RUSH put on it, and I didn't know where to find you."

Builder won't proceed without your OK

Dad married Mildred. I moved to your apartment.

Make haste getting home.

Emily

Adam was at a loss not knowing what to do. It would take most of the fifteen days to make a round trip to Montana. *For what?* A month's delay in starting the house would be small considering the bigger picture. Emily was frustrated, but she had a place to stay. Although she was not pleased, she had already agreed to live in the apartment after they married until the house was completed. *Had the house become the reason for marrying him?* He had to wonder.

Emily was sitting in Nate's office discussing what might be done to nudge the builder into starting Emily and Adam's house. It was near supper time. They had been to the hotel diner two evenings in a row.

Nate observed, "I suppose being seen at the diner together three nights in a row would start undue speculation."

"Yes, minds that have empty space and boring lives are inclined to fill the void to either tantalize themselves or justify their own behavior," Emily added.

"Ah, a philosopher, I hear," said Nate, then countered, "but those minds must first have a bit of evidence or intuition from which to extrapolate their theory."

His use of the word *intuition* stuck with Emily. She let it slide and informed Nate that she had sent a telegram to Adam telling him to get home immediately.

"Is there any legal way to force the builder to proceed without Adam here?" she asked.

"No, there isn't—"

There was a knock on the door.

"Telegram for Nate Clements," the delivery boy said.

"Excuse me for a moment. I want to talk to the boy about getting an opossum out from underneath the sidewalk in front of the building. Those things scare me."

Emily had noticed a few letters on his desk. With Nate out of the room, she picked them up and scanned them. One was addressed to Adam from the school in Denver. She slid it in her handbag before Nate returned and opened the telegram.

"It's from Adam," Nate said. He opened it and read it before handing it to Emily.

After reading it, Emily wadded it up and said, "Well, he's to be delayed because of an estate. Seems he didn't heed my request to return immediately. Let's go to supper at the diner. Why worry about what people may say?"

Emily had moved into the larger apartment Mildred vacated across from Nate's when Mildred and her dad were married. She considered Adam's too small for her. As a gentleman Nate walked Emily to her door when the couple returned from the diner. Once she had unlocked her door, she turned, reached for him, and kissed him.

"It is not inappropriate to kiss a man after three nights dining out," Emily declared.

Nate was stunned but found himself kissing her back before catching himself.

Emily felt no guilt. It was time to hedge her bets. Her dad was married in a fraction of the time she had been dating Adam. Nine years younger than she was, Adam did not have a dwindling amount of time to marry but she did.

In her apartment, she opened the letter addressed to Adam. As expected, it was from Lori. Emily fumed. Adam had stopped in Denver to see her. They had spent time together on a porch swing. It was signed, *your adoring friend*. Two could play the game.

She knocked on Nate's door and showed him the letter from Lorraine.

"You shouldn't have taken that. I promised Adam to keep them for him."

"Have you promised him anything else?"

*"The best effect of fine persons is felt after we have left their presence."*

Ralph Waldo Emerson

# ★ CHAPTER 30 ★

Adam had decided not to leave Terrell until he learned more about his father. After checking into the hotel, he headed to the saloon where his dad had been shot.

At the bar, he ordered a beer and was checking the place out when the bartender asked, "Don't believe I've seen you here before."

"You haven't, but I understand my dad spent time here."

"And who would that be?"

"Ted Duval. I'm his son Adam."

"I should have guessed—you're a shorter version of him. I'm Henry, I own the place."

"Glad to meet you. I hadn't seen my dad in years and would like to know more about him."

"I suppose you are here for the...you know."

"I came here to see why he didn't return to Montana this spring as he promised. I had no idea he had been killed or if he had money or property. Did you get to know my dad?"

"He was great for business in the saloon, although not so good for those who sat at the table with him. Never a cheat that I knew, but a shark, no doubt. And always courteous to those he lifted of their money. He never let someone leave his table empty handed. He'd toss them a few coins. And when the game was over, it was common for him to buy drinks for the house. Good for business, he was."

"Who else here might want to talk about him?"

"See the guy sitting at the table in the corner. He lost his cattle herd to your dad in a card game. He's a regular here. I'm sure he's looking for another game tonight, to the dismay of his wife."

"That's probably not a good thing," Adam said.

"Yeah, but I'm not a preacher. I'm just trying to make a living here," the saloon owner defended himself.

"What's he drink?"

The bartender did not answer, just handed Adam a bottle of whiskey. "That'll be a dollar."

"Is this seat taken?" Adam asked the man.

"Will be when you sit," the man answered.

"I'm Adam Duval, Ted's son."

The man seemed startled before he answered, "Birch Daniels, your herd foreman; that is unless you fire me."

"I understand you lost your herd to my dad at a table."

"Yep, foolish of me, but a man doesn't really live without taking chances. Good of your father to keep me on."

"Who would know my dad best around here that I could talk to?"

"That'd be Silvia—she owns the restaurant across the street. Your dad and her spent time together. Our herd, or your herd, is about seven miles southeast of town. Come on out sometime."

When Adam walked into the restaurant, a forty-something lady flipped a sign to show *closed* on the street side and *open* on the inside.

"You're the last customer tonight. So please don't order anything complicated."

"Coffee will do. Are you Silvia by any chance?"

"That'd be me. You look familiar."

"I'm Ted's son, Adam."

"Oh, my dear, I knew your dad for a brief time but miss him. You came from Montana, right? Who notified you of his death? No one here knew where you were, to my knowledge."

"No one notified me. I've come because he didn't show up at our roundup as promised. I didn't know much about him, and I'm looking to learn as much as I can."

"I know he was looking forward to heading north last spring and spending time with you before he was killed."

"Do you know what caused him to leave Montana when I came to the ranch?"

"Long story there, he told me. Seems as though you were living with your grandparents in Peoria, Illinois, since your mother and he split, and she took you. Then at some point your mother died and Ted didn't think the wild of Montana was a good place for a boy to grow up. When your grandparents died, he sent word for you to come to Montana.

"From correspondence with your grandfather, Ted learned that you were bright. He decided if he was gone when you arrived, it'd force you to learn cowboy ways quicker. It would throw responsibility on you that couldn't be done if he was there. Hank, his foreman there kept him abreast of your activities by mail. Ted was proud when he learned you gained a reputation as a wolf killer."

"What caused my dad and mother to split?"

"He was an adventurer, and she liked the peace and quiet of Peoria. After they married, they found not much in common."

Her comment gave Adam pause. *Did he and Emily really have enough in common, or was he bound to make the same mistake his dad did?*

"What was the trial of dad's killer like?"

"There was never any doubt how it would come out. Your dad was well liked. More than once he paid the tab for someone in this restaurant who didn't have the money to pay the bill. I believe the jury was thinking hanging before the testimony started and they found no reason to change their minds."

"Thank you for sharing all this with me. I've learned more about my dad than I ever knew."

The next morning Adam took papers from his leather bag lining and dropped them off with the judge, then headed to Silvia's restaurant for breakfast.

"What's your plans for the day?" she asked him.

"I met Birch Daniels last evening, and he invited me out to look at the herd. I'm curious about it."

"Birch is a nice enough fella with a great wife who puts up with a lot from him. I wish someone could convince him to control his problem for his family's sake."

Adam's inquisitive look caused her to continue, "He has a gambling problem."

Sitting at a table next to Adam was a family of four. The children looked to be around ten, clean but their clothes were worn. Their manners were good, but it was obvious eating in a restaurant was out of the norm for them. He overheard the mother and father talking. They seemed concerned as they counted coins and looked at the bill.

Adam handed Silvia his breakfast bill for seventy cents and a five-dollar note.

"Don't you have anything smaller?" she asked.

"Add the family who sat beside me to the bill and keep the change."

"Thank you. You are like your father."

On the ride to the ranch southeast of town, Adam could not help but wonder whether he would be like his dad in marriage also.

He rode over a knoll and saw a huge pasture as far as the eye could see with no brush and only scattered live oak trees. It was not a few trees that caught his eye; it was the gigantic Hereford herd, thousands he guessed, maybe two or three, a real Texas-sized herd. Many were bunched in shade from the Texas sun under the large live oak trees. At a great distance he saw a house and barn. He rode to the house thinking someone could direct him to what he assumed was a smaller Daniels ranch. When he stopped in front of the white clapboard house, a woman stepped out.

"Are you looking for someone?"

"I'm trying to find the Daniels ranch," he answered.

"Well, you found it, the Daniels property, that is. The cattle no longer belong to us."

Adam was dumbstruck. This herd was many times bigger than the one in Montana.

"Are you with the estate people?" she asked.

"I'm Adam Duval, Ted's son."

"Well, get down from your horse. I'm Racheal, Birch's wife. Birch told me he met you last night. I hope he told you we still own the property, house, cowhand quarters, barn and all the corrals."

"He didn't go into detail. You've quite a spread here."

"Yes, but it's worthless without cattle, and his bad habit took care of that."

"I'm sorry to hear that."

"Can't imagine being sorry about acquiring this herd," she observed. "Come on in. I just made a pot of coffee. Birch is gone looking for rustlers. He took our son, which I wasn't happy about. Hard to tell when they'll be back."

Adam went in, met her daughter, and ate a piece of freshly baked cherry pie.

"Hopefully, you're not of mind to alter our agreement. Birch is a great herd manager. He grew this herd to its present size."

"Birch didn't explain our agreement. He just said he hoped I would continue it."

"Your father and Birch agreed that in leu of foreman wages for Birch, they would split the income from the herd, but all expenses would be paid from our half, including supplies and cowhand wages. It doesn't leave us much, but we survive on it, if I can keep him from gambling."

"How long have you been on the ranch?"

"I was born here. The property has been in the family since before the great war. Birch joined his herd with ours when we were married. Dad and Mom are both gone, and I inherited the land and buildings. Over the years our herd had grown through hard work despite Burch's table pastime, until he lost it."

"Thanks for the coffee and pie. I should get back before dark. Tell Birch I stopped and tell him if I end up with the cattle when the estate is settled, I plan to make no changes."

Adam rode around the corrals on his way out. They were much more extensive than his in Montana. At the end of a funnel in the corral he saw a mustard-painted metal headgate on a chute. On closer observation, he saw "Adam's Chute, made in Iowa" painted in small letters on the right-hand bottom. Seeing the inscription over fifteen hundred miles from Great Falls made him prouder than owning the large herd ever would.

The next morning, he realized he had thirteen days before the judge would rule on the estate, and he had nothing to do in Terrell. At the restaurant, he asked Silvia what there was to see and do in town.

She suggested going to the newly opened museum, which was the original home of the city's founder, Robert A. Terrell.

"Why would that interest me?" he asked.

"It's called the 'Round House' although it is octagonal. It was built to provide better defense against Indian attack. It was the first house in Kaufman County to have glass windows."

Touring the place took the rest of the morning. Now only twelve and a half days to kill. He found himself restless. Lorraine told him her summer two-week break started tomorrow. Most girls went home for the break, but she planned to stay at the school. A long round trip to Montana and back would be too grueling. A round trip to Denver and back less so. He found riding a train without his attention on a horse and the direction they were headed gave him time to ponder life.

Adam checked the telegram office. No telegrams. He considered sending Emily a telegram but did not know what to say. He stabled the rented horse and took the afternoon train to Dallas. The next morning, he boarded the train to Denver.

Candace helped her husband, Stanley, unload the buggy. It was filled with rolls of wallpaper.

"Is it what you ordered?" he asked.

"Yes, it'll really modernize our house. I'm sure you'll love it when I'm finished."

"Looks like a lot of work to me. I can't help you put it up. It's our busy time of year at the plant. Do you know anyone who could help you? We could pay them a little."

"With what the paper cost, we can't afford to pay anyone, but I've an idea."

His look caused her to continue, "The girlfriend of the guy who rode the train with us is on break at the girl's school. She planned to stay there."

"You mean Lorraine."

"Yes, she would probably like to get away from the school for a few days. She could stay with us and help me hang wallpaper for meals and a change of venue."

"Sounds fine with me. Go ask her tomorrow."

Off the train in Denver, Adam walked to the nearest stable. He priced a week rental of a horse, then asked about buggy rental. He already had a horse rented in Dallas which he realized meant nothing concerning this choice, but it gave him an excuse to rent a buggy. He had brought ample money, could leave Texas with more, and what was money anyway?

At the girl's school lobby, he asked the receptionist, who had given him the runaround before, to see Lorraine.

"I'm sorry but she has gone to work for a local couple until school restarts. It is our policy to not reveal the location of our girls to any-one but relatives."

Adam moved his shoulders in an attempt to control his ire. "You remember me from last week when I picked up Lorraine to visit friends and had her back before curfew time."

"Yes, I do, but rules are rules."

Left with little choice, he reached into his pocket and laid a five-dollar gold piece on the counter. "Will this help?"

She gave it a look as if the coin might bite her and entered an office behind the counter. Miss Wolcott led the receptionist back into the lobby.

"Mr., whatever your name is, this is not Chicago. You cannot bribe your way around rules. We will protect our girls against harass-ment. Get out. If you are ever seen here again, the constable will be notified."

Adam turned and started for the door. "You forgot something Mr.," Miss Wolcott reminded him.

He grabbed the gold piece and returned their antagonistic looks.

Adam knew of only one local couple who Lorraine had met. At Roberts' home, he knocked on the door. With no answer, he was about to leave when he heard someone yell from a distance, "Who is it?"

"Adam Duval."

"Well come on in. We've our hands full and can't come to the door," answered Candace.

Adam entered and walked through the entry way to a den. Candace was smearing paste on a length of wallpaper laying on a table, while Lorraine was standing on a ladder waiting for the next paper strip. They both wore aprons which were smudged with paste.

Lorraine had moved to the lower ladder step when Adam em-braced her. They both laughed when he stepped away with paste on his jacket from her apron.

It was the look on Adam's face as he gazed at Lorraine and

her expression of delight that told Candace what neither Lorraine nor Adam had admitted to themselves. Lorraine had attempted to explain to Candace that Adam and she were only friends and that he was engaged to an older woman. Candace knew that if Adam's marriage to the other woman was to be successful, the other woman, Lorrianne and he would have to come to terms with his relationship with Lorraine.

"Have you ever placed wallpaper?" Candace asked Adam.

"No."

"There's another apron in the kitchen. Put it on and help us get this done. Then Lorraine and you can sort things out."

Lorraine was upset when Adam explained what had happened at the school. Candace said the staff could not be blamed as they had to protect the girls and that Stanley, or she could pick Lorraine up anytime Adam wished to see her.

For the next few days, Adam and Lorraine helped Candace hang paper every morning, and they went for a buggy ride in the afternoon. The first night Adam went to a hotel room. Stanley insisted that it was an unnecessary waste of money and Adam slept on a den sofa after that.

Given that the senior pastor was out of town, Stanley gave the sermon Sunday. He talked about God's direction to us and how to interpret messages. The points he made that stuck in Adam's mind were the statements "Sometimes God wants you to go with your gut. Our intuitions aren't infallible, but that doesn't mean we should ignore them."

*"If you know the Way broadly you will see it in everything"*

Miyamoto Musashi

# ★ CHAPTER 31 ★

"Your sermon had an inspiring message," Adam told Stanley.

"God gives us choices; the easy way is not always his way," Stanley answered, "but sometimes he paves the way with signals. Thank you for helping the women with wallpaper. It looks great. Too bad Candace and I can't enjoy it right now — we're leaving for Kansas City tomorrow on a business trip on which I promised to take her."

"We will drop Lorraine off at school for the start of her fall semester. It is not far out of our way to the train station," Candace said.

Lorraine spoke up, "Thank you for the offer, but Adam is going to drop me off before heading to the train station. Given how they treated him at the school, I want him to drop me off."

After goodbyes, they headed in different directions.

Adam pulled his buggy into the school lot. "Enjoy the next semester," he said, helping her from the buggy but thinking it better to let her enter the building alone.

"No," she said. "A gentleman would carry my bags to the lobby."

"But—"

"They will not treat you like they did. I will not stand for it. Follow me."

The receptionist bristled when she saw Adam enter the lobby.

"You've been warned. You are not to be here," she said to Adam, then turned and hollered to the office, "Miss Wolcott, come now."

When Miss Wolcott appeared, Lorraine said, "I'll have you know this man saved my mother's life, my innocence, set my mother up in business, and paid the big part of my tuition. He is not to be treated like he was by this school."

Adam was flabbergasted. Never would he have expected such a forceful rant from Lorraine.

"He also tried to bribe his way around our rules, which we cannot allow. And neither will we tolerate a lecture on how to run our school from a student, Miss Montgomery," stated Miss Wolcott.

"And furthermore," she added, "You are hereby suspended for three weeks. I suggest you study hard, or you will never catch up when you return and will flunk out."

"Very well—all for the better," Lorraine answered, turned, and walked out the door. Adam followed, never prouder of anyone he could remember.

In the buggy, Adam asked, "What are you going to do? Candace and Stanley are gone."

"I could go home to Montana, but I've always wondered what Texas is like. Is it as big as they say?"

After witnessing her teardown of Miss Wolcott and her gleeful acceptance of the penalty, Adam would not deny her a chance to see Texas, nor did he want to.

The conversation between Lorraine and Adam never stopped on the train ride to Dallas, then on to Terrell. Lorraine covered all the subjects she had learned in school. They discussed everyone they knew in Great Falls but avoided Emily. And Adam described who he had met in Terrell and the reason for his return. Later, the conversation shifted to life in general and their expectations. Upon reaching Dallas, Adam realized he knew more about the personality, aspirations, fears, and intellectual workings of Lorraine than he did his fiancée.

Off the train in Terrell, Adam secured two hotel rooms. While Lorraine unpacked in her room, Adam said he had business around town. He expected a frustrated telegram or more from Emily at the telegraph office. There was none from her, which he thought strange. Neither did he have any from Nate. Only one telegram from Hank. It was short in keeping with his character.

- Grass short, herd fine

- You should know; Emily and Nate married

Hank

Adam stepped outside, leaned up against a hitching rail and read the note a few more times. He felt no anger, or betrayal, only shock. He knew he should be infuriated; he was not. *Why should he be surprised?* Emily and Nate were of similar age. Out of curtesy, she had left her family home when her dad married. She had to feel in limbo in an apartment. Nate lived across the hall and would soon be moving to a new house which begged for a family, not a bachelor. Adam's house was a hope and promise in the future that she could not control, and her design input had been denied. If Emily had discovered the amount of time he was spending with Lorraine it would have only added to her insecurity.

Adam slid the telegram in his pocket, saw the saloon sign next door, and walked up to the bar. "A beer again?" asked the owner who remembered him.

"Make it a big one," Adam answered.

Halfway through the beer, the realization struck him that what was intended to be a beer to drown his sorrow was not; it was more a celebratory beer. God had tossed a curve in his direction, and he would celebrate it.

Birch Daniels entered the bar and offered to buy Adam another beer.

"No thanks," he answered. Another beer would not help his judgement. He had been unhitched from something he had stumbled into. Now was the time to pay attention to his gut, as Pastor Stanley said, *Intuition if you will, and ignore not the signs God has given you.*"

With his attention back to Birch, Adam asked, "Your wife invited me to dinner. How would tomorrow evening work? Would it be okay if I brought a friend?"

"That'll be fine. Perhaps we can play cards; my wife prefers that I play at home so she can limit my bets."

"Just curious, how did you get the name *Birch*?"

"Rumor has it that after my parents were married, they hung out under a Birch tree."

They both laughed. Adam found Birch to be a likeable guy with a great sense of humor.

Lorraine answered the second knock on her hotel door. "Does this look okay for the restaurant you told me about?" she asked, as she spun in a dress he had not seen.

"I think it is absolutely delightful."

"Do I smell beer?"

"Yes, you do, but it has nothing to do with how I feel."

Lorraine was introduced to Silvia, and they had ordered dinner.

"Did your business go okay?" Lorraine asked.

"I stopped at the telegraph station to pick up any messages."

"Did you hear from Emily?"

"No, only Hank," he answered and handed her the telegram.

Her look indicated she was as shocked as Adam had been. "I'm so sorry."

Adam laid his hand upon hers and said, "I'm not."

Their meals were served discouraging further discussion about the telegram, but not their thoughts.

Sleep did not come easily for Adam that night, but it was not for regret or discord. It was anticipation of the life he expected and tasks to do before he left Terrell.

Neither did Lorraine sleep easily. She was apprehensive about how the end of Adam and Emily's engagement would affect her relationship with Adam. She was concerned that he would be focused on pursuing another wife and no longer would there be a place for their special relationship. In the last ten days, there had been no kiss; their connection had obviously plateaued. She was happy to accept what was.

After breakfast the next morning, Adam entered the judge's chambers. The fifteen days had transpired.

The judge stated, "No one else has appeared to lay claim to the estate. I have three documents for you. An estate distribution letter acknowledging that you are the legal heir and are of age. A deed to a herd of Hereford cattle, known as the Daniels herd with the D-bar brand, and a bank draft for the amount found on your father and in his hotel room."

The amount of the bank draft shocked Adam. He had no idea it could be as much. The estate distribution letter he considered most valuable as it declared that he was of age. As for the deed to the cattle, he had a plan.

Adam rented a buggy and stopped in front of the hotel. He found Lorraine walking the street, not content to stay in her room. "Get in. I'm taking you on a tour of the countryside, and we've been invited for supper at a ranch."

"That sounds marvelous. I've checked out all the stores in town."

"We're going to see beautiful country, and I'm going to show you the largest herd of cattle you've ever seen."

"I don't know much about pasture and cattle, but this looks like a paradise for a herd. Could you ever see yourself living here instead of Montana?" asked Lorraine.

The buggy had no top, and the Texas September sun was still hot. Adam stopped the buggy in the shade under a large live oak tree.

"I believe there are much more important things to get out of life than where you live. There are nice and not so nice people everywhere. Much of it depends upon your attitude."

"And what do you think is the biggest determinant of your attitude?" she asked.

"A combination of your life experiences and who you are with. How about you? After school, do you think you'll go back to Montana permanently?"

"It just depends," she said, as they moved on and passed over a ridge and the herd came into view. The herd's appearance interrupted Adam's follow-up question about what she meant by *it just depends*.

"Wow, I've never imagined a herd this big. Who owns it?"

"I do," Adam answered, then explained why they were having dinner with the couple that owned the ranch.

The children saw a buggy coming and summoned their parents. Racheal and Birch greeted Lorraine and Adam from their front porch. Racheal had fixed a great meal with all the trimmings. Lorraine noticed Racheal's wedding ring as she passed the potatoes.

"What a gorgeous wedding ring. The design and engravings on it make it look special."

"Thank you, one of the infrequent payoffs from my husband's trip to Dallas."

As an awkward silence came over the table, Lorraine changed the subject. "What a lovely cake on the counter. Is it someone's birthday?"

"Yes, today is Jeremiah's birthday. He is now thirteen. Tell them what you've been working so hard for this summer."

"I'm saving to buy a horse and saddle."

"How much have you saved?" asked Adam.

"I've eight dollars saved now. Dad says I may find an old mare for twenty-five."

For a reason Adam could not explain, the boy's situation reminded him of saving for something when he was younger, but he could not remember what. Like Lorraine he changed the subject.

"I noticed you have a new contraption gate or chute in your corral. How's it working?" Adam asked Birch.

"Fine, we bought it last year from some manufacturer in Iowa. It's even got your name on it."

"The world started and remains full of Adams," Adam answered.

"Let me help you with the cleanup," Lorraine offered after smiling to herself at Adam's dropping the chute conversation.

"How about a friendly game you promised?" Adam asked Birch. Lorraine gave Adam a look of surprise as she didn't know he played poker. Racheal's glance at Adam was a scowl.

"You know what we agreed, Birch. No heavy gambling and this land is off limits," she cautioned him. Then to Adam she said, "Your dad already got the herd, isn't that enough?"

"Don't pay attention to her, Adam. You know how women are," said Birch.

The first two hands were uneventful as neither got any cards worth a heavy bet. Birch dealt the third hand. Adam picked up three jacks, a queen, and the four of clubs in his hand. He laid a five-dollar gold piece on the table.

Birch studied his hand met and raised the bet ten dollars. Adam raised it another five dollars.

Birch studied Adam, "I remember that look in your dad's eyes; I see the same in yours. It is not the look he had when he won the herd but the look when he was bluffing. I'll raise you one hundred dollars."

"Birch, that's all we have for supplies the next month. You can't do that," protested Racheal.

"I know what I'm doing, dear."

Adam reached into his pocket and pulled out the folded deed to the herd and laid it on the table. "I'll call you with this," he said.

"I can't match that," Birch responded.

"I think you better look at the condition I've written under the fold before you say that. It may not be worth much," Adam answered.

Birch unfolded it. Adam had written on the bottom of the paper above his signature.

I will convey all ownership is what is known as the Daniels cattle herd in three years if Birch Daniels has not placed a poker or other bet in excess of ten dollars in the time period. If it is reported to the judge and shown that he has broken this requirement, this conveyance is void.

"You better understand the terms of the deed conveyance if you wish to continue," Adam warned him.

Racheal stepped behind Birch, reached for the deed, and read the conditions. Lorraine stood behind Adam.

"I don't think I can accept that as cover for my bet," Birch announced.

Racheal tossed the deed in the middle of the table and said, "You'll either accept it or find another place to stay. My parents left this house in my name."

The gaze between the husband and wife was poignant until Birch said, "Okay, how many cards do you want?"

Lorraine watched Adam discard two of his three jacks and a queen. He was dealt a five, king, and an eight. From her work sweeping floors in the saloon, Lorraine had learned enough about poker to realize what Adam was doing. She laid her hand on his shoulder.

Birch drew two cards and laid down two aces. Adam had a king high.

"I knew he was bluffing," Birch exclaimed, "Look, honey, I got the herd back."

On the porch on the way to the buggy, Birch said to Adam, "That was pretty crafty of you."

"You know I will enforce the terms."

"I know. We'll send you your share of the profits every quarter for three years."

"I will be back before then," Adam said as they shook hands.

Adam looked at Jeremiah, "So you are looking for an old mare. You know I rented one in Dallas and rode here two weeks ago, stabled it in town, and now don't know how I'll get it back to the stable in Dallas if we ride the train. I was thinking I'd just buy it when I get to Dallas, save me the hassle of returning it. Your eight dollars would likely pay the stable fee in Terrell. If you pay the stable fee, and take the horse, it'd help me out."

Before they left, Racheal hugged Adam and whispered in his ear, "Thank you for everything."

On the ride back, Lorraine said, "You are a very good man, Adam."

He replied, "And you will make someone a great wife."

Lorraine knew the remark was meant as a compliment, but all she could feel was disappointment.

*"Dost thou love life? Then do not squander time,*
*for that's the stuff life is made of."*

Benjamin Franklin

# ★ CHAPTER 32 ★

Lorraine was waiting for Adam in the hotel lobby with her bags when Adam entered. Since he wasn't handy with a needle and thread, it had taken him longer to re-sew the lining in his leather bag which now included a bigger bank note.

"Shall we leave these in the lobby and return to get them after breakfast?" Lorraine asked, referring to their bags.

"I'll carry yours," he said carrying both their bags. He did not want his out of sight and did not want to alarm Lorraine that its contents were valuable.

At breakfast Silvia asked, "Will you be back soon?"

"I'll be back periodically to check on my investment," Adam answered.

"Will you bring your attractive partner with you again?" Silvia pried.

Adam had to admit to himself that he had thought of Lorraine in many ways but not as a partner. "We'll see about that."

On the train to Dallas, Lorraine said, "That was a very generous birthday gift you gave Jeremiah."

"Not really only thirteen dollars for his thirteenth birthday."

"That horse will cost a lot more than that," she observed.

"No, not really. Twenty-five dollars for the horse and saddle, the stable flier stated. Between the two-week rental fee and the cost of stabling it in Terrell I would have owed twelve dollars regardless."

"I was top of my class in Denver with numbers, but you're a real numbers guy, aren't you?"

"Speaking of numbers, how many days of school suspension do you have left?"

"I haven't given it any thought because I'm not going back."

"Why? I thought you liked it."

"I did but I've learned much of what they teach. Like the Great Falls school, reading at home put me ahead of most. And I believe after the incident that caused my suspension my attitude would not be to their liking at the school."

"Are you content to subject yourself to stereotypical torment again in Great Falls?"

"If Jimmy teases me again, I'll suggest his dad might discover his son is into his chewing tobacco. If Darren teases me, his dad may discover his wife is blaming him for disappearing cabinet whiskey due to his son's indulgence. If Alvin tries to kiss me again, I'll tell him I'd rather kiss a less verminous rattlesnake. And if Alvin's dad doesn't control his son, I'll ask him how homelife would be if his wife found out about him and the saloon girl."

Adam was impressed. In a few months, the school had caused Lorraine to stand straighter in more ways than one. Since she was on a roll, he asked, "What about Rosanne, your schoolmate in Great Falls who refused to sit near a saloon worker in class?"

"Perhaps her mother would be surprised that she spent a night in a tent with Jeremy, the town drunk's son, instead of at her girlfriend's house."

"Wow, you sound like a guy—better have you as a partner than an enemy," Adam answered, then the ramifications of what he said struck him and he diverted the subject. "What are you going to do in Great Falls?"

"My mother has taught me much about sewing. I shall help her in the seamstress business, but doing so will require we adjust our partnership with you. It would seem unfair for you to profit more because I started working."

"I think we can work out something. I was also thinking with more business dealings I should acquire an associate, someone good with numbers and a strong spine who I can trust."

Three times Adam had kissed Lorraine, but none on this trip. He had been the perfect gentleman, which Lorraine appreciated, somewhat to her disappointment. Theirs was to be a respectful deep friendship but no more. She could handle that. But if she was to be like an associate or secretary, she needed to set the parameters.

Although conversation with Lorraine was always enjoyable, Adam was glad when the train pulled into the Dallas train station. He had made a decision. It was one that he had contemplated for some time but now felt righter than ever.

"The Denver train doesn't leave for three hours. I've got to settle for the horse, mail the horse bill-of-sale to Jeremiah, and do other business. There are many shops around. I'm sure you'd enjoy browsing. I'll meet you back at the train station.

The stable owner tried to charge thirty-five dollars for the horse until Adam reminded him of what the flier stated. He mailed the bill-of-sale and found his way to the jewelry store.

"Ah, glad to see you. Here to pick up the ring, I expect," beamed a happy jeweler ready to finalize a sale.

"No, she married someone else."

"I'm so sorry to hear that. You must be very disappointed. I should have insisted that you take it and give it to her immediately," he sympathized, then turned. "You realize that the down deposit was non-returnable."

"No disappointment here. It was all for the best. I expect the down deposit could be applied to another ring."

"Well, yes." The jeweler's face brightened.

When Adam arrived at the train station, it was already boarding. Lorraine was waiting on the rear boarding dock. "I feared you wouldn't make it in time," she said.

"I had several errands. Let's go to the forward boarding station."

"Isn't this where we are supposed to board?"

"Not this time."

Adam showed the conductor his tickets and they were ushered aboard a car called *The Pioneer*. George Pullman of the Pullman Palace Car Company of Chicago designed it. They were shown a private dining area, a washroom, and their cabin which included a wall pull out cot and a bench seat that also served as a bed. The cabin had ornate woodwork, carpet, and leather upholstery.

"What do they call this?" Lorraine asked.

"First class and this train travels on to Helena. We will not need to switch trains."

Lorraine was enamored with the accommodations. After checking everything out, she asked, "What caused you to spend what must have been much for this?"

"I think it is appropriate that we discuss business dealings in comfort."

Her inquisitive look told him to continue.

"If you remember Silvia at the Terrell restaurant referred to us as partners. Then you said we should discuss a new partnership arrangement at the seamstress shop, and if you are to help me in business dealings, we should formalize our partnership. Does that make sense?"

"Yes, what do you have in mind?"

Adam reached for Lorraine's left hand and pulled it toward him.

"What are you doing?" she asked.

He slid a gold ring inscribed with etchings on her third finger and said, "I think this shall symbolize our new partnership if you will accept."

"It's beautiful," she remarked then it hit her like a gold brick what it meant. "Does this mean…?"

"Yes, I desire our partnership to be as husband and wife. The signs have been continuous since I first saw you in the wilderness. To ignore them would categorize us as clueless non-God following imbeciles."

Their fourth kiss was the best.

Lorraine took the ring off and said as much as she would like to leave it on her finger it was not proper until they were married.

"I want you to wear it now," Adam insisted. "You may take it off before the wedding, and I will not act in husbandly ways until it is properly worn."

The conversation on the rest of the trip took on a different tone as they made wedding plans, talked of children, and planned their future.

They deboarded their first-class car in Helena. The train was on time, allowing them to avoid a night in Helena. It was a two-block walk to the stagecoach heading for Great Falls. Adam asked Lorraine to hold her bag. He stepped off the wooden sidewalk, tossed his expensive looking leather bag on the dirt street, and kicked it a few times.

"What for the love of…are you doing?" she asked.

"Trying to make it look old, used, and unwanted," he said as he picked it up and wiped the dust from it. "The reason, I'll tell you later."

The stagecoach ride was uneventful, but with other riders it was difficult to talk. The company did not prevent contemplation of their future and a tantalizing exchange of knowing glances at each other. Fortunately, on the prior train ride they had step by step laid out their plans once in Great Falls. The first stop was the seamstress shop.

"Lorraine, what are you doing here? Haven't fall classes begun?" Mildred asked before catching herself and giving her daughter a hug. "I've missed you. Did this man here accompany you home?"

Before Lorraine could answer, her mother turned to Adam. "So sorry to hear about your father. Unfortunately, both of you lost your dads to brutal outlaws—just another thing you two have in common."

"Lots of questions there, Mom. In order, I've quit school. And yes, Adam did escort me home. As soon as possible he will also escort me to the church alter where we will be married."

She held out her hand and showed her what would become her wedding ring.

"I think that is marvelously wonderful. But I'll be frank, it's not the biggest surprise. I think it is written in a plan somewhere that the two of you should be together."

"Mom, we also want to congratulate Elmer and you. Where—"

"Gerald and I have moved to Elmer's suite above the general store. Emily moved to our former apartment, but yesterday both... I'm sorry Adam, I assume you know."

"Yes, I know, and I believe they will make a good pair. Go on."

"Yesterday they moved into Nate's new house, leaving that apartment empty for Lorraine, until you're married, of course."

"Mom, of course, we want you, Elmer, and Gerald at our wedding, and we are also inviting Emily and Nate, plus others. But we must leave for the church now and make wedding arrangements with Pastor Ken."

Pastor Ken, upon seeing Adam, said, "Losing your father and betrothed within a week must be traumatic. But we must always remember God has a plan. I'd be happy to set aside a time to talk about your disappointments."

"We stopped to discuss the future God has pointed us toward rather than the past. Lorraine and I wish to be married," Adam answered.

"Well three weddings in a month. I must be the busiest guy in town," Pastor Ken said. "When were you thinking?"

"Saturday afternoon, will that work?"

"You don't mean this Saturday—it's already Wednesday."

"Yes, we do."

Pastor Ken turned to the door and spoke loudly, "Ginger, what does our calendar look like Saturday afternoon?"

Ginger entered the room, "Sunday's sermon prep is all you have."

"I think a marriage will take precedence," Pastor Ken answered, then advised his wife of the couple's intent.

"Law says I'll need an affidavit, proof you are eighteen, or a parent's written permission."

"Mildred has agreed to give permission for Lorraine to be married, and I have an estate settlement signed by a judge stating that I am of legal age."

"That should suffice. How many do you plan to invite?"

"Few formally, but if it is okay, let's leave the door open to the public."

"We'll start preparation immediately," Ginger answered.

The next stop for the couple was the bank. Adam deposited the bank draft from Terrell, checked his royalty payments, and added Lorraine's name to his accounts.

With business finished first, as always for the banker, he said, "I wish to express both my condolences for your dad and congratulations on your upcoming wedding."

"The wedding is at three Saturday afternoon. We will not send invitations but would be happy for you and your wife's attendance."

It was nearing five in the afternoon when Adam knocked on the door casing to Nate's office. "Have a few minutes?"

Seeing Adam in his doorway, Nate jumped up and met him at the door. "I just want you to know—"

"I don't want to hear it. I wish Emily and you the best. In the long run you did me a great favor. Emily and I were never a good match."

Relieved that Adam's arrival was not confrontational, Nate noticed Lorraine standing with Adam just outside the doorway. "Oh, hi, Lorraine. Come on in, both of you."

Adam and Lorraine moved toward the chairs in front of Nate's desk. Nate, still stunned by what he feared would be nasty having turned cordial, remained frozen with relief in the doorway.

Emily had been stocking goods in the general store when she heard two customers whispering. They did not notice her moving closer to hear the gossip. Hurriedly, Emily went out the back door and briskly made her way to Nate's office holding her dress above her shoes to avoid tripping at her pace. As she entered the foyer, she saw Nate standing in his office doorway.

"Nate, Adam is back in town, and he is taking that girl, Lori, around with him," Emily announced with volume matching her walking pace.

Nate was stunned and at a loss for words. Emily breezed by him and saw Adam pulling out a chair for Lorraine to sit.

"Hello, Emily," Adam said, stopping Emily in her tracks.

Emily started to move her jaws, but words did not come out.

Adam broke the standoff. "Lorraine and I wish to congratulate Nate and you on your wedding, and we wish your attendance and blessings at our wedding Saturday afternoon."

Later at the hotel diner, Mildred and Elmer were sitting with Lorraine and Adam when Nate and Emily entered. To everyone's surprise, Adam stood and invited the couple to join them. Most of the conversation centered around Adam's experiences in Texas.

"Might you be moving there someday?" Emily asked Adam.

Lorraine answered, "We've talked about it, but we'll let nature lead us where it will."

When they were leaving, Adam took Nate to the side. "I'd like you to me my best man Saturday."

As the men talked, Emily said to Lorraine. "I'm glad you are marrying Adam; you two were destined to be together. You've changed so much. I knew Wolcott's school would bring out who you really were. I hope we can become the dearest of friends."

"And I have you to thank for the suggestion I go there. It gave me confidence I'd never have realized here."

"Come on Lorraine, we've much work to do getting a dress ready for you," Mildred pulled her daughter away.

The next morning in a buggy, Adam and Lorraine headed for the winter herd camp. She was apprehensive about the prospect of spending the night in a cabin with cowboys. But Adam had insisted that she see another side of him.

"You can use the bunk bed above me that Hairy vacated. I can't think of a safer place for my future wife than in a cabin with six armed cowboys all of whom are dependent upon me."

With only Hank in the cabin with them, Adam told him of coming changes. "As you know dad is gone, and I will be here only occasionally. You must take over responsibilities. As such, I'm making you a partner, one-quarter interest in leu of any foreman wages."

Lorraine and Adam spent the rest of the day riding around the ranch, spent the night, and were back in town the next day.

Appropriately, late Friday afternoon Lorraine told Adam she would not see him until the wedding. Her mother had final dress alterations to do, and Hank and the cowboys wanted Adam to join them at the saloon.

With Adam gone to what was assumed to be a bachelor party, Lorraine ran into Emily in the foyer. "Emily, you said you desired to become good friends. Since Nate is best man, would you stand with me at the wedding?"

"I would be delighted," Emily responded.

After two beers, and late-night teasing and taunting by cowboys and others at Montana Betsy's saloon, Adam lay in bed, contemplating the speed at which life was moving. Although he had clues, he still did not know from where he had come.

He had been in his present reality less than three years, becoming a cowboy, an inventor, nearly been hanged, a wolf killer incurring a reputation he did not deserve, found his soulmate, and soon was to be a married man at eighteen years of age. No one could accuse him of squandering time.

Life had been good for him. He tried to imagine where the next three years would take him. Like he could never have envisioned the past three years, the next three would be beyond his imagination.

As he drifted toward sleep, a light fell upon him, then a feeling of weightlessness overcame him, and he entered a universe of tranquil haziness.

*"A man does what he must—in spite of personal consequences, in spite of obstacles and dangers and pressures—and that is the basis of all human morality."*

John F. Kennedy

# ★ CHAPTER 33 ★

Hardly conscious, Adam felt both his physical self and soul floating separately in the unknown. It was not a floating one would imagine in a hot air balloon but a swaying as if dangling over a junction of numerous dimensions of time and space.

Suddenly, the floating stopped, and he felt himself proceeding toward a destination. His soul and physical self were rejoined. The sensation stopped when he felt himself on a mattress. Dreams came and went. He commonly would lay in bed and analyze a dream, but this was like only one other dream-like experience which he could remember which was three years prior.

In a few hours he would be a married man. The experience was anxiety, part of the transition to married life, he was sure.

"Adam, it's time to get up," he heard a voice piercing his thoughts. It was loud and real. The voice he recognized, but he could not place it.

Light was entering his room through a window. On his bed was a rectangle of light encased by the window frame. It was brighter than what would enter from the moon. Curiosity raised him from bed to the window. The light source sat on top of a large pole. He saw others spaced down what appeared to be a street. The artificial lights were unknown, but the more he studied them familiarity came.

Not knowing why, he moved to a toggle switch by the door and flipped it up. The room miraculously lit up. It startled him. It was like discovering yourself at the gates of hell or heaven. His head spun until realization struck him that he was no longer in Montana. He was in Peoria.

Answers to questions about his life prior to three years ago were downloading like a flash drive had been inserted. As they down-loaded, the last three years began to fade.

"Adam, get downstairs, you'll be late for school," again the voice came, augmented by a tap on his door. It was his mother.

It took a few moments standing in front of his closet to recognize his clothes. He reached for a pair of jeans and momentarily thought they had only been invented ten years previous until the thought left his head. He pulled on the cowboy boots he wore while riding his dad's horse.

"I've made you a big breakfast for the first day at school after spring break," his mother said.

"Where's Dad? Adam asked.

"He's gone to the shop. I see you're wearing boots. You've never worn them to school before, have you?"

"No, I don't know why, but they just felt right today."

Adam picked up a coffee cup and studied the coffee machine before he remembered its operation. He selected a Hazelnut flavored pod from the drawer until his mother stopped him.

"No, put it down. Your dad and I discussed it this morning. No more coffee before school for you. Your hyper-activity just gets you into trouble. Hopefully, your room confinement last evening taught you the necessity of going along at school. We don't live in this world alone, and things aren't always as we wish. You can't change the world."

All was coming at him too fast to challenge the new coffee forbid-dance. He sat down at the table where his dad had left the morning newspaper. It struck him that a newspaper was a relic of times past his dad clung to. He read the headline article that Peoria's population had declined three percent since the 2020 census and twenty percent since 1970, while the poverty rate was now nearly double the national average.

Recent history reading taught him that Peoria was once the epitome of middle America. Politicians would often ask "How will it play in Peoria?" while deciding on a position. Now no one paid any attention to the dying town in middle America whose vote would never affect the state's lopsided outcome.

"What's this sausage?" he asked his mother.

"It's a meat substitute. We're told it is the coming thing."

Suddenly, it struck him why he should be excited about school this morning. He had turned sixteen, and as promised, for his work cleaning the shop his dad had paid him with a car. It was a white ten-year-old Toyota Camry with a salvaged title which his dad had rebuilt. This morning there would be no two-block walk to the bus pickup.

"Lori will be here in ten minutes," Adam's mother said, bringing back more recollection about the conditions his dad had given him for driving the car to school. His dad had explained the reasons to help the Montgomery family the prior evening.

Mr. Montgomery owned a local taxicab business. The cab business from Mr. Montgomery had been instrumental in his dad's auto body shop becoming successful. Five years prior, when given a chance to manage a large taxicab company in Chicago, he sold the Peoria taxicab company. Earlier in the year, Mr. Montgomery was filling in for an absent driver when two men attempted to hijack his car. He was shot and killed in the process. With Illinois's new no-bail law, the shooter was released before Mr. Montgomery's funeral. His wife, Mildred, and daughter, Lori, moved back to the family home in Peoria, less than a block from the Duval's.

"I can't bring her home. I still have two weeks of after-school sensitivity training left."

"She has tennis practice after school, so it should work out fine," his mother answered.

"I hope she still doesn't say the silly things she did five years ago," Adam stated. "Friends will make fun of me if she still says she and I will get married someday."

"You haven't seen her since they moved back. She was only ten then. She has changed in the five years they've been gone. She's only one year behind you but pushed forward in classes as you were."

The doorbell rang. "Answer it, Adam. I must get ready for work. Just be nice, okay?"

Reluctantly, Adam opened the door expecting to see the little pesty girl that aggravated him years ago. She was not what he remembered. The red hair was all that remained of the kid standing at the doorway with a tennis racket handle protruding from her backpack.

"Let's go or we'll be late," he said, still thinking of her in the past.

On the ride to school, she tried to start a conversation. "My mom said you played tennis also."

"I quit last year." His answer was short.

They were within a block of the school when Adam pulled up to a stop sign. As he turned right to check traffic, he noticed something on Lori's neck below her red hair line. It appeared to be a mole a couple inches below her left ear. Familiarity struck him from where he did not know. He did not remember her having it five years ago, although he would not have noticed. He was trying to sort through the weird recollection from an unknown place when the car behind him honked.

"Is something wrong?" she asked.

"No, not at all," he answered.

As they entered school, each student was given a copy of the new rules. Adam noticed that Lori wadded and tossed her copy in the first trash can she passed. The brashness reminded him of someone he could not place.

Adam's parents had been notified of the new requirement for

those driving to school. Car keys needed to be turned in at the principal's office when students arrived to prevent them from leaving during lunch break. Adam reluctantly complied.

"How was your spring break?" Terresa asked Adam from her alphabetized adjacent locker. Few people were around including her basketball-playing boyfriend, which caused her to think it was an opportune time to be nice to the boy who she knew had a crush on her.

Terresa was a senior, an older long-time fantasy girlfriend of Adam's, who very seldom spoke to him in school and sometimes treated him as infectious. Infectious because his behavior was often countercultural, making it prudent for her to keep a distance from him. Her dad owned a hardware store and was adamant that she do nothing to hinder his business.

Adam was distracted by Lori at her locker down the hall when Terresa spoke to him. "Sorry, what did you say?" he asked.

"Never mind," she replied, thinking enough of being nice.

Students were required to leave cell phones in their locker. Adam grudgingly complied. Lori put hers in airplane mode and kept it in the backpack she now carried to class.

Between the second and third period morning classes, Lori stepped outdoors to enjoy the beautiful spring day. Making new friends was stressful and deep breaths of fresh air helped relieve her anxiety. She saw whom she was told was a new principal dressed more like a man than a woman walking to the student parking lot.

The principal stopped at Adam's white Toyota. She was sure it was Adam's because the front and back wheels did not match. The fob the principal was holding opened the door and she climbed in. Lori pulled her cell from her backpack, zoomed in on her principal driving away in Adam's car and captured the image.

Lori's mother had given her Adam's number. She texted him the image of the principal driving his car with the message, "Nice of you to loan your car out."

Lori walked up to Adam's table in the cafeteria. "I texted you an image you should see. Check it out," she said before leaving.

Curiosity caused Adam to open his locker and check messages on his cell phone. It did not violate school rules to check messages on a phone in your locker. Instead of placing the phone back in his locker, he slid it in his pocket and walked to a window overlooking the parking lot. His car was gone.

He stepped outside, dialed the Illinois Highway patrol, and reported his car as stolen. Before he entered the school, he saw his car reclaim the parking spot and the principal exit it.

Adam was standing in the hallway beside the principal's office as she returned. "We need to speak," he said.

"I have much on my schedule today, perhaps another time," she answered.

He ignored her and followed her past her secretary into her office. "This better be important," she spit at him as she sat.

He pulled his cell from his pocket.

"You should know that a cell phone outside your locker is a rule violation. What is your name?"

"And stealing someone's car is a felony," he replied as he showed her the image Lori had sent him. "Oh, I'm Adam Duval."

"No big deal. I needed to go to the post office, your car was close, and mine is nearly out of gas. Filling mine with gas would have kept me away too long."

"The highway patrol may think otherwise, since I reported it as stolen."

"You must call them and tell them it was a mistake, or life will be difficult for you the rest of the school year."

"I'll call them, only if we come to an understanding on my terms."

It was her first year as a principal. Technically, she was in a temporary position that would be reviewed at year's end. Allegations that she had driven his car would destroy her career.

She sat glaring at him, until his name rang a bell. In a list of potentially troublesome students, she had reviewed his file. He was often written up for inappropriate remarks and behavior. She was boxed in a corner until she realized that his infractions were negative marks on her administration. Scouring the record of his past and future indiscretions would make her look better. It would be a win-win.

"All right we have an understanding, but you must not go too far."

Adam called the highway patrol and withdrew the stolen car report, then said to the principal, "I've attended enough of those after-school sensitivity classes. I need you to sign a dismissal."

The principal gave him a look wondering how far this would go, but she had no choice. "I guess for the likes of you it would do no good anyway," she replied before she signed a slip.

Ms. Judith Johnson-Corinth's history class had started when the principal opened the door and summoned the teacher. When the teacher returned, the glance Adam received told him all. He was not called on that day, seldom the rest of the year, and his questioning hand up was most often ignored.

Mx. Bellamy, Adam's literature teacher, also conducted the after-school sensitivity training. Adam was one of eight students scheduled to give a book report that day. He was not called upon. Her stern look told him she knew of his excusal from training. He could have given her the principal's slip after class, but he needed to stay until Lori's tennis practice was over anyway. And it would give him satisfaction giving it to her in front of the training class.

After school at the training class, Adam waited until all the discipline-bound students were seated, then walked to her desk holding the slip of excusal. She did not look at him and mumbled, "Get out of here."

Most of the class noticed the smile he wore as he left the room.

It was a great spring day, and he could not leave until Lori was finished with tennis practice. Adam decided to watch the practice. He sat on the second row of the bleachers and saw the principal sitting at the other end.

The girl's tennis coach gathered the players and addressed them,

"We have two spots left to fill on the team and four hopefuls. The hopefuls will play off to see who joins the team." He studied a clipboard then said, "Lori you are to play Devon."

Adam could not believe it. Devon was last year's Darren. He/she was wearing a short white tennis skirt and was sporting a failed attempt to grow a mustache. Darren had been one of the few players on last year's boys' team that Adam could regularly beat.

The coach tossed Lori a tennis ball and said, "You can serve first."

Lori bounced the ball off the court in warm-up for her serve more than normal until the coach said, "Get started, we don't have all day."

She turned to the coach, and said, "I signed up for girl's tennis, not boy's tennis."

Adam noticed the principal leave her seat with Lori's comment. The coach started to say something, but the principal held her hand up, refraining the coach from speaking. "You will play this match or never play tennis at this school and start sensitivity classes."

"So be it," Lori answered, then said to Adam, "See you at the car," as she tucked her racket in her backpack and left the courts.

The principal had started to go back to her bleacher seat when Adam approached her and said away from the ears of others, "She will not go to that class, and this will be forgotten, understood?"

The principal did not acknowledge his demand, but she had no choice.

On the ride home, Adam said, "That was courageous what you did. I admire you for it. But if you're not adverse to playing a real guy, I'd like to play a match with you."

'You're on," Lori answered.

"How was school today?" Adam's mother cautiously asked when he entered the house.

"Great," Adam answered.

She was shocked, he never seemed elated about school. "See, school will be better with a new proper attitude."

"Is my suit back from the cleaners?"

"Yes, why?"

"I asked someone to the spring dance Saturday night."

Made in the USA
Columbia, SC
18 November 2024

46305042R00159